THE AGENCY FILES

BOOK 1

# JUSTIFIED MEANS

CHAUTONA HAVIG

Copyright 2013 Chautona Havig

Second Edition Copyright 2020—Chautona Havig

ISBN: 9798580822075

This eBook is licensed for your personal enjoyment only. This eBook may not be re-sold or given away to other people. If you would like to share this book with another person, please purchase an additional copy for each recipient. If you're reading this book and did not purchase it, or it was not purchased for your use only, then please return to Amazon.com and purchase your own copy. Thank you for respecting the hard work of this author.

Chautona Havig lives in an oxymoron, escapes into imaginary worlds that look startlingly similar to ours and writes the stories that emerge. An irrepressible optimist, Chautona sees everything through a kaleidoscope of *It's a Wonderful Life* sprinkled with fairy tales. Find her at **chautona.com** and say howdy—if you can remember how to spell her name.

**Edited by:** Cox Editing
**Fonts:** Garamond, Bank Gothic, Doppio One
**Cover photos:** depositphotos.com
**Cover art by:** Chautona Havig
**Connect with Me Online:**

**Twitter:** https://twitter.com/ChautonaHavig
**Facebook:** https://www.facebook.com/chautonahavig
**My blog:** http://chautona.com/blog/
**Instagram:** http://instagram.com/ChautonaHavig
**Goodreads:** https://www.goodreads.com/chautonahavig
**BookBub:** https://www.bookbub.com/authors/chautona-havig
**Amazon Author Page:** https://amazon.com/author/chautonahavig
**YouTube:** https://www.youtube.com/user/chautona/videos
**My newsletter (sign up for news of FREE eBook offers):** https://chautona.com/news

The events and people in this book, aside from the caveats on the next page, are purely fictional, and any resemblance to actual people is purely coincidental and I'd love to meet them!

All Scripture references are from the NASB. NASB passages are taken from the NEW AMERICAN STANDARD BIBLE (registered), Copyright 1960, 1962, 1963, 1968, 1971, 1972, 1973, 1975, 1977, 1995 by The Lockman Foundation

## For Lynn

I cannot express how grateful I am to have you for a neighbor and a friend. This book is for you.

## Lee

Thanks to Lee for her wrinkle-free joke.

# ONE

Jarred from sleep, duct tape stretched over her mouth, muffling Erika's gasp. She struggled, but someone swiftly bound her hands, before wrapping rope around her body twice to keep her arms at her sides. The man with the rope wore nothing to hide his face, and the woman with him worked quickly and silently, pulling clothes from her closet and drawers before dumping them in Erika's duffel bag.

Zip ties bound her feet together, and she wondered, illogically, why they hadn't used the duct tape for that too. Instinctively, she wanted to scream, fight, and flee but Erika knew it was useless. No one was home to hear, and she could never overpower two people while bound and gagged. Despite the utter ridiculousness of the idea, regardless of her mind fighting her to try it, her body screamed for her to try.

Emotions ranged from fear to confusion to anger. What would they do with her? Could she hope that the presence of the woman meant she wouldn't be physically assaulted? How dare they break into her home and take her like this! What could they want anyway? Her family wasn't wealthy; she didn't have a top-secret government job. Why would anyone want to abduct a coffee shop manager? She shuddered at the logical answer.

As the questions raced through her mind, the man pointed toward the door and threw her over his shoulder. Craning her neck to see what was happening, Erika watched as the woman nodded, grabbed Erika's bag, purse, and jacket, tousled her spiky hair, and walked calmly from the house swinging her things. Through the sheer curtains of the window, she stared fascinated as the woman tossed everything but the purse into the trunk of Erika's 1992 Honda Prelude. She started the car, pealed out of the driveway, and raced down the residential street presumably toward the interstate.

"*So much for keeping quiet,*" Erika thought to herself.

Silently, the man carried her out the back door, locking the door after rearming the alarm system that obviously hadn't been much of a deterrent for him. He opened the back gate, slipped into the narrow walkway between back fences, closed the gate behind him, carried her three houses down, and opened a gate to the backyard of the next street over.

The man moved quickly—each step a deliberate movement without any hesitation or strain—as if he carried bound women on a daily basis. Human trafficking? That thought made her shudder—again. He hurried across the backyard, slipped into the garage from a side door, and loaded her gently onto the floor of a small minivan with the first bench seat removed.

Once inside, he buckled himself, turned on an eighties rock station, and punched the garage door opener. Slowly and casually, he backed into the street and drove off into the night. "I just want you to know, Erika; we're not going to hurt you."

She couldn't see him. She couldn't answer. However, his words did little to reassure her. Who was "we?" How did "we" know her name? What did they want with her? And why did she have a sickening feeling that she'd never see her family again?

---

They drove for hours. For a while, it felt as if they were climbing—possibly into the mountains—but it leveled sooner than she expected. Light slowly filled the sky outside the windows, giving her hope. With light, perhaps people could see her and help. The van stopped for gas, and Erika banged her feet against the floorboard, hoping to attract attention, but the sound of the man's chuckle told her they were alone—no one near to hear.

As he jumped back into the vehicle, her abductor spoke. "We'll be there soon. Just hang tight."

Suddenly, every foul word she'd ever heard in her life

bubbled up inside her. Erika rarely used coarse language; she considered it evidence of a weak vocabulary and lack of imagination, but at that second, had she been able to, she would have sworn enough to embarrass the toughest biker or gang banger. For the next forty minutes, she ran through every filthy word she could remember, created a few of her own, and decided that the language she'd created as a child needed a few obscenities as well.

After what seemed to be an age, the van stopped. The pungent scent of pine and earth filled her nostrils as the man crawled over the seats and opened the side door. Erika tensed as he pulled her from the floor, snipped the zip tie around her ankles, and helped her walk into a small log cabin that seemed completely surrounded by trees.

She couldn't even see where they'd entered the tiny clearing of a yard. Her green car sat near a pine tree, and Erika wondered—some sort of defense mechanism, she supposed—if sap would drip on it and ruin the paint. As if paint on a ten-year-old car was a concern anymore.

"You took long enough!" The woman's voice sounded impatient. "Her stuff is in there—food on the counter. Better get the perishable stuff in the fridge. I'll call."

Without another word, the woman grabbed the keys from the man, hurried to the van, and seconds later, shot between trees that looked too close together to drive through. The man sat her on a chair and stared at her as though frustrated. "I don't know how to get the tape off without hurting you."

Erika glared at him. *There, lie one. You said you wouldn't hurt me. Ha!* She tried jerking her head to tell him just to tear it off, but he stared at her confused. Again, he tugged at one corner but stopped when she winced.

"I'm sorry, I don't under—" He paused, watching as Erika jerked her head toward the bathroom. "Do you need in there? Let me get your hands."

That was too easy. *Are you really going to untie me?* Erika ran through her self-protection course in her mind. Jab the nose, kick him into opera, and run. The sight of him placing a gun on the table next to him stopped those thoughts. She probably shouldn't irritate someone who could likely run faster and shoot straight.

"I have to keep you here, so the gun is out when you're not secured. You can go in the bathroom and stay there as long as you want, but I'll be out here with the gun to keep you from running. Understand?"

Erika nodded. As much as she tried to hide it, fear washed over her, and with her expressive face, he'd see it. *Drat.* Then again, for a split second, she thought she saw him wince. That could be a good angle. If he didn't like this job, she might be able to talk him into letting her go.

The ropes fell from her hands at approximately the exact moment he picked up his gun. "Bathroom's in there. Take your time. We've got more of it than either of us wants."

Erika reached for the tape and jerked it away from her mouth. "Ow!"

"You didn't have to do that! I was going to get vegetable oil—"

"You steal me from my house, drag me out here bound and gagged, hold me at gunpoint, and you're worried about getting the tape off me gently? You've got some nerve!"

Erika stormed into the bathroom and slammed the door. He could just sit out there for a while. She intended to stay in the bathroom for as long as humanly possible. Her stomach rumbled. Great. Her hypoglycemia wouldn't let that happen. *I need protein... and soon.*

Light filtered into the bathroom, making it rather well-lit. She'd expected a dark place with a tiny window for ventilation with a slim-to-none chance of escape. Instead, glass blocks between the shower and ceiling and a long narrow window on the opposite wall let in all the light you could need—and none of the space she wanted. She tried to measure the window but knew she'd never get her head through it, much less her body.

Resigned, Erika finished, washed her hands and face, grabbed a new brush lying on the sink, tore off the package, and tamed the snarls in her hair. Time to face the ogre-in-training. She opened the door and glanced around her hesitantly. Where was he? *Maybe I should make a run for it...*

"Don't even think about it, Erika. I've got cold cereal here. Clamp that thing by the doorway around your ankle, and I'll put away the gun."

"You know my name," she began as she looked for the *thing*, "but I don't know yours." The *thing* was some kind of shackle—well-padded enough to avoid rubbing her skin. What was with this sadist? Keep her in a pain-free prison? Seriously?

"Keith. Keith Auger. Sorry we had to meet like this...." his attempt at humor failed miserably.

"Well, you could let me go and then it wouldn't be so bad...."

She clamped the shackle around her ankle and tried to open it again. It wouldn't budge. There seemed something seriously wrong with making a person tie themselves to their captor's house. "All snapped. This is a really long chain."

"It'll let you go anywhere in the house or on the front porch. Your room is that one in there." He pointed to the room to the right of the bathroom.

"My room? How long will I be here? You know, we don't have any money. No one can pay any kind of ransom, and my dad is the kind of man who wouldn't even if he could."

Keith passed a bowl and a box of cereal across the breakfast bar. "Eat up. We don't want money. You're here for your own safety."

"You kidnapped me for—what the—? My own safety?" The derision in her tone would have cut a weaker man. *Guess he's not weaker.*

"Something like that. Eat up. Your blood sugar is going to give us fits if you don't."

"How did you know—?"

"I know a lot more than you want me to. Let's just leave it at that."

Erika frowned. The man was awfully curt for a guy who had the upper hand. "When will your partner return?"

"Karen?"

"Whatever her name is." Erika poured the cereal, noting that the gun was out of sight.

"She'll be back on Saturday with more food."

So, she'd be here for at least the week. Who would handle the bank drops, get change, make orders, schedule the crew? What did her mom and dad think? "What happens when my parents report me missing?"

"You left a note saying you needed to get away. You'll call in a couple of days to assure them that you're fine, but you haven't decided when you're coming back."

"You're going to let me call?" This seemed odd. How did he know she wouldn't scream or say something to give away her situation?

"Eventually. We can't have them getting too worried. This has to look like your choice."

"Why?"

"For your own protection."

There was that word again. Protection. What did it mean? "Why do you keep saying that?"

"Look, Erika, the less you know, the better. All I'm allowed to tell you is that it's for your own protection."

"You're d—"

Keith wrinkled his nose almost imperceptibly. "Swearing won't change facts. You're here. You're here for your own good. I'm here to protect you. That's all you need to know."

She eyed him curiously. What kind of guy kidnaps women for their "own good" and takes special care to see that they're as comfortable as possible in that situation? What kind of guy is he if that same man obviously doesn't like women to curse?

"Okay, let me try that again. Maybe you can't appreciate this from your vantage point, but I am petrified, furious, and bordering on maniacal." The look on his face hinted that she might have crossed over that maniacal line. Exasperated, she threw up her hands. "Can you tell me who you work for?"

"Eat." The word accompanied the negative shaking of his head.

She took a bite. "Okay, so why are you here instead of the woman—Karen?"

One eyebrow rose. As it did, she sighed. He stayed because he had the strength, and possibly the speed, to ensure that she didn't escape.

"Eat some more."

"You sound like an Italian mama."

With a perfect hyperbolic imitation of an Italian accent, Keith passed her a plastic cup of orange juice.

"Drink-a-your juice-a."
 "Very funny."
 "You're awfully calm."
 Keith sounded annoyed by it. His frown irritated her. "I'll fall apart later. Right now, I'm still hovering on disbelief followed by a little bit of 'I must be dreaming.'"

# Two

He slept. One minute he'd been reading his Bible, an idea that she found revoltingly contradictory, and the next, a snore escaped. Erika glanced swiftly around the room again, looking for anything to help her escape. His hand covered the gun, much to her disgust. There was no way to get it away without waking him and, yet she had to take advantage of the gift of "blindness" in order to try to escape. Sitting around until they decided that she no longer needed "protecting"—stupidity at best. She had to try to get out of there.

With her first step, the chain rattled, causing Keith to stir slightly. She couldn't walk. She'd have to find the keys or something to pick the lock without moving her leg, but Erika had no idea how to pick a lock or what kinds of objects worked to do that sort of thing. *Neglecting my career as a lock picker—epic fail.*

Her eyes scanned the room where moments before she'd sulked on the floor by the wall. Deliberately, and much to Keith's chagrin, she'd refused to be comfortable. She considered herself a prisoner and would act like it.

*Why don't I wear buns like people in books or movies?* She continued to seek something, anything, that she could use to attempt to pick the lock, and almost gave up in defeat, until her eyes saw the old pinched-pleat drapes. Erika's grandmother had drapes like that—she'd hated re-hanging them after laundering, the pins jabbing into her thumb. Now, however, she mentally thanked her grandmother for distasteful tasks that might possibly ensure freedom.

Inch by inch, she moved up the wall, forcing her left foot not to move. Her hand stretched as far as it could reach, but she wasn't tall enough. If she could just move her foot.... Erika scooted her foot closer, one centimeter at a time, until she finally managed to push the hook out of the pleat.

Frantically, she worked the lock. All efforts seemed ineffectual as she jimmied, wriggled, twisted, and ignored the looming feeling of insanity-laced doom. A memory—an image from an *Alias* episode, no less—prompted her to try bending the hook into a u-shaped object and she tried again. Seconds ticked past—minutes. Sweat poured down her face and soaked her shirt, pooling into her bra. Her breathing grew more rapid with each failed attempt until the cuff finally fell from her ankle with a soft thud.

Erika's eyes flew to the couch where Keith still sat sleeping. Once more, she inched her way into the bedroom that held her things and slipped on shoes. The work Crocs that Karen brought wouldn't be the best for protecting her feet, but they would be quiet. Peeking around the corner, Erika saw that Keith hadn't moved and tiptoed quietly across the floor. It was now or maybe never. *Definitely now.*

She expected an alarm to blare the moment she opened the door, but nothing happened. Feeling a little more confident, she stepped across the threshold and then bolted as a cheerful chime, one similar to a small store might have, sang it's little "ding-dong."

She flew across the small clearing that surrounded the cabin. Only fifteen feet to the trees around the back of the cabin—closer to twenty in front. Erika sprinted toward the back, hoping to get lost in the trees before Keith could catch up to her. Footsteps grew closer—louder. He couldn't have left the cabin more than three seconds behind her. How—?

"I'm going to tackle you unless you stop now. It'll hurt."

His voice sounded curt—angry, even—and though she knew she *should* stop, Erika couldn't bring herself to do it. The trees loomed. Just two or three more feet—a leap! Surely if she made it she could dodge him in the relative darkness.

Blinding pain followed her fall as he threw himself at her. Keith pulled her hands behind her almost before she hit the ground. In seconds, her hands were bound in front of her and he'd flipped her over on her stomach. She tried to kick, but he simply straddled her legs and inched his way down them until he had her pinned at her ankles. With swift, and much too well-practiced, movements, he pulled zip ties around each calf and looped one between them to hold them together. If she hadn't been sobbing uncontrollably, Erika might have been impressed. *Not hardly.*

A new fear arose in her as Keith stood and walked away from her. Would he just leave her there? If she walked long enough, she might find a sharp rock or something to cut the zip ties. Those thoughts dissipated as his footsteps returned. Fresh sobs wracked her body as she felt his hand brush the debris from her foot. He awkwardly shoved her shoe back on her before helping her to her feet and giving her a gentle shove toward the cabin. Erika tried to choke back her tears. *When did I lose a shoe?*

She missed his first words, but even as she struggled to gain control over her emotions—control that she grasped at as if a lifeline—the tone changed from matter of fact to gruff and stern. "—told you not to do this, and now look. You're hurt."

Stubbornness welled up in her as she realized any step toward the cabin meant compliance with her captivity. Erika stopped short, refusing to take another step. Though she didn't expect to make much difference, she was surprised when Keith hefted her over his shoulder, carried her back to the cabin without another word, and laid her on the bed.

When Keith didn't remove the zip restraints, fresh fear and grief washed over her. She imagined herself locked in the room—bound and gagged—with five-minute food and bathroom breaks. That grief intensified when he left—again, without saying anything. Erika would never have admitted it, but she hated the aloneness even more than being with her captor. Seconds passed into minutes as the realization that she couldn't go anywhere—do anything without him. She was dependent upon the very man responsible for her situation. *Revolting.*

She rolled onto her side, back to the door, and allowed the tears to roll down her cheeks, tickling them in that irritating way that tears have when we can't wipe them. A shuffle behind her told her Keith had returned. Without a word for the change in position, he carried a bowl of water, first-aid kit, and a washcloth into the room. And rolled her onto his back.

Despite the terseness and accusation in his tone, she heard it again—that split second where he sounded almost sorry. It disappeared so quickly that Erika couldn't decide if it was her imagination or if she had actually seen it. Had regret flickered in his eyes? Despair settled over her as she realized that what she had likely seen was irritation—anger prompted by her flight. *Great. He'll probably be even less likely to listen to reason.*

"I think you need stitches."

Hope did cartwheels in her heart and landed in a face plant as he pulled a familiar tube of surgical glue from the kit. The school nurse where her sister taught was an expert with that stuff. So much for a trip to the ER where she could try to escape. A new thought made her try again. "I'm allergic—"

"We know your medical history, Erika. You're not allergic to anything but walnuts and even that is mild."

"Had to try—"

He gave her a wan smile. "I know. It just won't work."

"I got out of here," she whispered to herself softly. Erika sniffled, closed her eyes, and berated herself for not being faster.

"Took you long enough."

---

Her surprise amused him. Perhaps it wasn't professional, but it had already been a long morning. The extraction had gone off without a hitch. The drive had been long, but without incident, and as the psychological profile had suggested, Erika Polowski wasn't an easy weeper.

As he prepared to deal with her wounds, Keith mentally relived the morning, reevaluating every decision— every movement that both of them made. Mark would want to know. The trip to the cabin left no questions. If an error had been made, it came after Karen left.

After breakfast, Erika sank against the wall, refusing to sit anywhere that one could deem comfortable. If things stayed the same, it would be a long assignment. The hours ticked past, until he finally brought her lunch and smiled in satisfaction as she shuffled to the bathroom—twice. Maybe she'd come around.

Her resignation discouraged him—very unhealthy. A perfectionist at his job, Keith decided to do something about it. She needed to fight for herself, or this would be an even longer ordeal than it already promised to be. He sneaked a glance in her direction and sighed. *Time for plan B.*

Keith grabbed his Bible, opened it in his lap, and read. Slowly and thoughtfully, he turned pages as he read, until at last, he let his hand fall and his eyes close. After a minute or two, he attempted a soft snore that, to his immense relief, captured her attention. *Good. What will she do?*

He listened as Erika moved her foot and forced himself to stir slightly. Agonizing minutes ticked passed as she tried to examine the room, looking for ideas for escape. He should have left the keys within reach. There were bobby pins in the bathroom. Would she try that? Fabric brushed against a wall leaving him to wonder what she was doing until he heard the sound of the drapes moving. *The hooks. Smart.*

Once Erika finally managed to secure a hook, he nearly groaned audibly. Every second passed slower than a monotonic sermon, but he waited—mentally urging her onward and forward—until he realized that she must have bent the hook. Any minute now she'd open that lock. Would she bolt out of the cabin panicked and in her bare feet, or would she be cautious? What would she do?

The shackle fell from her ankle with a soft thump. *Showtime.*

What she did next decided everything. He heard her feet shuffle quietly into the bedroom, and his rigid shoulder muscles relaxed. Just a little. At least she intended to be reasonably intelligent about it. It would keep the assignment interesting.

Several steps, a slowly opening door, and then the pause—Keith readied himself. In seconds, the chimes would ding… there they were. He jumped up as if disoriented. It took every ounce of strength not to react as though awake. He glanced around the room, bolted into the bedroom, and then dashed out the door behind her, praying all the way. He'd promised not to hurt her, but if he had to do it...

"I'm going to tackle you unless you stop now." Beneath his breath, he added, "It'll hurt."

The moment the words left his lips, Keith knew it wouldn't make any difference. She'd keep running until she dropped from exhaustion unless he took her down. As much as he resisted, he also needed to stop her immediately. With the slightest increase in speed, he jumped, tackled, and tried to soften the blow, but she leapt at the same time he jumped, striking her head against a tree. *That'll leave a gash—maybe a scar.*

This part of his job—he hated it the most. The fear in her eyes, the helplessness, the vulnerability—it was all so natural, and yet he couldn't alleviate any of it. Instead, he was the cause—in her eyes anyway. As much as he wanted to, Keith simply could not make her see that the safest place in the world for her was with him right where she was.

---

"What did you just say?" Erika's voice shook.

"Took you long enough."

"What—you were awake?" Sniffles overshadowed prior sobs for several seconds as incredulity triumphed over despair.

"Yep." He watched terror fill her as he carefully folded her shirt in flat "rolls" displaying the ugly scrapes and scratches. "I'd leave this to you, but most people can't force themselves to clean their own wounds thoroughly enough. Infection would make this little 'vacation' of yours even more unbearable." He poured a little peroxide on his cloth. "It's going to sting a bit."

"Aaah! A bit!"

"Sorry." Could she see—hear—the honesty in the words and in his expression? Did she have any idea how much he hated what she must think?

"I'd believe you if I knew who you were, why I am here, and wasn't lying uncomfortably with my hands tied behind my back!"

"Well, I'd unbind you, but I need to fix these first." Carefully he coated a double piece of gauze with a thin layer of anti-bacterial cream and taped it over the scratches. "It's a bit of overkill, but those'll drive you crazy if your shirt rubs them." As he spoke, he unfolded her shirt and tugged it gently over the bandage.

He cleaned her knees, a couple of facial scrapes, the bottom of her foot, and an elbow before he decided she was fine. He carried the bowl of water into the kitchen, replaced the first aid kit, and locked the cupboard before he returned to the room with the shackle. An attempt at a joke fell flat again. "It seems almost rude to put a chain on an injured woman…"

"Then don't," she spat out bitterly. "I won't complain."

"It's—"

"Your job. Yeah. So I've heard."

Keith locked and unlocked the shackle several times before he finally decided it was undamaged by her escape attempt and refastened it to her ankle. He ignored the horrified expression on her face as he flicked out his favorite oversized pocketknife and cut the ties around her ankles and wrist. Prepared for a physical attack, he nodded satisfied as she rolled over, face the wall, and began crying softly to herself once more.

---

Despair washed over her as Erika realized the full impact of her situation. She was alone, with a strange man, in an area so remote that they didn't feel the need to hide or gag her. They'd made it look as though she left voluntarily. So far, everything that happened seemed preplanned and carefully analyzed. No one would doubt for weeks maybe. Weeks. Could she stay alert and focused for weeks? How long would it take him to make a mistake big enough for her to capitalize on it?

Even if she did escape, she had no idea where to go. It was "not that much farther" to the gas station—and that was by car going who knew how fast or slow. That's what he'd said. How long could she evade them on foot when she had so far to go? It seemed hopeless.

On the other hand, she considered between bouts of weeping and sniffling, perhaps she could stay antagonistic for a day or two—maybe even three. Then she could slowly let him think she was relaxing and letting her guard down. He was a man, wasn't he? She'd play up her womanhood to the 'nth degree if necessary. If escape wasn't a successful option, perhaps psychology was.

Hours later, she heard his knock on the door. "What is it?"

"Stew. You hungry?"

"No. I'm not."

He grinned. "Well, if you're planning on trying to escape again, I'd recommend keeping up your strength. Starving yourself only makes my job easier." With that, he set the tray on a chair and left the room leaving the door open.

Erika glared at the bowl as if it had betrayed her. She wanted nothing more than to kick it across the room and through the window, but she'd likely succeed only in ensuring she froze at night. Even worse, he was right. If she didn't eat, her blood sugar would—that thought was a good one. If her blood sugar got too low, she usually just felt weak, and sometimes people said she acted a little drunk, but she'd heard that some people actually had seizures.

Before she could turn over and ignore the bowl, Keith's voice called out from the kitchen, "I can force juice down you if I need to. It won't work, Erika."

"Arrogant know-it-all," she muttered and reached for the bowl.

# Three

Nighttime meant she was locked in her room and shackled to the bed. As much as Erika hated it, something in the look on Keith's face made her unwilling to show it. He looked almost fierce as he waited with arms crossed outside the bathroom door while she prepared for bed. She brushed her teeth for a full three minutes, washed her face, hands, and feet and slathered lotion all over her. Just to be obnoxious, she even brushed her hair for "one hundred strokes" just like the ancient storybooks she'd read as a kid mentioned. It wasn't easy with her short spiky haircut, but the annoyance factor made it worth every single stroke.

When she could think of nothing else to drag out the inevitable, Erika opened the door and glowered at him. "You ready to chain me up in my dungeon?"

Keith jerked his thumb at her room and waited to follow. After ensuring the lock around her ankle was secure, he shortened the chain on her bedpost ensuring that she couldn't reach the window. Her plans to wake him up every hour to "use the bathroom" crashed when he carried in a bucket with a lid that opened to a toilet seat. "Just in case you wake up. I'll see you in the morning. Sleep well."

"You enjoy this job too much to be normal. My dad always said you had to be just a little crazy to be in the military or law enforcement. I never got it, but I think he's right. You're nuts."

His expression never changed. "It probably seems that way, yes."

Curiosity drove her to ask a question. She'd promised herself she wouldn't make small talk, but Erika couldn't resist. "Do you like your job?"

"I'm good at it, it helps people, and that's all I've ever wanted to do."

As sincere as his words sounded, he looked furious. Whether it was because she'd asked, or he answered, Erika couldn't be sure. She also couldn't resist another dig. "If you wanted to help people, you could have become a doctor or a teacher."

"Someone has to do the hard stuff, Erika. A doctor saves a life when they are broken by the wrath of man. I try to make his job easier or unnecessary, so he can focus on helping a kid with cancer or a guy who decided to do an impromptu finger reduction while making a fort for his kids."

Erika felt her face softening as he spoke until she remembered where she was. "By kidnapping an innocent woman. Yeah, that makes loads of sense." Frustrated, she rolled over on the bed, pulled the covers over her, and stared at the wall.

"Goodnight, Erika. Try to sleep."

All the anger, frustration, and fear welled up in her heart and spilled over into wracking sobs as she heard Keith slide the deadbolts into place—the sounds taunting her with her prisoner status. A loud crash in the kitchen startled her. At the second crash, she forced herself to staunch the flow of tears. Her throat swelled and strained as she choked back the impulse to cry. She strained to listen, but her body betrayed her, and soon she fell into a fitful sleep.

---

Dread of locking Erika in her room settled over Keith, smothering him with it. He hated this part of his job. The woman was terrified, and who could blame her? The longer she delayed in the bathroom, the tenser and more fidgety he became, until he thought he'd go crazy. That she'd decided to take her time just to annoy him, he had no doubt. A wry smile tried to make an appearance on his lips, but his angst stamped it out again. Keeping up her little games would probably keep her mentally aware and resilient.

"You ready to chain me up in my dungeon?"

Keith stamped down a wince and tried to manufacture a deadpan expression. Still, couldn't she see how much he hated having to do it? And shortening the chain? He had no choice, but it cut. Deep. If she tried to get out of the window, she could hurt herself, and Erika Polowski was just desperate enough to try it. "Sleep well." Even as he said it, his mind cringed. Right. Like that wasn't a kick while she was down.

"You enjoy your job too much to be normal."

Another piercing dig through his armor. Keith did enjoy his job, but certain aspects, like the rare time he had to protect someone against his will, weren't on his list of highlights. However, once the ordeal ended, Keith knew he'd be glad he could protect her, and he hoped she'd be able to forgive him—someday. His agency rarely employed abduction as a course of action. Some of his coworkers had been involved in similar things over the years, but Keith had only been on one other "protective abduction."

The memory of one of his earliest cases brought a smile. The man, elderly, had an irrepressible sense of humor, even when annoyed. He'd spent the four and a half weeks of involuntary sequestration working on a stand-up comedy routine, trying to get Keith to smile. He'd succeeded more often than Keith liked to admit. In the end, while still not happy about so much time chained to a cabin, Donald Bruner had been thankful to exchange a month of his life for the *rest* of his life.

"At least Donald didn't have to lie on the other side of that wall, terrified of the horrible things I might do to him," Keith muttered, furious at the necessity for keeping even the most basic information from her. She'd handle things better if she knew. She'd understand if she knew, but that was the worst of it. Erika Polowski couldn't know—not if they could help it.

All the frustration of the day and the lack of sleep the previous night welled up in Keith as he wiped out the cast-iron frying pan. He'd never learned to be as detached as he appeared, and the frustration it brought welled up inside until he snapped. With more force than he intended, Keith slammed the frying pan down on the stove.

Five seconds of silence in the bedroom told him he'd scared her. Great. As if the poor woman weren't terrified enough, he had to make it worse. He grabbed the Dutch oven from the drying rack, opened the oven door, shoved it in, and jumped when the door slammed shut with a crash that was almost as loud as his abuse of the frying pan. This time, the silence hovered over the cabin like a suffocating blanket.

Anxious to escape the stifling atmosphere, Keith grabbed the gun from the counter, double-checked the safety, and then slid it into the holster but didn't strap down the cover. The night breeze, brisk and working up to a full-blown storm, seemed to blow the angst from his heart. "Lord, she doesn't even have You to get her through this. How do people stand it?"

Mark had provided a very thorough dossier on Erika Polowski. People who had nothing to hide tended to be very open about themselves—especially in the age of electronic information. Between her blog, her Facebook page—why didn't people use their privacy settings more often?—and her posts on several message boards, he had a fair idea of her political, religious, and ideological positions on most things. Jesus was nothing more than a euphemism for "my goodness" to her. Her politics leaned strongly in the liberal camp, and she had a soft spot for lost causes. She'd fight to save the cockroach if by some miracle the things neared extinction.

A shiver washed over him. Instinctively, his eyes scanned the trees, and he patrolled the perimeter of the cabin as a precaution. Nervous, he pulled his gun from the holster and rested his thumb on the safety. A flick of the safety, a pull of the trigger... that's all it would take.

The shiver traveled down his spine once more. Was it the cold? Did he sense something? Did something enter his peripheral vision? Why the heightened awareness now? Training kicked in as he kept to the shadows and strained to see something—anything—in the shadowy darkness just a few yards from him.

Chagrin crept in on tiptoe. It was the cold, surely. They hadn't been there long enough for anyone to have a clue where to find them, but he had to be sure. His job was to protect Erika, and ignoring anything, no matter how improbable, could get her killed. At the front door, he slipped inside, holstered his gun, and ran for his night-vision binoculars. Thermal imaging was amazing stuff, especially with a blanket of fog settling in around them.

Working counter-clockwise, Keith crept from window to window—even peering through the glass blocks of the bathroom—until he was forced to decide what to do about Erika's room. If he went in, he'd scare her. If he went outside without checking things out from her room, he'd risk himself, and subsequently, her. Remembering her terrified face when he stretched the duct tape over her mouth sent him back toward the front door. He couldn't do it.

Holding the binoculars in one hand and his gun in the other, Keith crept from the house and began his sweep around the structure once more. Nothing. A glance at Erika's car reminded him that someone could hide behind a tire. If he stepped away from the cabin, he'd be even more vulnerable, but he had to check. A drawback to his job.

With another prayer for Erika's safety on his lips, Keith raced to the trunk, gun drawn, thumb resting on the safety, and took one last deep breath before he stepped around the bumper to the other side of the car. Empty. A rush of air escaped his lungs as he relaxed. All his imagination. He'd take one last sweep, just to be sure, and then get some sleep. Erika wouldn't be happy if she was forced to use the potty-bucket.

As he rounded the corner of the house, a movement near the tree line to his right sent him diving behind the propane tank. "Not exactly a comforting place to take cover, Auger," he muttered to himself as he tried to peer around it with the binoculars.

There it was again. Just a flash and then nothing. He waited. Whatever was there hid... and well. Sweat beaded on his forehead, and his heart pounded in his chest as he waited, each second passing slower than a minute to his adrenaline-riddled body. Just as he thought he'd go insane with the wait, he dropped the binoculars, holstered his gun, and marched back into the house, disgusted.

"Of all the stupid rookie things to do, that has to be the worst. I can hear it now. 'Yeah, Mark, I spent half an hour protecting her from a ferocious raccoon.'"

Keith set the gun back on the counter before replacing the binoculars back in his duffel. Erika's dossier lay tucked beneath his spare jeans and t-shirts. Grabbing it and another pair of socks, he made a cup of cocoa and prepared to relax for a few minutes to let the adrenaline settle before he tried to sleep.

Spread out on the couch, he opened the folder and stared at the photo. Like most people, Erika Polowski's driver's license photo did not flatter her. She still wore her hair in the same short, dark, spiky style—the style that had required Karen to buy a wig for the extraction—but it was much more attractive in person than on the photo before him. An attempt to avoid the mug shot-look gave her face a grimace that made her look immature and bad-tempered, and her eyes, though the license claimed they were green, looked inky black in the photo.

He pulled a small manila envelope and shook out a small stack of photos taken of her at work, the grocery store, and a local bar. Keith paused at one picture of her laughing at something a man with her said. Just from that picture, he could tell she was flirting. The dossier said no boyfriend, but the pictures were only a couple of weeks old at most. Had that changed?

Another picture, this one of her talking with an elderly customer, made him smile. As he flipped through the stack, he realized that in nearly every one, she smiled. Frustrated, he shoved the photos back in the envelope. How long would it be before she'd feel like smiling again?

Once again, his eyes scanned the list for anything he'd be able to use to make her feel more comfortable. A B.S. in Anthropology didn't give her many job opportunities, so she'd taken the job managing a popular café and had doubled the business. She was popular with the customers and played softball during the season.

Twenty-six years old, five-feet-five inches tall with perfect eyesight and two upper dental implants as a result of one of those softball games. Six months out of the year, she lived at home with her parents, presumably saving to buy her own house, and the other six months were spent house sitting for a woman who spent the winter in Australia to enjoy their summer season. She'd been in Helen Franklin's house when they took her.

He sighed. There was nothing. Erika was an avid political activist—a champion for justice for everything from trying to eradicate the death penalty in all fifty states to preserving the natural habitat of the Mojave ground squirrel in California. "Seriously, Erika? A squirrel?"

Keith snapped the folder shut and dragged himself from the couch. Shoving the dossier under his clothes again, he grabbed his toothbrush and went to brush his teeth. His nighttime "ablutions," as his grandma always called it, took a fraction of the time Erika's had. "Just like a woman. Even trying to be obnoxious, she used the bathroom to do it."

That thought made him smile again. The girl had grit—was feisty. He had to give her that. He rinsed his toothbrush, dried it, and laid it on the sink, snapping the light off as he left the room. Seconds later, he flipped the switch again, grabbed the toothbrush, and left the room again. Leaving his toothbrush for her to contaminate would be something someone like Erika could not resist.

He paused at her door, listening. Nothing—not a single sound emanated from the room. He hoped that was good. A roll away cot pulled from the closet, a pillow, and a sleeping bag made up his bed. His own yawn startled him. "Okay, Lord. Things are okay, so far. Let's just get through this first night, okay?"

# Four

Keith flew from the cot, tripping over his own feet, and grabbed his gun, swinging it in an arc as he tried to discover the source of the pounding. Relief washed over him as he realized it was just Erika. Maybe he'd been wrong. His confidence that he could protect her without needing someone to take watch while he slept almost seemed misplaced as he stumbled toward her bedroom. If someone had entered the house, he'd be dead. Erika would be dead.

After several fumbles, he opened the door and removed the cuff from Erika's impatient leg. "There you go. Sorry."

The nasty look she gave him hardly registered. Instead, his mind scrambled with a dozen thoughts at once. The agency was spread very thin. If he called for backup, someone else would be removed from an equally or more serious case. Several protective agents had volunteered to work without someone to take a night watch, and the result might be disastrous. On the other hand, it was the first night. Maybe he should give it another day or two before requesting a partner. The chances of anyone finding them in the first seventy-two hours were slim.

The bathroom door opened. "So... got food? I'm starving."

"Scrambled eggs or cereal?"

"Seriously?"

Opening the fridge, he frowned. "There's more stew, lunch meat..." A glance in the freezer added a few more options. "Frozen burritos, pizza, hamburger patties..."

"Did you think about things like salads? Vegetables? Fruit?"

He shoved a bowl of bananas, oranges, and apples across the short counter. "Eat up."

"I don't believe this!" Erika opened cupboards, fridge, freezer, and glanced around her. "I thought you said you knew everything about me." She jabbed a finger at his chest. "Well, I don't eat like this."

"Everything in this cabin has been on your grocery receipts for the past month, so don't tell me you don't eat any of this stuff." A grin tried to edge its way onto Keith's lips, but he fought back the temptation. "You'd give anything to slap me, wouldn't you?"

"It is now my most cherished dream." If her expression could be believed, it was true. "I don't think there's anything I wouldn't love more."

It was a risk, a calculated one but still a risk. Keith chose to take it. "Go ahead."

"What?"

He had to force himself to stay nonchalant when he saw Erika's stunned expression. "I'm serious. I don't hit women, so go for it." He shrugged as he watched her stare agape at him. "I just thought it might give you a bit of relief."

Erika turned in disgust, took a step and then whirled and slugged him. "If my hand didn't hurt so bad," she gasped, "I'd say that was the best feeling in the world."

As he watched her retreating form, Keith rotated his jaw. He'd have a bruise— a nasty one. For a split second, he'd been tempted to step aside. He'd agreed to a slap, not a slug, but just as he'd seen her stance and realized she intended to punch rather than slap, he knew he should just take it. His father's words echoed in his memory as he watched the door slam behind her. *Men have a duty to be the buffer that protects women from the harshness of the world.* "Well, Dad, I don't know if that's what you meant, but okay."

By the time Erika returned, Keith began spooning perfectly cooked scrambled eggs onto the plates. As he passed her a plate and a fork, Erika caught his eyes. "I'm sorry. As much as I wanted to do that, my father taught me that violence is never the answer, and I threw that away for a few seconds worth of personal satisfaction."

"I offered."

"You offered a slap, and I took advantage of it. This is the only apology you'll get from me, so you'd better accept it." A glance at the eggs made her groan. "Do we have salt? Ketchup?"

"Oh, great. A ketchup on eggs person. How did we miss that one?" Even as he spoke, Keith retrieved the bottle from the fridge and handed it to her. "Eat up. Oh, and don't even think about using that to hit me over the head. Plastic isn't effective, and it just irritates me."

---

Lunch passed, with its thrilling entrée of chips and deli sliced turkey breast sandwiches. Erika ate an orange with it, but still felt dissatisfied. "What was wrong with salad greens? Fresh vegetables?"

"They go bad quickly. We had to have things that last."

"They don't go bad," she spat, "if you actually eat them! Did Karen say she'd be back with food on Saturday?"

"Yes."

"I want food. Real food. I want fresh spinach, romaine, even *iceberg*, cabbage, carrots, celery—"

"Got it. I'll let her know."

Her brow furrowed. "That was easy."

"Look, we're not trying to make your life miserable." The stony look was back on his face. "This can't be comfortable—I know that, I do—but we'll do the best we can."

"Because you're here to protect me."

"Right."

"But you can't tell me from who or what or why?" She couldn't keep the skepticism from her voice, no matter how hard she tried.

"No, I cannot."

"And you've done this before?"

Keith nodded. "Not as much as others— I'm new in this branch—but yes, I've done it before."

"And when it was all over, what did your last prisoner—" She swallowed hard when an undecipherable look flashed in his eyes. "Okay person— whatever—what did the last one think of your 'protection?'"

"He didn't like it—"

"But you expect me to."

"But," Keith continued as if uninterrupted, "he was grateful. I believe his words were something like, 'I didn't like losing a month of my life, but I am glad to have the rest of it to make up for that.'"

"And someone was really going to hurt him?"

"Someone was really going to hurt him."

"Did he think anyone would?" She hurried to explain as Keith shook his head. "No, I mean when you first took him. Could he think of anyone who wanted to hurt him?"

"No. Like you, he had no idea of the danger he was in or why."

"And you didn't tell him why?"

Again, Keith shook his head. "No. Like you, telling him why would have, in all likelihood, put him in more danger."

"Me knowing why someone wants to hurt me is going to put me in *more* danger? That makes no sense!"

Keith grabbed an apple and jerked the stem from it with one twist. Her stomach twisted at the sight of the muscles in his forearms flexing with the movement. He could cause some serious damage if he wanted to, and she'd hit him. *What was I thinking?*

"You're right."

Erika's eyes widened as she looked up at him. "What?"

"You're right. It doesn't make sense."

Hope welled up in her and she nodded. "Just tell me. I won't be as afraid of you, where I am, and what is going on if I just understand."

"I can't." Keith's face almost looked fierce as he said it. "If it would help you, I would—even if it meant facing an inquiry at work. I'd do it. But, you're just going to have to accept that sometimes things that don't make sense happen. Telling you why will potentially—probably really—put you in further danger. I won't do it."

She watched, confused and curious, as he double-checked his gun and then grabbed his key ring. "How about a walk out in the yard?"

"I can go out there?" Her eyes lit up as her mind considered a dozen ways to trick him and escape. "Without the chain?"

"I've got the gun. I'm faster than you are. Yeah, you can go out there." Just as she stepped on to the small porch, his voice interrupted her scheming. "Erika, I know you're an intelligent woman. I know you are strong and courageous." She turned, ready to blast him, but he continued. "But you need to remember something. This is what I'm trained to do. I'm trained to anticipate what you're thinking and prevent you from doing anything that deviates from the plan."

"You're not God."

"That's for sure," he agreed. "However, I am a professional. People behave in predictable ways. I can probably give you more successful ideas for how to escape in thirty seconds than you can come up with in a month."

"I'll take any one of them."

Despite himself, Keith laughed, his sides shaking as he tried to repress it. There was something less ominous—more appealing even—about Keith when he relaxed. "You're persistent. I'll give you that."

It was too cool for sunbathing, or she might have been tempted to rip her jeans into micro-shorts and tear up a t-shirt into a tube top. It'd be a perfect time to get a tan— and annoy the guy who was supposed to be guarding her.

Instead, she decided to use the time to get a little bit of a workout, jogging back and forth across the clearing, well aware that Keith watched every move. He looked asleep as he stood leaning against the porch post, but he couldn't fool her. Either he really was as bored as he pretended, or he was too cocky for his own good.

She'd spent the past thirty-six hours going over every person she'd ever met, ever talked to, and ever had any disagreements with and found nothing that could remotely be construed as a danger. Customer after customer flitted through her mind, but even those she didn't know well enough to know what they did for a living were still too innocuous to be remotely considered a threat.

Erika had narrowed her theories down to the two she considered the most plausible. The first was the most obvious. Keith worked for the FBI and they had her mixed up with some other Erika Polowski. At first, she'd dismissed the idea when she remembered how detailed their information was about her. However, when he had mentioned her shopping habits in the last month, she decided that they'd simply found her and based their "intelligence" on her rather than the Erika Polowski they really needed to help.

The second option terrified her. Thus far, Keith had been everything he'd claimed to be. Yeah, they'd kidnapped her and dragged her out into the middle of nowhere, but even with Karen gone and no one to know, he hadn't given her a look or touched her in any way that could be considered inappropriate. She'd initially assumed that this meant she was reasonably safe from the proverbial "fate worse than death," but a new idea had been brewing that churned her stomach. Predators were sick people. If this was all just a part of a cat and mouse game....

She glanced back at the porch once more. Trying to imagine that the guy now sitting there—with an open Bible in his hands no less—was really the kind of pervert that would do something like that.... Not hardly. As she stopped jogging to watch him, he tensed. She saw the change in his posture long before he set the Bible down and strode across the grass.

"Something wrong?"

"I was just trying to decide if you're a sick perverted creep or not."

"Not."

"That's your opinion." A tiny part of her felt a twinge of remorse at the venom she spewed, but it didn't last. Regardless of why he did it—altruistic or grotesque—the guy was a kidnapper and held her against her will. That constituted a crime—in all fifty states and probably nearly every country in the world.

His phone rang. After staring at it for two more rings, he finally turned from her and answered. "'sup, Karen?"

Every instinct told her to take the distraction as an opportunity to flee. She glanced around her, looking for the thickest area of trees, but as her eyes passed over him, she saw his head shake. Covering the phone, he called, "It won't work, Erika."

Even though unable to hear, she knew he was telling Karen about her attempts to escape. Well, if she couldn't get away, and Erika was sure he was too alert to let that happen yet, she'd try to listen in on his conversation. Any information was better than none.

Feigning irritation, Erika stormed to the porch and dropped to the steps, crossing her arms over her chest and leaning against her knees. When she heard Keith mention her "tantrum," she nearly came unglued. However, she couldn't hear the conversation if she ranted at him, so with every ounce of self-control she could muster, Erika tossed him a dirty look *without* the string of expletives that she so desperately wanted to spew.

"Did you locate that target?" Keith rolled his eyes at the blatant interest she showed at the word target. "I haven't heard from Mark. I don't think he planned to contact me."

Was Mark the target? The only Mark Erika could remember was an employee who had quit when he transferred to Texas A&M. The kid was an accounting whiz but completely harmless. Surely, they didn't mean him!

"Erika thinks she knows who either the target or Mark is. I can't tell which."

"I'm surprised you'll admit that there's something you don't know."

Another grin split his face, and he chuckled. "Apparently, I come off as an insufferable know-it-all." His laughter increased. Covering the phone, Keith said, "Karen says she's going to start calling me Hermione."

Erika rolled her eyes. "I think I'd like Karen if she wasn't in on this plot to ruin my life and get me fired."

"You won't be fired."

"I—"

Keith shook his head firmly. "Your job will be there when you get back."

Those words filled her with fresh interest. If he told the truth, then that had to mean her FBI theory was most likely correct. Only the government could pull those kinds of strings. She couldn't imagine anyone else having the clout to make something like that happen.

"Either way, I'm going to lose a few paychecks, and Helen is going to be livid that there's no one there to make the house look lived in."

"We're taking care of it all," he assured her, before returning to his conversation. "She's worried about the bills now," Keith relayed to his co-conspirator.

The phone call lasted another five minutes, but she heard nothing useful after the comments about a target and "Mark." Once he pocketed the phone, Erika turned to him. "You have the wrong Erika Polowski. I think that's the real problem here. I get that you're supposed to protect an Erika Polowski, but you got the wrong one. Just tell your other FBI agents to find the right one and do some research. You'll see."

"FBI." Keith picked up his Bible again, turning the page. "Donald thought US Marshalls. Now FBI. Cool."

# Five

"We'll call when you get here. It'll be fine. Don't forget her produce."

Erika waved her arms to get his attention. "Games, books, anything. I'm bored stiff. I think I could play Solitaire for hours!"

"Apparently, I'm not an interesting companion, and she wants something to occupy her time. Bring badminton."

"Croquet?" The studied air of innocence didn't work, and she knew it.

"I am also, obviously, quite stupid. She thinks I'll request a croquet set so she can bash my head in while I'm trying to pop the ball through a wicket or four." He nodded a few times and then slid his phone shut. "She'll bring stuff. We had to come get you earlier than expected, so there was no time—"

"Whatever."

Keith wandered across the room and sat on his heels, waiting for her eyes to meet his. "She's been texting your parents. They're not worried about you at all. As far as you're concerned, the pressure at work just got too bad so you asked a friend to come stay at your house, and you went on an impromptu road trip."

"In my car? They believed that?"

"Karen can be very convincing. It's a perfect cover story, because if you are delayed, we have a reasonable excuse." Keith stood and moved to his favorite chair. It looked miserably uncomfortable to her, but he always sat in the wood rocker as if it was his dream chair.

"And I can call today?"

"We'll see. We'll either call for you and let you listen to the conversation, or we'll let you call. It all depends on how cooperative we think we can trust you to be."

"I'll do anything—"

"I'll bet." He shook his head. "Sorry, Erika, but Karen is the determiner. Basically, if you want to talk yourself, you're going to have to convince her that you don't plan to do anything to make them doubt the story they've been given."

"Come on, do you really think that any reasonably intelligent normal person wouldn't? Give me a break! I'm a captive in a cabin with a strange man! I'm gonna try to get help if I think I can. Even if they only get enough information to know that the texts are lies, they'll go to the police for help." She knew she was throwing away her chances, but Erika was too keyed up to care. "Do you really think I'm that stupid?"

"Erika, think about it. What happens if you do let them know somehow that something is wrong? Now they're worried and waste police resources trying to help you when you're already as safe as human beings can make you. If we hadn't taken you, you'd be dead right now. As it is, you can let your parents worry and fret or you can truthfully let them believe you're perfectly safe. You're actually safer here than the average single woman driving around the countryside in a car that has seen much, much better days."

"Just leave me alone."

"Happy to oblige." The curtness of his tone surprised her. Though he often looked like he lived with perpetual anger management issues, he usually sounded pleasant enough. Sometimes he annoyed her by sounding amused by her, but that was the worst of it. Curt was a new one.

"Hey, when is she going to be here?"

"She's on her way to get the stuff on your list and then she'll come. So probably by dinner." He glanced down at his Bible. "I didn't even offer. If you want to read—"

"No." Guilt washed over her as she realized how ungracious she sounded. "Sorry, I'm just not interested."

"I didn't think so, but I had to offer."

The anger—it felt like it would kill her from the inside out. She'd begun to see how things like the Stockholm Syndrome developed. After a week of nearly constant angst, she was emotionally exhausted. Erika wanted nothing more than to call a truce but had determined not to capitulate.

Realistically, she knew eventually she'd have to exchange anger for a less demanding emotion.

"How long was Donald the old guy angry?"

"I'm not sure. He spent the whole time creating a stand-up comic routine, and I think that masked his true emotions. Looking back, I think it was his way of ensuring that we couldn't quite tell his state of mind."

"The whole time? As in from day one?" Erika didn't even try to hide her skepticism.

"Once we reached the cottage, he took a shower, came out freshly shaved, and said, 'When I get out of here, I'm going to invent dryer sheets for the body.' I asked if there was something wrong with his towel and he frowned at me and said, 'You're supposed to ask why.'"

Erika hated herself for it, but she couldn't resist asking, "Well, did you?"

"Yep. He said, 'So people my age can get clean *and* wrinkle free.'"

A snicker escaped before she could prevent it. No, it wasn't hysterical, but it wasn't bad for an old guy who had just been taken hostage by strangers. "Did they get better?"

"Much. I had a hard time keeping a straight face."

"I bet he would have enjoyed it if you'd just relaxed and been a cool guy rather than a warden. Older people usually are really cool with great stories about when they were younger, and not very many people like to listen anymore."

"Who said I didn't?"

"I know what you're like. I've been here for a week with you. You look like the pictures I've seen of Hitler's prison camp guards—all stone-faced and harsh." She shook her head. "The guy probably couldn't stand the stress of being around someone so negative for so long."

"He told the joke three hours after our meeting. I wouldn't call that too stressful, and yeah, I tried not to laugh. He liked feeling like he got one over on me. Sue me for giving the guy something to look forward to." Keith jerked his head at the shackle. "Clamp that around your ankle. I've got to go check something outside."

Stunned, she stood in the doorway, one ankle attached to the chain and watched as he scoped out the trees. At one

39

point, he glanced back at her and frowned. She watched as he jogged back to where she stood, double-checked the ankle cuff, the place where it was mounted to the wall, and then stood. "I'll be back in five minutes. Don't do anything stupid. Just—just don't."

The moment he disappeared into the trees, Erika raced for the curtains. She could do this. How he'd been so stupid, she didn't know, but she had every intention of getting out of there the minute she could. Even as she fumbled with the hook, her eyes darted around the cabin, looking for the keys to her car. She could afford to hit him with it if she had half a chance. With Karen coming, even if he was hurt, he'd get help.

She watched through the window as she fumbled with the lock until finally the shackle fell from her ankle. He was still gone. There was no sign of Keith anywhere. Excited, she fumbled around the counter, in the drawers, in his duffel, nearly coming unglued when she found the dossier, and then gave up. She'd have to skip the idea of the car. Grabbing her jacket, Erika tied it around her waist, stuffed the pockets with fruit, grabbed a couple of water bottles from the fridge, and peeked out the door. Still no sign.

For a moment, she wondered if it was a test—of what, she couldn't guess. The idea that anyone wouldn't try to leave if given half a chance was ridiculous. She had to go. The choice came down to now or never. Remembering her last attempt, this time she crawled along the floor, barely raising her head, in an attempt to avoid the incessant ding of the alarm. Who knew how good his hearing was? It worked. As she stood, she glanced around the cabin and relaxed—confident that he hadn't seen her.

She hurried to the back of the cabin, took a deep breath, and then dashed for the trees. She'd go about twenty yards in and then start walking in a wide circle to get back to the road. It was impossible to walk in plain sight but sticking to the road should get her to some kind of civilization at some point.

A twig snapped, causing her to jump. Erika's eyes darted around her, panicked that somehow, she'd either been followed already, as unlikely as that seemed, or that some animal was wandering too close to their cabin. Fury overtook her as she realized the plural possessive of the idea of "their" cabin. She'd fallen prey to the idea that she was a part of this mess. It was just wrong!

The temptation to climb a tree and wait until dark nearly overwhelmed her. She tried to imagine getting high enough not to be seen and without her stupid Crocs slipping off and shook her head. Not likely. Staying put would be a better choice. Keith would have to comb every inch of the woods to find her. Surely, the odds were slimmer of that than her making it to the top of a tree.

For the next two hours, she kept moving, pausing every few minutes to listen before pressing onward. Her plan to retrace her steps back to the road backfired as she found herself walking in circles, one that took her too close to the cabin for comfort. After dark. She'd try hard to find the road but not until after dark. Each rustle of leaves, cry of a bird, or crunch along the ground sent her heart racing, but Erika refused to quit. The all-knowing and arrogant Keith Auger had made a serious mistake, and the chances of that happening again were highly unlikely. She needed to capitalize on it now.

Night fell much more quickly in the forest than it did in town. It seemed as if she'd been walking for hours and that she'd just escaped—simultaneously. What that meant, she didn't know. Was the darkness due to another storm coming? Was it a sign that time passed much more quickly than she'd realized? A sound, one definitely man-made froze her in her tracks. With every ounce of will left in her, she forced herself to hide behind a tree, nearly praying that whatever was coming would come from behind rather than in front of her.

With each second, it grew louder until Erika was ready to cry. It had to be them. They'd found her. The noise was that crazy van; she was sure of it. Just as she was ready to risk losing a shoe to climb the tree, the noise became quieter. It seemed as if the vehicle was going away again. Understanding followed a relieved sigh. She had found the road. Perhaps if she got close enough, she'd be able to see how close sunset really was.

Stumbling almost frantically, though she knew it was foolish, Erika finally reached the edge of the trees. Sundown would be there soon. That meant Karen had probably arrived already. Now two people, from two different directions, could be a part of the search for her. Would they call in reinforcements? How many people could they get up there and how quickly? Should she risk hitchhiking? The idea revolted her, but so did going back to that cabin.

Erika winced at the look she could almost see in Keith's eyes. He'd gloat. It wouldn't matter that she'd gotten away, he'd gloat that he forced her back, and this time, they'd remove anything that she could use to open the locks. They'd probably go with a combination or something. What had been a horrible week would stretch into an even more terrible month—or more.

She needed to get out of there fast. Hitchhiking might be her only option. She'd have to take her chances. Once she was home— Realization struck like a Mac truck. She couldn't go home. If she went home, they'd find her. If she went to her parents' house, they'd be there. They knew her friends, her family, and probably were monitoring her accounts already. The minute she took out a penny, used a card, anything, they'd find her.

Torn, she waited just inside the tree line as she watched the occasional car drive by. It grew dark, and still she watched, deliberating between staying on the run, a prisoner of circumstance but free or going back and enduring whatever was left of this incarceration. Both seemed like impossible choices. The only way to stay out of their hands was to keep moving. She couldn't do it without money, and to contact anyone for it meant they'd find her.

The idea of going to the police with her story flopped once she realized that Keith and Karen would still find her once she was out of the police station. Even if the police considered it serious enough to protect her, she'd end up in "protective custody" and it'd be the same thing that she already had. Sure, it'd be voluntary, but a prisoner is a prisoner when you get to the root of it.

Each moment that passed intensified the inner torture. To go or to stay—that became the real question. She just couldn't ask it—no one around to answer. Illogically, she tried to imagine what Keith would do. The guy was trained in the kind of scenarios she faced, so how would he handle it? Her problem—she didn't know.

As she polished off another of her water bottles, Erika frowned. She'd taken three bottles. Two were gone. Her brilliant idea of staying hydrated while walking would fail—unless she found more water. One bottle wouldn't last long. She glanced up and down the highway. Which way was back to the cabin anyway?

"That's it," she muttered to herself. "I'm picking a direction. If I see the entrance to the cabin, I'll go back. If not, I'll figure it out when I get to wherever I end up."

Approximately a mile down the road, she found the turnoff to the cabin. If you didn't know where it was, it'd be hard to see. Located on a curve, either direction would miss the slight parting of trees and grassy drive unless they looked at those exact few feet. Disappointed, Erika turned in.

Shoulders slumped, she dragged her feet up the long drive to the cabin, dread increasing with each step, and tried not to imagine the fierce look on Keith's face when she returned. The only thing worse than his obvious irritation would be the gloating. Oh, how she hated the idea of that gloating.

Karen stepped from the shadows as her foot reached the front step. "Are you okay?"

Erika jumped, a squeal escaping her before she could stop it. "Yeah."

"If it makes you feel any better, I'd have done the same thing."

"It doesn't."

The woman pushed the door open to the cabin and returned seconds later with a cold bottle of water. "Drink up. You might want a bath too. You're going to be sore."

"You might as well call Keith and let him know I'm back. There's no reason to keep him out looking anymore."

"He's not looking."

Her head snapped up at Karen's words. "He's not?"

Compassion, pity, or something equally ambiguous and distasteful flooded Karen's eyes. She pointed toward the trees and shook her head. "No. He's there."

Turning, Erika saw Keith. He strolled silently across the small clearing wearing camouflage and with filthy hands and face. Pulling out his phone, he punched some keys, causing Karen's to vibrate. She read the screen and then passed it to Erika.

SHE ALMOST CAUGHT ME AT LEAST FIVE TIMES.

# Six

"Go take a shower, get cleaned up, and then we'll call your parents."

"I guess," Erika said with a despondency she couldn't hope to hide, "this means that I get my mouth duct taped again. Can you give me time to suck in my lips so they don't lose another layer of skin?"

"You can call. We'll go over what to say and how to do it when you get out of the bathroom. Take a long hot bath. I'll go make dinner. I've got the stuff for a great salad in there." Karen smiled at her—the opposite of Keith in every way.

"You okay, Erika?" Keith's voice over her shoulder, despite hearing his footsteps as he approached, still startled her.

"I'm fine."

"I didn't scare you?"

"Probably—I just didn't know it was you if you did." She glanced back at him. "Why did you let me go? Why stalk me like that?"

"We had to test you, but we also had to protect you, Erika." Gently, Karen pushed Erika inside. "You passed the test."

"I didn't," Erika admitted. "Not really. I only came back because I realized that you'd just find me and take me away again."

"That's good enough. Just—" Karen's phone rang, and she turned away to answer. "Stenano here. Yeah, she made it back. We'll call after dinner. Mmm hmm."

"Go on in, Erika. Just relax in the tub until you can't stand to be in there anymore." Keith's voice sounded almost compassionate. "You did really well. You made smart decisions before and after you left and didn't let your emotions drive your decisions. You did great."

"I did, though." As if unable to handle a gentler Keith, Erika struggled to fight back tears. "I was at the road and looked both ways. I decided to pick a direction and if I saw the opening to get to the cabin, I'd go back. Otherwise, I'd walk to civilization and figure out how to keep hiding out when I got there."

Her eyes widened. Panic set in before despair. "Oh, no!"

"What."

"I shouldn't have told you that."

"Why not? Keith was visibly confused.

"She's letting me talk to my parents because I came back. I 'passed the test,' but now she won't. Now she'll—"

"Take a bath. You'll talk to them later."

With tears streaming down her face, Erika shuffled into the house, grabbed her duffel bag, and carried it into the bathroom. She cranked the water on full-blast, and then began undressing. Just as her foot hit the water, she realized she hadn't locked the door for the first time in the longest week of her life. Tracking water across the bathroom, she hurried to lock it and then returned to sink into the water. Before long, the scent of broiling beef drifted into the room, making her stomach growl. "I think Saturdays are officially my new favorite day of the week," she murmured, trying not to fall asleep in the water.

---

"I didn't ask if Christians were a bad example of what Jesus taught. I asked if what Jesus taught makes sense."

"And my point," Karen countered, not even raising her eyes to acknowledge Erika's return from her bath, "is that if his teachings were so wonderful, people would actually do it right. If a political party spouts high-sounding ideals but produces garbage, people quit voting for their candidates. The same is true of Christianity."

"Apples and oranges."

"That's a copout. Jesus taught forgiveness, but His followers don't forgive. So, His grand ideas about forgiveness are untried."

"So, you've never met a true Christian who lived what they claimed to believe."

"Other than you, no."

Keith's head snapped up as Erika snorted. "Yeah, because we all know Jesus taught his people to kidnap people from their beds and hold them hostage in the middle of nowhere."

"He taught to take care of others, protect them, and do what we would want others to do for us. If I was in your position, I'd want someone to protect me, however they knew how, if it would save my life."

Her eyes rolled as she turned to Karen for support. "Yeah. Like we believe that."

"He means it, Erika. I agree with him there. When you've seen the other side of the coin, when you've walked into a house too late and seen people's bodies ripped apart by bullets and watched their families try to cope with that loss—" Karen swallowed hard. "Yeah, you learn that sometimes the uncomfortable ways are the best."

"Until you've walked a mile in my shoes, don't tell me—"

Karen dropped the knife she was using to slice cucumbers and turned to leave. Keith, ignoring the confusion on Erika's face, tried to stop her, "Karen, are—"

"Let me go, Auger."

Sadness filled Keith's heart as he turned back to Erika. "She's walked that mile, and then another. She knows firsthand just what those bodies look like. Her father was one man the agency didn't get to in time, so be careful when you shoot off your little proverbs."

"I—"

Had the knife in Karen's soul not pierced her so deeply, he might have felt a sense of satisfaction in the shock on her face. He took a few steps toward the door and turned back. "When she comes back, don't bring it up. If she wants to talk about it, she'll say something."

Stepping out onto the porch, Keith found Karen gripping the railing. "You'd think," she ground between clenched teeth, "you'd get used to it, but you don't. You just don't. Every single time someone makes a snarky comment about how I don't know what they're going through, I see black and want to wrap my hands around their throats and scream, 'You don't know how lucky you are! Just be grateful and shut the—'"

"I know." He knew it was rude, but Keith's deep revulsion for women and any hint of foul language overrode his conversational etiquette. Even the milder words that many of his Christian friends used bothered him and, when spoken by a woman, revolted him. He tried to keep his opinions to himself, but he couldn't help but try to stop it before it happened. "I should have guessed she'd be one of the ones. She's feisty. It's keeping her sane, but it also means some pretty sharp barbs."

"I gotta get in there and get that salad made. We need to prep her for the call. Hey!" Karen's eyes grew wide. "We left her alone in there with the knife."

Keith shook his head. "It'll be fine. She's not going to use it. Not now."

"You're always so confident. Aren't you ever wrong?"

"Yes."

Ignoring his confession, Karen flattened herself next to the doorway, hand on her gun, looking through the screen to see if Erika had taken the knife, but it lay on the cutting board where she'd left it. "Dang! You're right. She didn't."

Keith laughed. "Dang?"

"I know how much you like your words sanitized. I tend to forget, but I know."

"He likes his words what?" Erika frowned, obviously trying to follow the conversation.

"Keith doesn't 'do' swearing. You should hear him sing 'Bad, Bad, Leroy Brown.'"

Disbelief flooded Erika's face. "Don't tell me he sings, '...the whole *dang* town.'"

"Nope. He just hums loudly there."

"I'm right here!" he protested, glaring through his grin at the women.

"He just doesn't do furious well with a smile on his face, does he?" Karen picked up the knife and waved it. "Do you want tomatoes? Keith doesn't touch 'em."

"Love tomatoes," Erika agreed. "And yeah, I didn't know he could smile. I was starting to wonder if I shouldn't take up stand-up comedy."

"You told her about Mr. Bruner?"

He flushed. It wasn't customary to talk about other cases with those under their protection, but it had seemed important. "I thought—" Shrugging, Keith popped a slice of cucumber in his mouth and then mumbled around it, "It just came up."

"Okay, let's prep her for the call while we finish up." Karen pulled steaks from the oven where she'd put them to keep warm. "Medium, rare, or well?" The question was directed at Erika. Keith prayed she said well.

"Well."

"Yes!" Grabbing a fork, he stabbed the well-done steak, popped it on a plate, and passed it across the counter. "Can we give her a steak knife? I really hate having to cut people's meat into bite-sized pieces as if they're five years old."

Karen passed a steak across the breakfast bar and jerked her thumb at the table. "There's a table, Auger. Use it." Once seated, she spoke again. "Okay, we need to prep her for the call."

Inwardly, Keith groaned. Erika wouldn't like it, and he knew it. Turning to her, praying feverishly that she'd be cooperative, he said, "Just try to keep an open mind about it, okay?"

"Why? What's going to happen?"

"Well," Karen was in her element. Prepping people for contact was a particular talent of hers that others, Keith being at the top of the list, found horribly difficult. "You see, it's a controlled conversation, but you can't let it seem like one. That takes some acting skills, and not everyone has those."

"I can act. I did Community Theater right after I got out of college."

"Good. I was hoping that'd come in handy—but if I remember correctly, you were on the props committee." She winked before continuing. "So, there are three things you need to know." Karen popped a bite of steak in her mouth and sighed happily. "It didn't get overdone. Whew."

"What three things do I need to know?"

The way Erika inhaled her salad told Keith that fresh greens were essential. As much as it seemed like a pain, they really needed to make it a priority. A pointed glance at Karen and her nearly imperceptible nod told him she'd noticed and agreed.

"Well, first, you have to prepare yourself to lie. It's highly probable that someone will ask you something that you can't answer."

Erika frowned and then nodded. "Oh, right, like if they ask if I'm in the mountains, I need to say that I went to the lake or something."

"Actually, no. You mention the mountains as where you were, but you're headed to the lake now or something."

"Why say it at all? It seems like asking for trouble." The skepticism in her tone frustrated Keith. It was as if Erika couldn't stand not to question and push everything.

"Because," Karen explained patiently, "and this is point two, you need to try to tell as much truth as possible without giving anything away. You make things less complicated and more believable when you stick to the facts as much as possible. Basically, you're going to embellish truth rather than avoid or change it."

"Okay, so first, be ready to lie. Second tell all the truth I can without giving us away. Got it. What's the third?"

"Change the subject without it being obvious you did."

Erika's eyes rolled. "And just how do I do that?"

"Okay, for example, if your mom asks where you're going next, be frank and say something like, 'Well, I'm not sure, but I thought about seeing if the car would make it to Nashville and places around there. Where would you go if you were me?' Change that subject in a related vein and then slowly move it to something totally different like a movie you supposedly saw and then comment on how you don't miss celebrity gossip. Anything to get the subject away but not so fast that it's noticeable."

"That's insane!"

"It's the natural flow of conversations. I'm going to have a pen and paper here ready to give you ways to change it up, so you're not going to be alone in this."

Disappointment flooded her features as Erika shook her head. To Keith's surprise, she refused to call. "You'll have to do it. I can't do that. Maybe if I listen, I'll feel more comfortable, but this just won't work for me."

Keith and Karen's eyes met across the table, concern etched in hers, suspicion in his. After waiting all week for the chance to talk to her family, it didn't make sense that she'd be unwilling to try. Just as he was going to question her, she added, "Besides, any voice changes might be noticeable. At least if Karen talks it'll sound like it has been. She sounds nothing like me anyway. They might notice the difference."

"There's more to it than that, Erika. I can see it in your face." He sounded accusatory and he knew it, but Keith didn't care. Something was not right.

"I don't know how to be someone I'm not. That's what you're telling me to do, and I don't want to. Just hearing that my family is okay is enough for now. Maybe next week."

"She's hitting phase two faster than I expected." Karen leaned across the table as she spoke. "Don't give up fighting. You have to keep fighting."

"I'm tired! It's exhausting. I'm angry that this is happening, I'm angry that I escaped and then really didn't, and I'm livid that I'm stuck in a cabin with the biggest hypocrite on the planet. It's wearing me out."

Pain registered in Keith's eyes just long enough for Karen to see before he shut down again. He knew it the minute she asked, "Why do you say he's a hypocrite? I don't agree with his religious views, but I've never seen him claim to believe something he doesn't at least try to practice."

"The Ten Commandments. Whatever happened to 'thou shalt not lie?' He's practically ordering me to lie. There's one."

Keith shook his head. "The Ten Commandments do not say, 'thou shalt not lie.' It says not to 'bear false witness.' We're not to perjure ourselves in court. I think the point is not to do it to someone's detriment since we're told not to 'take the Lord's name in vain' and that also has connotations of swearing in court on the Lord's name."

"So, lying is just okay for a Christian? I don't think so."

Again, he shook his head. "Well, I don't know about that, but I do know that it wasn't condemned when done to protect others."

"Name once." Erika's disgust grew visibly with each refutation.

"Rahab. She brought in the spies, hid them, and when told to tell where they were, she lied and sent the king's men to the wrong place. The Bible only commends her for saving the spies. It never condemns them, and people like Corrie ten Boom lied about having Jews hidden during WWII to protect them from the Nazis. It was a lie, but it was done for the protection of others. I don't think God was in heaven, shaking His finger and saying, 'tsk, tsk.'"

"Argh! That's what I can't stand about you people. You've got glib answers for every objection. Do they brainwash you until you can spin your verses like that in your sleep?"

He could see that she wanted to rattle him and almost felt badly that she would be so disappointed. Rejection of Jesus wounded him, but derision of his faith hardly registered. Christianity wasn't about him. If people couldn't see that, well, they'd be disappointed if they thought they'd use it as a weapon against him. "You'd think so, wouldn't you?"

"I never get you, but," she pushed her plate away, "I just think it's a wasted discussion. You don't think you're a hypocrite. I do. We don't agree on much else, so why would we on that?" She turned to Karen and nodded to the phone on the counter. "I'll be over there listening."

It took every ounce of Keith's self-control not to try to comfort Erika. He watched, almost tortured by the pain in her eyes, the way she buried her face in her pillow when sobs wracked her body at something her mother said, and then the stoic—nearly numb—look on her face as the call disconnected. Without a word, she stood and strode into her room, shutting the door behind her.

Although he knew the answer, Keith couldn't help but ask, "Do I *have* to lock her in tonight?"

"You know you do."

Sighing, he nodded. "I know."

"How close are we to nailing him?"

"Not close enough. He has too many men searching for her. Even if we managed to get him, there's no guarantee that'd end it. We have to get them all, one at a time, as usual."

---

Erika listened to the voices on the other side of the wall. So, he didn't want to lock her in anymore. That surprised her. She was also intrigued to discover that Karen seemed to have seniority over him. Though her mind wanted to replay the conversation with her mother, she kept listening. Who was he? Why did Karen talk like there was more than one person after her?

Just as she was tempted to open the door and demand to know what they were talking about, she heard Keith say, "Careful. She's listening, I'm sure."

How did he do that? How was he always right on top of whatever she planned? Yeah, he was a professional; she'd give him that, but even professionals don't know everything. Karen's next words stunned her.

"I'll come back Wednesday if I can. I might be within forty miles or so. If I am, I'll bring more produce. Also, find out what kind of movies she likes. I just brought the three recent releases."

"What are they?" That was interesting. Keith didn't sound interested.

"*Back to Romance, Cry of the Heart,* and *The Girl Who Cried Sheep.*"

Erika snickered despite herself, and then choked back guffaws as he groaned. "Romantic drama, romantic comedy, and a politically correct cartoon. Great."

# SEVEN

Sunday morning, Karen let Erika out of her room. "Shh. He's still sleeping."

"Why—"

"He's tired. We're used to having someone to split day and night watch with. He's not used to being 'on call' even when he's sleeping."

Erika shook her head as if trying to clear it. "Why don't you have someone here then? Why aren't you staying? Oh, wait. You were going to leave last night. You are staying. Duh."

Karen waited until Erika left the bathroom and shuffled into the kitchen for a glass of juice, and then said, "I'm not staying, Erika. I might be back Wednesday, I don't know, but I had to let him sleep last night." The woman poured a bowl of cereal as she spoke. "Want some?"

"Why not have someone to help him then?"

"We're shorthanded. There's a lot going on right now."

"You'd think an organization like the FBI could pull people from offices or something!"

An enigmatic smile spread across Karen's face. "We're not FBI, Erika."

"What are you?"

"I can't say, but we're here to protect you. That's all I am allowed to tell you."

Understanding dawned. "NSA! Wow. You so have the wrong person. You really need to do a search for other Erika Polowskis. Find the right one before someone gets hurt." As Karen began to protest, Erika nodded understandingly. "I know; you're not NSA. They're never allowed to admit it."

Karen gulped down the last of her coffee and set it in the sink of dishwater before she turned back to their "guest." She waited for Erika to meet her gaze before she forced every ounce of seriousness into her features and tone as she said, "Listen, Erika; we have the right person. I can't tell you how I know that you're the right one, but you are. There is absolutely zero chance that we've made a mistake. It has happened before—we're not perfect—but this time, there is no doubt. You really need to trust us on this."

"It just doesn't make sense!"

"Violence never makes sense, but it happens." She looked toward the door where Keith slept, in a comfortable bed, for the first time since their arrival. "Look, I know this is miserable. I know it's confusing and you feel like everything is being stripped from you. I know you're scared and the last thing you want is to be stuck here with a strange guy, but go easy on him. He's the best at what he does. He gave up the chance at a lot more money to work for the Secret Service to work with us because he believes in what we do."

"He's so grumpy!" Her confusion must have shown, because Erika protested, "Seriously? Have you not seen him? He practically bites my head off, scowls at everything, and I swear all he wants to do is lock me in a closet, feeding me bread and water, until this is over. Why can't he just be nice?"

"Don't know. I've never heard anyone complain about him, but maybe that's because he's usually on Jerry's watch. I get brought in with a woman. Normally, we don't leave a man alone with a woman like this, but—"

"You're stretched thin."

"And we needed a guy with military experience. We needed the best, so we got Keith."

"I got the best? What did I do that rated me the best?"

"You got in the wrong place at the wrong time and got a price put on your head." Karen began packing her things in her duffel bag as she spoke. "It's part of the process."

"Wow."

"Look," Karen began in a much more business-like tone. "I don't expect you to understand this or even to like it, but the fact is, you're here and you're not going anywhere until we know you're safe, so you can be miserable about it or you can try to relax and commune with nature or something—anything. Just don't make his job any harder than it already is."

---

"If I came back, why the locked door, the gun, shackles, and stuff? Why can't we just exist without the prisoner-slash-guard scenario?" She slapped down a card and drew from the discard pile.

"Sorry, Erika. It's just how things are done. People could easily pretend to cooperate. That puts everyone in danger. We just follow protocol, and everyone is safe—" he grimaced, "if not completely comfortable."

"So even your comedian had to be locked up? A little old man?"

Keith took her discard and dumped one of his own. "Yep. And this 'little old man' had biceps that most American men would kill for."

"Not you."

He froze mid play. "What?"

"Not you. Your biceps have biceps."

Unsuccessful at stifling his snicker, Keith played his last cards. "Add up the points." Smiling to himself, Keith added, "Thanks."

"It was an observation, not a compliment."

"In this case, it works out to the same thing."

"So, I take it Mr. Hilarity was a lot easier to handle than me, eh?" She knew her voice betrayed insecurity, but Erika couldn't help but ask.

"In some ways, yes. I mean, he was fit for an old guy, but he was still old. I had to be careful of his medications, and the elderly just don't have the stamina of a younger person, so in those respects, you're much easier."

"I have the whole blood sugar thing, but I'm reasonably fit."

Laughing, Keith collected the cards and began shuffling. "I'd say you're fit. You gave me a decent workout on Saturday."

"What's the worst part of me?" At the exaggerated look of horror on his face, Erika laughed. "No, really. I want to know."

"You're a woman."

"Gee, I didn't know that was a crime."

His attempt to smile failed. "Seriously, it's an issue. At least Mr. Bruner was a man—an elderly one at that. I knew he wasn't on the other side of the wall, terrified of the horrible things I might do to him."

For a moment, she softened. Despite her mistrust of Keith, she had become confident that he wouldn't attack her. She started to say so, but knew it was too early. She needed to remain outwardly antagonistic whenever she could—just in case. "Yeah, well, I don't have that luxury."

The second her words were spoken, she regretted them. Despite his attempt to hide it, Keith's eyes registered shock and then pain. "You'll have to take my word for it, Erika. I couldn't—" He sighed. "I just couldn't."

His cell phone rang before Erika could respond. His hello was cut off by a firm order, "Get out of there. *Now.*"

Erika could hear Karen's voice from across the room. Her eyes grew wide with panic as Keith shoved the phone back in his pocket and raced for her room. All curiosity as to why he kept their clothes in the duffel bags evaporated as he threw the few things left around the room and bathroom in her bag and zipped it shut, racing to the car with it. In the space of time it took her to process that Karen's call meant danger—to them or her she wasn't sure—Keith dumped his clothes, the first aid kit, his Bible, and a huge sweep of food into the trunk of the car.

"Need the bathroom?"

"No, just went." Erika grew fearful. Keith knew every move she made. She'd joked to herself that he probably knew when she needed to relieve herself before she did.

"Right. Okay. I've got to put those cuffs on you for a minute."

The words didn't scare her nearly as much as the hesitation. Her normally confident captor seemed flustered and uncertain, making her wonder what kind of danger he—she— they might be in. "Are we okay?"

He snapped the cuffs on her and sat her in the chair. She'd expected roughness, but in his haste, he was just as gentle as ever. "I'm so sorry, Erika. I'm going to have to drug you."

"Drug me! What kind of drug?"

The stern Keith returned. "Heroin."

"What!"

"I need to be able to have a reason that there is a woman passed out on my seat. I have to have a reason you might tell an officer that I kidnapped you."

Bile filled her throat, and she shook as he brought a syringe near her arm. "I hate needles. Please! I won't tell. I promise."

---

"Trust me; I don't want to do this." Even as he spoke, Keith held her arm immobile with one hand and injected the heroin with the other. In an unprecedented move, he smoothed her hair away from her face, wiped her expectorate from his face, and waited for the drug to take effect.

In less than a minute, her skin grew slightly flushed, and he saw the glassy look of euphoria cover her eyes. Feeling like a failure, he unlocked the handcuffs and led her to the car, tossing a pillow in before he urged her into the back seat. "Let's go, Erika. I've got to get you out of here."

She didn't respond. He could see the terror intensified in her eyes. Fear, confusion, and growing cotton-brained effects of heroin mocked him from her eyes, and it tore at his heart. Keith hated this part of his job. It didn't happen often, but when it did, he inevitably felt like a failure. His job was to protect his people, not create more fear in them than they already felt.

Without a second glance at the cabin, he bounced through the trees as fast as he dared push the car and breathed easy again once he saw the highway. He only needed ten miles to feel confident. A glance at the back seat in the rearview mirror told him he'd made the right choice.

He'd have to admit to Allison that she'd been right. You did need to know the intricate details of a person's life—even every drug she'd ever taken—in order to effectively protect her. According to her file, all morphine products made Erika Polowski excessively drowsy and incoherent. A perfect choice, "If I do say so myself," he added under his breath.

For thirty minutes, he drove back toward the gas station he'd used the last trip and grumbled at the lack of darkness. Why couldn't Karen have phoned after dark? The station was busy, but no one seemed to notice Erika snoozing in the back of the Prelude.

With a full tank of gas, he turned around and drove back in the direction of the cabin. This was the genius plan of the head of the nerd trio. If you have to leave, retrace steps and then backtrack. You look like you're going in the direction of where you should be fleeing. Who would expect it?

Twenty-two miles from the gas station and five from the old cabin, Keith pulled off the road and let the car crawl its way a few yards into the brush before he turned off the motor. A glance at Erika told him she was still out, so he hurried back to the entrance, brushing over tire tracks and broken shrubbery until no one would guess anyone had driven in there for weeks. For three miles into the woods, he stopped the car every few yards and hid what traces of their driving that he could. A true tracker wouldn't be fooled for a moment, but the average Joe might glance, and seeing nothing blatant, allow his eyes to move along, missing the glaring clues of their presence.

Just before he arrived at the mini clearing around the second cabin, Erika flung herself from the car and stumbled wildly through the trees. What Keith would have considered as a diversionary challenge the previous day, was nothing less than irritating today. He didn't have time for this kind of cat and injured, hardly crawling, mouse game.

It took less than a minute to catch her—the delay being that he didn't feel like running. He simply walked to where she stumbled back and forth between the trees muttering about kidnapping, ransom, and the NSA, turned her around, and led her to the cabin. The door wasn't locked, but considering no one could know the place was there without extensive exploring in just the right place,

Keith didn't expect to find anything off. Filthy, oh the place would be filthy, but not amiss. He'd miss the electricity most.

While Erika slept off the rest of her drug-induced somnolence, Keith went to work. He hid her car, brought the food into the cabin, gathered as much water as he could, and jury-rigged a new shackle for her out of the handcuffs. That solved, he went to work on fighting the filth of an abandoned cabin.

As he swept the single bedroom, he called Karen, hoping for news. Just as she told him the old cabin had been torched, he heard the screams of sirens as they wound their way up the hill. He hated this part. Keeping close to where you escaped always seemed scarier when the danger brushed past on its way home.

"Will you be dropping anything?" Karen assured him that a food and supply drop would arrive as soon as they could appropriate a fire helicopter, which prompted him to add, "Make sure you add an air mattress. There's only one bed. Oh, and new sheets. I don't have time to wash these before she wakes up."

"We're sending cheese, beef jerky, a solar battery, kerosene, and personal items for her. They'll be in pink saran wrap."

"Oh great. It's that time again."

"Just about."

He knew better than to ask, but Keith couldn't help but hope. "Are we any closer to nailing these guys?"

"If we were, would I be sitting here exchanging pleasantries? I won't be coming back for a few weeks, though. Until we know how they found you, we're not coming close." She covered the phone and then seconds later, said goodbye. "Chopper's moving out. I'm going to make sure they get the right place. See you in a few weeks."

"Call me."

"Keep your phone charged. Don't waste that battery on curling irons for Miss Priss."

"I can't let her have a curling iron and you know it."

The noise of the helicopter made it difficult to hear, but Karen's last words sent a new wave of dismay over him.

"... and don't let her call again. If somehow that's how they found her—"

The line went dead. He knew she was right, but he didn't want to think about telling Erika. He also didn't want to think of the long trek he'd have getting a letter from Erika to the nearest mailbox in the middle of the night. He also didn't like the realization that it'd mean restraints while Erika slept.

She stirred on the couch. He felt guilty for putting her on the filthy thing and made a mental note to request dustsheets for all unused safe houses. If she had been asthmatic, they'd have been in trouble. As if taunting him with concerns that didn't even apply, the smoke in the air thickened somewhat.

In what felt like minutes but almost an hour later, helicopter blades cut through the air. A glance at his watch showed that time had uncharacteristically flown. He glanced at her and decided to risk it. Once fully awake, she'd still have lingering effects. He'd be able to catch her even if she did run. He hurried outside and watched as the helicopter hovered a few feet from the ground before Karen pushed the pack from the edge and gave the signal to go.

From his peripheral vision, he saw Erika's movement and waited, forcing himself to remain relaxed, until she decided to pounce. Would she choose to try to hit him over the head? The thought caused him to shift slightly as he waved— better to be safe than sorry. He stifled a snicker as she rushed at him with every ounce of her one hundred twenty-two pounds. The split-second question was, step aside and let her rush the air or catch her and swing her around like a child and save her from an almost certain fall?

As tempted as he was to catch her, he knew the swing could encourage vomiting. Just in time, he stepped aside as Erika rushed to tackle him. She stumbled, fell to her knees, and scraped her chin. *"Great, another injury to clean and keep from infection."* Guilt tried to take root in his heart, but he couldn't help the twitch of amusement at the corner of his mouth.

"You knew I was coming!" Erika's accusation merely stated the obvious.

"I did."

# Eight

Fury exploded in her heart until Erika was sure she'd kill him. "I can't believe you let—" She grabbed her head, spun in a disoriented circle, and vomited.

With a grumpy face that contradicted the gentleness and tenderness he displayed, Keith helped her into the house and grabbed a bottle of water. While she retched into a dishpan, Keith rubbed her back, handed her water, and wiped her face and mouth with a wet washcloth—none of which endeared her to him. More irritable than ever, Erika lashed out at him, but to no avail. He seemed immune to her tirades.

"Drugs! Do you know how addictive drugs are? I can't believe you did that to me! I *said* I wouldn't be a problem! I begged!"

"I know. I'm sorry. It's just what we have to do." She slapped his hand away as he tried to wipe her mouth after another bout of vomiting, but it didn't seem to faze him.

"Feel so weird."

"It's the side effects. Drink some more."

"I don't want to drink more! I'm puking here!"

"You'd rather puke with something to come up than have dry heaves. Besides, dehydration means we have to sedate you and give you an IV. That's really not what you want to happen." He pushed the water bottle into her hand and then wiped his face with his sleeve when she used the "sport top" to squirt him with it. "That's not helping."

"But I feel better." As if unable to ignore the opportunity for irony, her stomach heaved again. "Ugh, why do people think this is so wonderful?"

He shook his head. "I don't know, Erika. Drink up."

"I don't *want* to 'drink up.'"

Before she could squirt more water at him, her body rejected the last infusion of liquids and spewed it all over his feet. He unwound a few paper towels from the roll Karen had dropped and mopped up his shoes. "I'll wash them later. Come on, Erika. Take a drink. Squirt me if you think it'll make you feel better, but get some more liquids in you. If you get dehydrated, you'll vomit from that too, and it'll just make it worse."

She broke away from him, furious that he acted so nonchalant about having drugged her and the misery it produced, but at the door, he stopped her. "You can't leave the cabin right now, Erika. I'm sorry."

"You are not! What a hypocrite! So, I don't like your method of keeping me quiet, and now you're going to lock me up even tighter? What kind of—?"

"We were just evicted from our cabin because they found us. Do you get that? Erika, they found us! That cabin is on fire right now. They burned it, probably assuming—or at least hoping—we were still in it. Dead. If we hadn't left, we'd be dead. Do you hear me? Dead."

"But you still drugged me!"

"Yes, I did, and if we had to leave right now, I'd give you a half dose and do it again, so don't think that me being sorry I *had* to do it means I am sorry that I *did* do it. There's a difference."

"You—" Another wave of nausea crashed over her. Dizzy, she stumbled in a semi-circle and then sank to the floor holding her head. "Oh, man…"

"Come on, Erika," Keith encouraged, trying to get her to stand. "Let's get you back to the couch."

"I can't move. Leave me alone. I want my dishpan."

At the sink, Keith pumped the lever on the hand pump at the sink, rinsing the dishpan. Erika started to complain, but seeing him working to give her a clean pan made her hesitate. When he returned, he lifted her in his arms and carried her back to the couch. When she eyed the dishpan once more, he handed it back to her and apologized. "I didn't use the soap. It's in the bundle, so I can if you want me to, but I thought—"

"You thought I could clean up my own puke. First you make me sick, and now you want me to clean it up. What a guy."

"I thought you might need it," he restated as if she hadn't just ungraciously attacked him for trying to be nice. "Want me to wash it out to kill the smell?"

"Yeah. Might want to clean the rest of this place while you're at it." She tried not to look at the door as she spoke, but it was as if her eyes refused to obey her brain. Even still, he didn't seem to notice.

As he stood at the sink scrubbing, she crept toward the door, trying not to make any sudden movements that he might notice. She had to get away. These people were crazy. Drugging her? What kind of "protector" drugs the person he's responsible for? The same word that seemed to define the entire experience blasted her brain again. *Insanity.*

Just as she reached the door, he spoke from the sink, and she bolted before the words registered. "I wouldn't run—" Still unsteady from the effects of the heroin, Erika fell flat on her face before he could finish his warning.

"Aaah! What the—" She stared at her feet as if they'd betrayed her. Handcuffs combined with a towing chain that was locked to a ring in the floor were hooked around one ankle. "When did you? I know I made it—"

"It just took a second when I put you back on the couch. I'm sorry, but you can't be seen in the yard right now. The car is hidden, but if someone sees us out here, it could get back to A—all the people who are looking for you."

With every ounce of mental strength she possessed, Erika forced herself to think about his words repeatedly, until she fell asleep. He'd started to say something with a short "A" sound. Whatever that meant, she didn't know, but it was a start. She couldn't let the drugs take that away from her. A. How hard could it be to remember the first letter of the alphabet?

As she sank to the floor, Keith realized that she'd need help. It'd be impossible to curl up next to that dishpan unless it was empty. Stuffing down the impulse to gag, Keith dumped the contents down the toilet and pumped a bucketful of water to pour into the tank. This no electricity thing would get old quickly. As he handed her the rinsed dishpan, he slipped the handcuff around her ankle, hoping she was too upset to notice. As miraculous as it seemed, it worked. Now, if she'd just stop puking so he could give her detox capsules for her liver.

Just as he warned her not to run, Erika tripped. As expected, a new string of insults followed a fresh wave of anger and culminated in a torrent of foul-mouthed expletives. After trying to explain why she couldn't leave, Keith gave up and led her back to the couch. "Just rest. I—" he sighed. "Just rest."

When she didn't awaken to vomit again, Keith sighed, relieved. He had too much to do and little time to do it before she woke up again. With the first sweep of the broom, he realized that she'd wake up coughing in no time unless he did something to filter her breathing.

Tearing a strip of cloth from the bundle that Karen had dropped, Keith wet it, wrung every drop from it he could, and then laid it carefully over her head. Seconds ticked by as he waited for her to swing at it or shove it off, but she seemed unbothered. He started in the bedroom, sweeping the ceiling, walls, and choking from the dust himself until he was forced to open the windows. Once he brushed down all surfaces, he slowly—trying to avoid stirring up any more dust than necessary—swept the floor until he couldn't get enough to be worth the fight.

Without a mop, wiping the floor meant crawling around on his hands and knees, but thanks to small spaces, he had no trouble getting the floor cleaned in a reasonable amount of time. The sheets, however, were the worst. Coated with months and months of dust and dank odors, he carried all bedding, including the pillows, into the bathroom and began pumping, filling the tub full of water. Though Keith would have preferred hot, he didn't want to take the time. Besides, wringing out those sheets would be workout enough for him.

At the bottom of the bundle, beneath the "pink package" that Keith stored in the bathroom vanity with a shudder, two fresh packages of sheets and two air mattresses waited. He unwrapped the mattresses, inserted the foot pump, and worked away, trying to fill it quickly. If he could just move her into the bedroom, he'd be able to work on the main cabin room. Finishing before dark would be hard, but he certainly did not wish to sleep in filth—with the critters.

As another mouse scurried across his toes, Keith jumped and shook his head. If Erika saw that, she'd never let him live it down. "Must. Not. Get. Startled," he muttered to himself as he worked.

Once he inflated the air mattress, Keith pulled the old musty mattress from the bed and put the air mattress on the box springs. Wrestling with it every step of the way, Keith dragged it to the living room. He could beat it after dark. By the time he finished making the bed, over an hour had passed, and he still hadn't rinsed or wrung out the other bedding.

The cloth over her head already looked filthy, and he hadn't even been working in there! As much as he hated to risk waking her, he scooped her into his arms and stepped around the chain as he carried her to the bedroom. Erika stirred, still groggy and feeling the aftereffects of the drug. At this rate, she'd be ready to start detoxing when she woke again.

"Wha—?"

"I got your bedroom cleaned and fresh sheets on an air mattress. The room is free of critters and ready for a good night's sleep."

"Is it night already?"

"It will be soon. Just knock when you want out again."

Erika fumbled for the dishpan he carried, and then sighed in relief as her body settled again. "'kay."

It felt like an insult to lock her in the room, but clearly something they'd done had given away their location. They had to return to strict protocol, regardless of how unnecessary some of it seemed. He stared at the mess before him for a moment, wishing for the cushy Secret Service job that didn't require housekeeping skills before he went to rinse his rags. Time to attack the kitchen.

The mouse droppings in the cupboards and along the baseboards nauseated him. Bugs, spiders, and even a couple of harmless snakes ended up flattened or tossed through the door as he worked. The tasks, though tedious, inconvenient, and sent him into fits of coughing at times, had a cathartic quality to them. As he worked, his mind went over everything he could imagine that could have given away their position.

His first thought was her escape. Had they somehow been followed in the beginning and lost whoever was pursuing them? Had she been seen and followed? It didn't seem likely. They'd waited too long to strike for that to be the case. Even if she had managed to evade following, anyone with any experience could have sent a helicopter over that part of the area to find where she likely went. However, it was an option. He'd have to be vigilant to avoid being outside during the day. Period.

His second option seemed the most likely. They'd managed to trace her phone. If that was the case, they'd watched Karen for a week before she made that call from the cabin. It didn't make sense that they'd put a trace app on her cell phone. Why wouldn't they have just killed her instead? However, it seemed more logical than his third option.

As he scrubbed the table, he fought the idea that someone within the agency had fed the information to someone in Anastas' organization. If it wasn't so unlikely, it would be his best bet. It ticked all boxes and filled all holes. His only comfort was that they hadn't lost a witness in over two years. It seemed unlikely that this case, as serious as it was, would inspire any of his coworkers to betray not only those in their care, but each other as well.

Once he finished scrubbing all surfaces within the cabin, Keith went to work securing anything that could be used as a weapon against him. Now that he'd had to drug her, he needed to go back to treating her as a potential threat to their safety. The thought frustrated him. He didn't expect to be friends with her—that was unreasonable. However, pleasant cohabitation during their incarceration wasn't too much to ask, was it? *Yeah, well it is now.*

Before he finished, her knock came in the form of pounding. Outside, the sun slowly set, giving them little time to eat before it was too dark to see. Flashlights were now impossible, and the lanterns would be worse. From now on, they had to avoid anything that drew attention to the cabin—particularly light.

"You feeling better?" he called as he unlocked the bolts on the door.

"Yeah. A little. I need food."

She might have felt a little better, but Erika looked pallid—almost grotesque. "I've got some beef jerky and some of your greens, which we need to eat before they go bad, but we have to eat quickly."

"Why?"

"It's hard to see what you're doing in the dark."

"We don't even have a flashlight?" The look on her face—priceless. Erika stepped into the bathroom, jerking the chain behind her, and slammed the door. "Why is this happening?"

"I don't know. I can't talk to Karen unless it's absolutely necessary. I have a few theories, but no good ones. Either they are too flawed or too horrible to trust."

He kept talking through the door as he dragged out their produce and rinsed everything. The salad would be crude, but that they had it had to be a plus—certainly better than none. Well, better to a girl like Erika anyway. He had his doubts.

"Hey, how do I flush this toilet? It doesn't work."

"I'll get it." That was another part of this change he wouldn't like. *Toilet duty. Oh, joy.*

Erika stood in the doorway, watching as he pulled the lid off the tank and filled it with water. "You've got to be kidding me."

"Sorry. I didn't refill after I flushed your lunch down. Just let me know when you've used it, and I'll fill it up again."

"I can fill it. I'm not that pathetic."

He started to argue; after all, it was his job. One look at Erika's face and he changed his mind. Women like Erika had something to prove, and Keith Auger wasn't up to the "Anything you can do" duet. "Fine. Just fill that bucket halfway, and you'll be fine." He pointed to the kitchen. "Better eat. The light is going fast."

As she chewed her beef jerky, Keith weighed the pros and cons of offering the herbal supplement designed to help speed the eradication of the drug from her body. Should he just tell her to take it and hope she listened? Could he sneak it into her salad dressing? She was contrary enough to make insisting on it a battle, but if she caught him sneaking...

"Okay, we've got an herbal supplement that helps detox your liver. If you want to get the drugs out of your system quickly, I'd recommend it, but it's up to you."

"What's in it?"

"Dandelion, milk thistle, fennel... I can't remember it all. I'd give you the bottle, but I don't have it."

"Will you take one if I do?"

"Sure. Liver health is important for everyone, right?" He pulled out the small baggie from his jacket pocket and handed it to her. "Take two out and pass them over. I'll take 'em first."

Apparently, he'd done something right. She hardly hesitated once he'd downed the ones she chose for him. Of course, it meant a dose she wouldn't get, but it was better than her getting nothing. "Once it's dark, I'm going to go out and beat that mattress and the couch. I didn't notice any signs of animals chewing on them—how I am not sure—but I'll look closer tomorrow. Once the dust is gone, it won't be so nasty to sit or lay on them."

"But you're doing it after dark so no one can see you."

"Right."

"This is insane," she muttered as she speared another bite of salad.

"I agree."

"Can I take a bath?"

Without answering, he stood, grabbed a large pot, and pumped it half-full of water. Once the flame lit, he frowned. A roll of aluminum foil in one of the drawers gave him an idea, and Keith used it to make a shield around the flame. He moved the mattress in front of the kitchen window and opened the door wide enough to block a view of the flame. "That'll have to do."

"You're serious about this, aren't you?"

"Because I'd do it for fun otherwise, right?" Sarcasm wouldn't help things, but he spoke before he thought. Then again, it might help his mental attitude.

Erika stood, shoved her chair away from her, sending it crashing to the floor, and stormed to the bathroom. Seconds later, she burst through the door again in search of her duffel bag. "The tub is full. There's something soaking in it."

The temptation to swear had never been quite so strong, but Keith resisted. "Then I'd suggest you help me wring it out, or you can forget the bath."

# NINE

The soft rhythmic whap, whap of an unknown origin woke her in the wee hours. Panicked, she pounded on the door, begging and crying to be freed from the prison that she was sure would become her tomb. Keys rattled in locks before she heard the bars slide sideways. Erika jumped as the door bumped her in the head. Heedless of her previous disdain, anger, and fear of Keith, she threw herself at him, trembling. "What do we do?"

"For what?"

"Didn't you hear it? It woke me up— a helicopter!"

The tension in his features, neck, and arms became instantly noticeable. "Stay right here. Don't move until I come back."

Clutching his shirt, Erika pleaded with him not to leave her. "I won't run. I won't do anything. If they shoot you, I'll be locked—"

Furious that he ignored her pleas, Erika glowered as he dashed outside, stayed out for what seemed like half an eternity, and then strolled back in again. "I'm going to see something. Tell me if you hear it again."

Seconds later, the sound returned, but this time, Erika recognized it. "I can't believe he's out there beating the mattresses and furniture while he should be sleeping."

Disgusted, she slammed the door behind her and crawled back up on the bed, feeling betrayed. She'd done her part, and Keith had abused her trust with the injection. Remembering the way she clutched at him, revolted her. *Oh, how could I be so pathetic?*

After a gentle knock, the knob turned, and Erika forced herself not to stiffen. "Erika? Was that it?"

"You know it was."

"I'm glad you called for me. Thank you."

She sat up and stared at the faint shadow in the darkness. "Thank you for what?"

"If I'd been asleep, I might have missed it. I appreciate it." She saw his hands move and winced, dreading the touch she expected, but it never came. In the near blackness, she saw the faint outline of his arms bent as his hands rested on his hips.

"Great, you scare me to death, and then you thank me for overreacting. Yeah. That makes sense."

Even with as little as she could see, Erika knew he stiffened. His jaw had probably gone rigid and the cold, steely look must have overtaken his eyes—as always. Keith turned as if to leave, and then sighed. "I'm sorry, Erika. I'm doing everything I can to make your stay as comfortable as possible. I know it's not enough, but I'm trying."

"You should be sleeping." She'd tried to make it a dig, but it sounded like concern, and she knew it.

"I know."

The door started to close. Though she knew she should let him go, the impulse to ask overtook her resolve. "Why?"

"Why what?"

"Why are you out there beating the furniture?"

"Because I can't do it during the day."

"But why do it at all?" Erika made a note to learn to curb her curiosity.

"If you have to be here for a few more weeks, without electricity, the least I can do is try to make the house comfortable." The door shut quietly behind him.

Staring off into the inkiness, Erika forced herself to do the one thing that rankled most. "Keith?" Her voice was quiet—too quiet, really. The chances of him hearing her weren't—

The door opened. "Yeah?"

"Thanks."

---

Her apology stunned him. After a week of antagonism, he hadn't expected the side of her personality that forced her to go against her personal comfort zone in order to do what she thought was right. Of course, she was irritated and distrustful. Who wouldn't be?

After another half hour of batting practice on the furniture, Keith sprayed it all with Lysol, and while it aired, took a quick, cold bath. As he slid down into the sleeping bag, his muscles sighing with relief, Keith slid his phone open and peeked at the time. Two-thirty. He'd get four hours sleep— if he was lucky.

An envelope lit up at the top of the screen told him he had a text message. He deliberated for several seconds before he gave up and read the message. Corey Knupp would arrive by morning. Backup. Sleep. The ideas were wonderful. So why did her coming feel like an intrusion?

---

At the first knock, Keith threw himself from the air mattress, grappling for his gun. He peeked out the door, but a second knock immediately relaxed him. It was just Erika. He felt like a fool. No intruder knocks before entering.

"Coming, Erika. Hold on."

"Sorry. I really gotta go."

As he slid the locks open, he pushed the door. "Hey, no worries. You hungry?"

"Do we have anything worth eating?"

"Oats."

"Cinnamon?" The hopeful sound of her voice made him wish he'd thought to ask.

"Don't think so." He knelt to unlock the handcuffs. "There. Don't try to run, okay? I'm beat." Her smile answered for her, prompting him to ask about the oatmeal again

Her shoulders slumped, but she nodded. "Yeah, it's good for you—cholesterol and all that stuff. I'll probably need it after so few greens."

The moment the door shut behind her, Keith strolled back into the kitchen, pumped some water into a pan, and set it on the stove. The change should have been a relief, but he knew a pleasant Erika meant something wasn't right. The question was, what?

Keith jumped as he caught movement behind him in his peripheral vision. Before he could ask her to dig out the sugar from the bundle on the table, Erika spoke. "It looks great in here. Thanks."

"You're welcome. Can you look for sugar in that pile? It should be in a Ziploc bag."

As she handed him the bag, she shook another one at him. "I think it's cinnamon and sugar mixed! Would Karen do that?"

"Only if there was already some from something else. Did you sniff?"

She stared at him— hurt shrouding every part of her. "What did I do now? Is it possible to say anything to me without scowling? Am I really that repulsive?"

"Don't do it, Erika. I'm trained to suspect the worst. So, either you're wasting your time trying to make me think you are softening and trusting me, or you're going to be hurt when I'm suspicious of you."

The flash of pain in her eyes before she turned away told him all he needed to know. She'd been at least partly genuine. The anger that followed had been real, but a glimpse of her wounded feelings told him she was relenting just a little. He couldn't risk that. It was dangerous for all of them.

"I got a message last night." After several seconds, Keith concluded that Erika had no intention of asking what it contained. "They're sending Corey to help. That must mean her last case is wrapped up. "

"Corey is a she?"

"Yep." The desire to ask questions was impossible for her to hide, but Erika managed. Taking pity, he poured the oats into the pot, turned off the burner, and replaced the lid before he added. "I'll get her to take day shift if you like. That ought to give you a break anyway."

"I just wanted to be cordial."

"And wanted me to let down my guard. What you were going to do, I don't know, but I can tell you, it'd be dangerous—whatever it was."

"I want to know why I am here."

"I can't tell you. I know you're sick of hearing it, but I can't. Even if I did, I doubt you'd get it. You don't have to like me, and you don't have to trust me even. You just have to listen and let me do my job so you can get back to your life and never have to think of me again."

"As if that'd be possible," she muttered, filling a glass of water."

No one would mistake the dread in his tone as he asked, "What?"

"Come on, do you honestly think I could forget being kidnapped and held hostage—even if I came to accept that it was for my own good. And," she added before he could protest, "I can see that the burned cabin probably means it really was for my own good. I'm stubborn and too independent for my own good sometimes, but I'm not stupid."

After stirring the oats once more, Keith jerked his thumb at the bedroom. "I've got to go lengthen your chain. Corey won't understand you being unshackled. I'm sorry."

"Whatever."

It took a couple of minutes to unwind the chain from the bed, and just as he reached the bedroom door, he heard, "Put it down and step away from the stove." Keith rushed out of the room, chain in hand, and bellowed, "Put the gun down, Corey."

"She was going to fling the contents of that pan at you."

"How—" The stunned expression on Erika's face confirmed Corey's accusation.

"I'm trained—"

"You guys are worse than people with PhDs. It's ridiculous. Every single time anything happens, you remind me, 'I'm trained to be smarter than you, so deal with it.'" Her high, mocking falsetto would have been amusing had Corey not still had her gun aimed at Erika's head.

"Put the gun down, Corey!"

"Not until she steps away from the stove and you put her restraints on. It's a wonder she's still here."

"Hey!" Erika and Keith grinned at each other as they spoke in unison. Wanting to defuse the situation before it got worse, he tossed the cuffs to Erika. "Put 'em on."

"She needs to get away from the pan."

"Fine!" Furious, Erika stormed past Corey, sending her looks that could torture, and sank onto the couch to hook up her makeshift restraints.

Keith felt a strange sense of satisfaction to note that no dust puffed into the air as it had the previous day. "Gun, Corey?"

"I didn't hear it snap."

"Sheesh! I got away from the stove."

The second the cuff clicked around Erika's ankle, Corey holstered her gun, reached outside the door, grabbed her backpack, and dropped it next to the couch. "I have some things you need to see, Keith, but privately. Now, I gotta pee."

The second the bathroom door closed, Keith turned his gaze to Erika. "Oatmeal?"

"I am going stir-crazy. I want out of here," the woman hissed. "I thought if I got away, I could stay somewhere that no one would expect me to go."

"Such as?" He couldn't help but be amused as she struggled with whether she should tell him or not. "You're not getting out of here, so you might as well tell me."

"Fine. I was going to try Stafford House in Brunswick. I thought no one would expect me to go to some place so public, and I have no connection there."

"Those are excellent points." At the sight of her happy smile, he almost didn't continue. "There is only one problem."

"What's that?"

"If they managed to track you, then not just your life, but the lives of everyone in that establishment would be in jeopardy. Instead of one life, it could be half a dozen gone. Stop being so selfish and just try to be patient while we do our jobs."

She seemed to accept that, but a second later, Erika jerked her head toward the bathroom. "Is she always so delightful?" Her tone told him that she suspected the correct answer.

"Corey is very good because she sticks to the book. She's one of our best. You're lucky to have her."

"Yeah. I feel lucky."

A voice interrupted them. "Good, because I brought M&Ms and I'm ready to whoop your sorry tushes at seven card stud."

Shaking his head, Keith poured bowls of oatmeal and said, "Bring it on."

# TEN

The pile of M&Ms next to Corey was only slightly larger than Keith's. Erika, a novice who couldn't seem to remember a flush from a full house, made crazy bets that made no sense and munched happily—in a manner of speaking—on her "chips." Aside from occasional questions or reminders, the game was silent. Keith knew it was a matter of time before the women pulled out their claws and things got interesting, but in the interim, he waited.

As he replenished Erika's "bank," his phone buzzed with a text message. He passed it across the table for Corey to see, pretending to hide it from Erika. She'd misunderstand what it meant, but it would reassure her. Sometimes that was more important than anything else. TARGET LOCATED.

"Good. Now we wait."

He saw Erika shift, and reached under the table with his foot and touched her leg. "Raise or fold."

"I—" she frowned. Shaking her head, she folded with a King and Queen on her face up cards. "Fold."

"I don't think you understand the game, Erika. This is only the second street. You should—"

"She's probably tired. Let's finish this round and play tomorrow."

Disgust and irritation etched into her features, Erika glared at both of her "protectors." "Erika thinks it is just so fun when Keith and Corey decide to talk over her as if she wasn't even present. She wonders why they don't just tell all secrets since they seem to think it's cool to talk around her."

"Third person," Corey snickered, "how quaint."

"Cut it, Corey."

Being the equivalent of a female linebacker, Keith's size didn't intimidate Corey, but he could see that his anger hit home. "Fine. Whatever. You need to sleep."

Unwilling to let the battle happen, Keith went to brush his teeth and take a quick bath. When he returned, Corey pointed to the bedroom. "You need real sleep, Keith. There's no way you'll be able to sleep well with us making noise out here."

He started to protest, but the expression on Corey's face was a familiar one. She'd fight him until he did what she wanted, and he didn't have the stamina left for it. Grabbing the air mattress from against the wall, he dragged it to the door of the bedroom. As Corey started to protest, Keith lost his patience. "Enough. Don't even go there."

"What?" Erika stared at both them, frustrated."

"She was trying to be helpful, but she's going to mind her own business now," Keith growled as he returned for his sleeping bag. "Wake me up when she's ready to go to bed."

He hadn't been out for an hour when a screaming match jerked him from sleep. Listening to the insults and accusations hurled in the other room, Keith tried not to smile. Erika managed to shred Corey in both insults and logic. The combination was brilliant.

"—stop and think for a moment, you'd realize that talking to me instead of over me might get you just a little cooperation."

"I don't have to cooperate with you. I have to protect you until we know you are no longer in danger. That's it."

"What ever happened to freedom? I mean, even the Witness Protection program is voluntary! I swear I'm ready to sue the US Government for everything that I can!"

"Go ahead. I'd like to see you try."

He stood and moved toward the door, ready to jump in and put a stop to it, but Erika's next sentence stopped him. "You really think I'm weak, don't you? At least Keith shows me courtesy and respect. You're just a bully, and I won't stand for it. I'm going to go public with this thing when this is over and make sure that the government answers for violations of my constitutional rights."

"It won't work, Erika."

Corey's voice was so revoltingly patronizing that Keith wanted to slap her upside the head himself. He took another step toward the door and waited. Would Erika back down, or go for the jugular? Or worse, would Corey lose what professionalism she had left?

"Yeah, it will. I plan to make sure that this doesn't happen to another person again."

"The government will look, but they will not find us. Your accusations will be silenced. Seriously, are you really that naïve? You forget that you're not the first. Do you watch the news?"

"Yeah."

"And how many public accusations of kidnapping by the government or any other agency do you hear about?" Even from the other side of the wall, Keith knew what Corey's face looked like as she added, "You'll keep your mouth shut and be thankful for your life like the hundreds of other people that we've helped. You'll quit whining about how horrible we are, and if you're not a completely self-centered jerk, you might have the decency to thank us."

"Thank you! Thank you for *this*? You've got some nerve!"

Realizing that they would never agree to disagree, Keith stormed out of the room, grabbing Corey's arm as he did. He ignored the light outdoors as he pulled her outside and unleashed his pent-up fury. "What do you think you're doing?"

"She's completely unreasonable. Talk about a diva!"

"Even if that were true, who cares! Since when do we take rejection of our protection personally?"

Corey glared at him. "What protection? We're standing out here exposed, you idiot! You've gone soft with this one! What, she's too cute to ignore? After all the millionaires' daughters, with their perfect complexions, bodies, and model looks, you go goofy over some snotty barista? You've lost your perspective."

"You've lost your mind and your professionalism. I expect you to go in there and treat her with the same care and courtesy that you showed that actor's agent." He frowned, a discouraged look on his face. "I'm going to have to report this."

"And I'm going to have to report your loss of perspective. You can't fall for your assignment."

"I've fallen for no one," he said quietly, realizing that Erika probably heard every word. "I have no objections answering for every decision and action I've made since Mark assigned me to this case."

"You are so delusional."

The venom in her tone stunned him; Keith didn't know how to respond. "I can handle the accusation. Can you handle the inquiry?" Without waiting for her reply, he turned and returned to the cabin.

Erika looked distressed. "I'm sorry—"

"You have no reason to be. You've done nothing wrong—nothing that every client we've ever helped hasn't done. I'm going to bed. If there's a problem, of any kind, come get me."

Just as he closed his eyes and pulled the bag over his shoulder, the door opened again. Erika's face peeked through the door. "Keith?"

"Yeah?"

"If you get in trouble, just tell whoever is in charge to talk to me. I'll back you up."

---

The argument replayed itself in Erika's mind until she thought she'd go crazy. The dagger looks that Corey sent her made no sense. She paced the floor until her irritable captor demanded she stop "making all that racket," and then looked for something to read.

Corey's snort of disgust when she picked up Keith's Bible made her want to throw it at the woman, but instead, she forced herself to be as pleasant as she could muster. "Do you have a problem with me reading this?"

"He'll see through it. Keith isn't stupid."

"You sure treated him like he is. What kind of garbage was that?"

"He's going to make stupid mistakes thanks to you. Just leave him alone!"

Corey stormed into the bathroom and slammed the door behind her. As quietly as she could, Erika picked up her chain and held it as taut as possible as she crept into the bedroom. "Keith?"

"Yeah?"

His being awake surprised her until she remembered the slammed door. That'd wake anyone. "I think I know what's eating Corey," she whispered.

"Good. Just avoid it at all costs."

"I can't."

"Why?" He raised himself on one elbow to look at her.

"It's me. She's jealous. She has it in her head that you're interested in me."

"Yeah, I got that much, but why the—" Understanding wrinkled his face in confusion until he shook his head. "No, I don't think so, Erika."

"Look, it's that or she's got some kind of 'Post Abduction Stress Syndrome' or something."

"PASS. Cute. I'll call Mark. Thanks." He jerked his head toward the bathroom. "Better get back in there before she returns. If you can't take it, just come play cards on your bed or something. You won't bother me."

"Like she'd let me do that."

"Just do it. I'll back you up."

As she shut the door behind her, Erika saw him pull out his phone. This was interesting. First, the target was located. That was fascinating enough. Did it mean that they'd be able to take him down soon? Isn't that what happened when you located a target?

More than that, though, the idea of not being associated with the government intrigued her. What did Corey mean? Was it true, or was it some cover story used to prevent people from exposing the American government's illegal activity?

Additionally, was he calling to report her, Corey, or himself? Erika had no doubt in her mind that Corey saw her as a threat to whatever she hoped to cultivate with Keith. Actually, the more she thought about it, the more she realized that Corey wouldn't have anything to do with him now. In the agent's odd way of seeing things, he'd been compromised. He'd lost value in her opinion, and in doing so, Erika's opinion of him grew more favorable—slightly.

The moment Corey returned from the bathroom, Erika knew something dreadful had occurred. Corey looked exultant. Murmurs on the other side of the wall grew slightly louder and forceful, but something else filled Keith's voice—desperation. She tried not to look at the woman across the room, but Erika couldn't seem to control her eyes. Corey sat, fingers interlocked with an assumed air of calmness. Silence grew so intense that it nearly deafened her, and still the agent spoke nothing and communicated everything.

At last, the bedroom door opened, and Keith appeared, jacket in hand. "That was low, Corey. You're just delaying the inevitable."

"You could have red-lined me if you considered me a danger to the assignment."

"After you red-lined me, that'd leave her unprotected while they flew someone in, and you know it. Despite what I think of your behavior, I think more of our responsibility to protect her. Once this case is over, you will be called to answer for your misuse of your position and your treatment of our client."

He turned to Erika, who sat stunned as she realized what his words meant, and said, "If there's any problem at all, I'll want to hear about it during debriefing. Do you understand? No matter what she says about anything, if there is anything that makes you feel mistreated or unsafe, make sure we know."

Keith passed her a pad of paper and a pen. "Before I go, I thought you'd want to write a note home. I'll have it mailed from somewhere down by Nashville."

"What do I say?" The question asked itself before she realized she didn't want to be told how to write to her own family.

"Tell them you're fine, that you saw two squirrels fighting over a nut, and that you're amazed at how well your car is holding up—only two flats and a dead starter so far." He grinned at her snicker. "Oh, and make sure you let them know you love them."

Those words sent a chill through her heart. Why had he emphasized that? It sounded as if— "Okay."

She wrote each line carefully, making sure every word was exactly what she wanted it to be, and then, at Keith's insistence, rewrote it quickly, copying it from the original in order to make it look quick and carefree. He folded it, slipped it inside an envelope, and had her write her parents' address it before slipping it inside a pocket inside his jacket.

"Take care of yourself, Erika. Just don't do anything stupid. Corey knows her job. She can and will protect you, even if it seems like she won't. It's her job, and she'll do it right. You don't have to like her, but don't be afraid to trust her."

At the door, he turned back to both of them. "I'll get these guys as soon as I can. Try not to kill each other while I do it."

# Eleven

With each step away from the cabin, Keith grew more nervous. Everything he knew of Corey told him to trust her, but his suspicions about a mole made him question everything he'd assumed to be true. As he reached the point where he knew he'd be unable to hear her if she called out for him, Keith's stomach churned. What was more important? Obeying orders and finding Alek Anastas and his crew, or risking everything—including his job—to protect Erika from what might be a new threat?

He paused, one hand leaning on a tree as he prayed for wisdom and guidance. Despite his deep desire to return, he felt unsettled at the thought of disobeying orders. A verse from Romans, "obey those who have rule over you" mocked him. Sure, the Scripture spoke of government authorities, and technically speaking, his entire job was a violation of that verse.

The official stance of the government was that his agency was subject to prosecution; they were, by legal definition, criminals. However, the government also looked the other way at their activities. As long as people did not raise a public stink and complain, his employer made the jobs of the FBI, CIA, NSA, and Homeland Security much easier—and at no charge. With each change of presidential administration, the tension within the agency became nearly palpable, but in three decades, not one president had made the choice to take the information public and shut them down.

"Lord, which authority do I obey? My boss? The Constitution? The President of the USA? I'm lost here."

As if a Divine finger illuminated the memory with a switch, Keith remembered how the Magi refused to return to Herod and tell him where to find Jesus. They'd ignored the commands of a powerful ruler like Herod, and in doing so, saved the life of the Savior of mankind. Mark said to come in. He'd go.

"Take care of her, Lord. Just—just take care of her."

---

Refreshed after a long, enforced nap, Keith met with Mark in the office of the Mayflower Trust building in Rockland. The plaque on the outer door read, "Acquisitions," which always amused him. Mark Cho watched him from across the desk, his fingers toying with a pencil as he made his initial assessment.

Despite his Asian sounding surname, Mark's broad-shouldered, tow headed, piercing blue eyes belied the hint of any Asian heritage. Rumors among the agents ranged from adopted to dominant Scandinavian genes. Keith just assumed he'd changed his name for personal protection and privacy.

"What happened with Corey? I could tell from your tone that you were calling to red-line her."

"I was."

"So why didn't you do it?" Mark continued when Keith didn't speak. "My guess is one of two things. Either you thought you needed to have yourself evaluated to assure you were still objective, or you were concerned for Erika."

"Both, but primarily Erika." He swallowed. "Frankly, Corey seems to have cracked, but her being there was better than risking a replacement drop for both of us."

"What happened?"

With a detachment Keith assumed at every debriefing, Keith told of Corey's arrival, of the snippy comments, the verbal catfight, but he hesitated when it came to Erika's perspective. "I—"

"Keith, you've been with us for five years. You're one of the best agents we have. I want the facts, yes, but I also want your impressions. I need your instincts."

"Erika seems to think Corey had a thing for me."

"I've thought that for a couple of months."

When he felt surprise creep over his face, Keith shut down. His job was to keep his emotions hidden. Exposing them now could mean his job. "I—I didn't know."

"Well, at least now you guys can do something about it—if you can get past yesterday anyway."

*He knows,* Keith thought to himself. *I should have known I couldn't hide anything from him.* "I can't, Mark. Not after what I saw today—um, yesterday."

"Why not?"

"If you'd seen her yesterday..." he shook his head. "Not possible, and besides, even if I was willing, Corey would consider it a betrayal of whatever. It's weird, Mark. It's just weird."

"Do you trust her to protect Erika?"

He thought carefully before answering, wanting to be sure his answer was unsullied by his thoughts and opinions. "I trust her with Erika's physical safety. She won't let Alek get to her. I don't trust her to treat Erika well. She's already been just nasty. I'd managed to make Erika feel safe. She hated it, but she felt safe." He kneaded his knees with his hands before meeting Mark's gaze. "Look, Mark. I assessed the client, discovered how to keep her fighting, but feeling reasonably well-protected, and was on the top of my game. I allowed no more laxity in rules than Karen did and approved of. Corey walked into that cabin and destroyed weeks' worth of hard work in minutes. By the time she was done, Erika was threatening media exposure and lawsuits."

Though he didn't say them, a string of foul words flew across Mark's face. "I'll send Karen in to relieve Corey."

Disappointment washed over Keith, but he nodded. "I think it'd be best."

"You don't want to go back?"

"If you thought I should, you'd have mentioned it." The words were hard to swallow, but they were true.

"You'll replace Karen in a week, but I don't want you and Corey in the same space until we meet here."

Keith nodded and asked about his assignment for the week. "I assume I'm not on vacation." The attempt at a joke fell flat.

"No, can't spare you yet, but good try. You'll be assigned to the taskforce on Alek Anastas."

"Have you located Helen Franklin?"

Mark's face answered before he opened his mouth. "She's officially on a 'walkabout,' but we actually have her in a hut in Fiji."

"Who here knows that Helen is who Anastas is really after?"

"You, me, Karen, and Corey—and of course Jill and Tony in Fiji."

"No one else?"

"No, why? Something is bothering you. I want to know what it is."

"It's—" Keith frowned, searching for words that didn't sound accusatory. "Well, did we ever figure out how they found the cabin?"

"No. All of the scenarios we considered were refuted—except one that is impossible."

"What was that one?"

"A mole."

"That's the one that's concerning me," Keith admitted. "I had a few theories myself, but all of them would have meant Erika would be dead right now."

"Our list of moles is short." Mark flipped through a file on his glass and chrome excuse for a desk. "Yep, it's just you, me, Karen, Corey, Jill, and Tony."

"Well, it's not you, and it's not me. Jill and Tony would have to have accomplices, but it might explain the misses."

"Okay," Mark was already pulling up files on his computer. "What about Karen?"

"I can't see it. Karen, more than all of us, couldn't do it."

Agreeing, Mark moved to the next option. "Okay, Corey. What do you think?"

"I don't like it. It's too easy. I mean, honestly, if she was a mole, she'd know we'd suspect her the way she was behaving. She'd have been more like Karen than the crazed person she was."

"And, as your boss, I have to consider you. After all, you just left the client with someone who showed clear distaste for her."

Keith's stomach plummeted for a moment. "That doesn't make sense either. If I am the mole, there's no way Erika is in physical danger from Corey." He kneaded his palms together, thinking. "I should tell you, Mark, I almost didn't come back. I started to hide in the woods and keep an eye on them."

"Why did you come then?"

"I thought my presence could be noticed and it put them in danger." As much as he didn't want to admit it, Keith added, "And I really don't think Corey will hurt her. Yeah, after what she just put Erika through, and after messing up all the work I put into making Erika feel safe, even if she did hate it, I wanted to think Corey was it, but I don't. I think she needs a month off to decompress and to get the idea of her and me out of her head, but otherwise, no. I just don't think she's the one."

"That leaves Karen, Jill, and Tony." Mark stared at his screen before he turned back to Keith. "Okay, I'll start looking into them more closely. I may need you to do some investigating. Meanwhile, I really want you to go to Columbus and check out the Hard as Nails chain of salons. Take your cousin with you—the pretty one. Have her go in for a set of acrylics or something."

"And what on earth am I supposed to say to make going to Columbus make sense?"

"You'll buy a boat. I'll have one there for you. You want her opinion. Let me know what kind of boat she'd be crazy about."

"Um, Claire hates the water with a passion second only to snakes."

"Car?"

"She loves mine. She'd kill me."

"What don't you have that she'd go crazy over?"

"Motorcycle. She's always loved Harley Davidsons."

"And you hate them." Mark closed his eyes for a moment, and then asked, "When is her birthday?"

"Next month, why?"

"That'll do. Get me a picture of a Harley that you know she'd want and take her to pick out her birthday present."

"She knows I can't afford—"

"You officially have a bonus, and you want to use some of it on her. Now make it happen." Mark's tone was dismissive.

Keith stood, shook his boss' hand, and strolled from the office, dialing his favorite cousin. "Hey, Claire. What are you doing this week?"

---

"He's not going to fall for you." Corey couldn't keep the venom from her words.

"I don't expect him to. I expect him—and you for that matter—to do the protecting thing you keep insisting is necessary. That's it."

"He's a Christian. Christians don't get involved with non-Christians."

"So, that means you're a Christian?" Erika didn't give Corey a chance to answer. "Figures. You're exactly the kind of person I've always associated with Christianity. Arrogant, self-righteous, vicious. Yep. Fits you all to a tee."

"Unbelievers love to excuse their rejection of Jesus with accusations. It's revolting."

Laughter bubbled over until Erika was gasping for breath. Corey sat, arms crossed, and shook her head at the display of hilarity. Once under control again, Erika stood and threw one last barb at her guard. "I don't think your Jesus would recognize himself in the nastiness that you keep displaying. I'm pretty sure the songs we sang in Sunday school at Grandma's were about love, forgiveness, and mercy. You disgust me."

Corey watched her leave, the angst welling over inside until she wanted to follow, lashing out at the stupid girl. They were saving her life, and she spent the whole time attacking. What kind of idiot did that?

Though she didn't want to admit it, the accusations stung. Her faith was young—untested. She'd seen what it did in Keith, and she liked it; she wanted it. After a long session with a pastor near her home, she'd followed the scripted prayer he offered her, promised to read the Bible every day, and pray in the morning and evening. All she had to do was do those things and she'd be saved from the wrath to come. It seemed pretty straightforward, and it didn't seem to be asking too much of her. God's Son dies for her, she prays and reads. Simple enough.

But it wasn't. Nothing was. The ache in her heart grew stronger with every line of text read and every sentence of prayer uttered. Corey chalked it up to being like exercise—hurting more in the beginning until you got your muscles in shape. She was just conditioning her muscles, and then things would be easier—they had to be. The joy that Keith showed when apart from his job was infectious. Everyone in the Agency respected him for it and sought him when they had problems.

Problems. Those problems were the reason she'd talked to him in the first place. She'd been sure her boyfriend was cheating on her—signs were evident everywhere—but she hadn't wanted to confront it. How someone could be so thoroughly masculine, so good at taking down the bad guys, so untouched by the accusations and violence of some of their clients, and then so gentle and understanding when a weeping woman confessed that she felt betrayed and lost in the wake of her boyfriend's infidelity?

A prick, so light she hardly noticed it, touched her conscience. Her job was to protect those in danger, yes, but part of that protection process was to make the experience as less of an ordeal as possible. She hadn't done that. Erika got under her skin, and Corey couldn't deny that.

"It's her fault," she muttered. "She made him lose his perspective, and now look. He's ruined. He'll lose his job. He's become weak, and for what? He can't even consider a relationship with her. A good man lost because some girl has a cute butt or spunky personality. It's sickening."

# TWELVE

Claire stiffened as Keith pulled up in front of a nail salon, Hard as Nails, and parked the rental car. "The owner of that bicycle shop has something I want you to see."

"Bicycle shop?" She studiously avoided even a glance at the large fingernails in the window that beckoned her. She wasn't handing her cousin over to Alek and his goons. She'd give information as she got it, but family was family. You didn't help people kill them.

"Yeah, I thought it was odd too—kind of ironic, y'know?"

"No," she said, forcing herself to laugh as natural-sounding as possible, "I don't know. I have no idea why we're here."

"Your birthday present."

"Since when do you give me anything but a package of Ding-Dongs? That's been the standing gift for the past twenty-three years or so."

"You'll still get them."

"Keith, you can't afford to give me much more than a book or a movie. Stick to the Ding-Dongs. The plane—"

"Was free. Frequent flier miles." He led her toward the back where Nate was working on bicycle brakes. "I got a bonus, and for once in my life, I'm not going to do the responsible thing and put it all in my savings. Half goes to making dreams come true. Come on."

Nate wiped his hands on a greasy rag and greeted them. "What can I do for you?"

"We're here about the bike."

"The bike? We've got dozens—"

"No, *the* bike."

"Oh! Come in back and check 'er out."

Guilt began to form, sending bile into her throat, as Claire realized what kind of "bike" her cousin had planned for her. How could she stand to betray that kind of generosity? He'd always been so kind to her, even when she'd been a pesky little kid—always trying to involve herself in everything the big kids did.

The motorcycle stood in the center of the room and shone so intensely that it looked brand new. "There she is."

"Do you like it?" Keith asked with unmistakable eagerness.

"It's incredible, but you can't—"

"If it's not what you want," he interrupted, "we'll find another one."

"I'd love it, but—"

"We'll take it. I need it shipped to Brunswick."

The man nodded. "It'll just take me a few minutes to dig out the papers. Do you have a cashier's check?"

"I—I just thought you'd be able to use my credit card."

"That's only for the business. I can't take it for this." The guy sounded apologetic.

"I'll find a way. Give me an hour, will you?" Keith pulled out his wallet and handed the man two hundred dollars. "That should hold it until I can get back."

Without waiting for a receipt, Keith led Claire out the door and glanced around them. "Why don't you go in the salon and get a manicure? There's no reason for you to ride around with me while I find a bank and get the check."

"I don't want a manicure."

"What! You love manicures." He punched the unlock button on his key chain and hurried to slip into the driver's seat. "I'll be back in just a bit."

She stood staring after him, stunned. What had gotten into him? Since when—? Then again, he was excited about the motorcycle. She had to cut him some slack. Especially since he'd expect to find her in the salon, and if she went in, she'd practically be handing him over to Alek and his men.

Erika Polowski had information Alek couldn't risk getting out, and she understood that, but letting them know he was there put Keith in trouble—not Erika. Claire deliberated and made her decision. She'd lie. The fact that Keith had brought her here to buy her the motorcycle proved he wasn't protecting Erika anymore, so she'd spin that her way, and then she'd get information on the way home.

Putting on a confident air, she shoved open the door and entered the salon. Before she could ask if they had an open slot for her, the girl behind the counter swallowed hard and picked up the phone. "Hey, yeah, can you tell Alek that Claire is here?"

---

Keith drove around the corner and parked. He popped the trunk, grabbed the cashier's check stowed there, and slipped it into his wallet. His watch assured him he had at least half an hour—thirty minutes to find the scum of the earth and ensure that Erika could return to her life, unhindered by the threat that now hovered over her.

All because of an address. If Helen Franklin hadn't been such a stickler for protecting her property, there'd be no issue. They could have taken down the Anastas ring on their own without worrying about the well-being of anyone, but because she was conscientious and persnickety about her possessions, Erika was in just as much danger as Helen— simply by address association. Alek Anastas was not a man to take chances. If Helen had to go, then anyone in her house would too, and that anyone was Erika.

He could hear her questions as if she stood next to him. *Why does knowing that hurt me? You're going to get him, so it's not a problem.* Alek was the least of her problems. His small piece of the business would be the least of her worries. Someone like Erika wouldn't keep her mouth shut if she knew how nauseating the stuff Alek's salons hid was. That meant she'd have to be kept in the dark. Agency policy said not to share—just in case. With Erika, ignoring that could be a life or death fail. If the other men and women involved in the trade knew she was aware of their activities, she'd be dead. That he couldn't risk.

Pictures flooded his phone after he sent a quick text message stating he'd arrived. The first three were of possible cars to look for, and the last three were people. Two men and a woman, none of whom he'd ever seen before stared back at him. The woman was identified as exceptionally dangerous and that she had the potential to recognize him.

"Great," he muttered as he found his way into an alley and crept from doorway to doorway until he had no doubt he was one away from the salon. Initially, he had luck with finding the vehicle, but a man stepped out the door, talking on a cell phone, and then returned inside once he snapped the phone shut again. Keith sent an empty reply to that picture, acknowledging he'd verified location.

Taking a deep breath, he hurried past the salon, and hid behind the garbage cans as he waited for a car to pass. The color was right, but the model seemed off. Then again, that had happened several times. The shadow follows, sees the target get out, it's right next to a car with similar color, and the shadow takes a picture of the wrong car. It wasn't common, but Keith never ruled out anything. Ever.

As the car door opened, he sucked in his breath and punched the reply button on a picture of Alek Anastas that Mark had sent him weeks before he'd abducted Erika. He had twenty minutes before he'd have to walk in the front door of that salon. Twenty minutes was plenty of time to take down a man like Anastas—if he was alone. If the salon was crawling with the man's army of bodyguards and silencers, then he'd be unlikely to escape and his cousin—

Keith shuddered. He couldn't risk leaving his cousin in the hands of these people. As he sent another empty reply to signify urgency, he hurried down the alley, keeping to the doorways and ducking behind dumpsters and large cardboard boxes.

A noise, a familiar one, sent a chill up his spine. His first instinct was to jump in the dumpster, but he'd have to walk in the salon in fifteen minutes. Being filthy was a great way to look suspicious. He had a choice of between flattened large refrigerator boxes or stepping inside the back door of the appliance store. Each second that he deliberated meant exponentially increased danger.

There it was again—the sound. The click of a walkie talkie. Why didn't they use cell phones on vibrate? Footsteps. He knew that gait. Whoever was coming was checking out the alley with a gun drawn and sweeping the area for a threat. Did they know he was there? Was his phone monitored somehow?

He had thirty seconds to move. Keith decided. Taking one of the biggest risks of his career, he opened the back door of the appliance store and walked boldly inside, calling out quietly for anyone. "Hey, excuse me? Is anyone here?"

An elderly man stepped from a storeroom with hands full of boxes. "Um, I didn't hear you come in."

"I was in the alley and it sounded like someone was following me. Kind of creeped me out, so I came in here. I'm really sorry."

"Hey, no problem. There's some seedy characters around these days. I'm considering retiring."

"Hey, thanks. I appreciate it." Keith glanced around the showroom as he walked through. "Nice place you have here. You don't see these old mom and pop type places very often anymore."

"Yeah, that's true. Everyone keeps telling me I can't compete with the big boxes, but I've made a good profit every year anyway—not enough to be rich, but enough to live comfortably."

"I bet you give great customer service."

"That's the key."

He wanted to stay and talk. Something about the guy reminded him of Donald Bruner. "If I decide to replace any appliances, I'll be sure to give you a call."

"Thanks. We deliver and install—free."

"I'll remember that." Keith had to force back a smile. *I bet he wouldn't deliver to Rockland free.*

His phone buzzed as he stepped out the front door and jogged across the street, dodging cars as he hurried into a costume store. "Hey, I was wondering if you have anything that reads Jack Sparrow or Captain Hook."

"Sure. Just step into that changing room and I'll bring it. Waist?"

"Thirty-two."

"Gotcha."

Behind the door, he slid open his phone. "ETA, 5. Get out."

A glance over the top of the changing room door showed the woman digging on a rack near the front window. He slipped from the room, crept through the swinging doors to the back, and dashed out into the alley. He ran, dodging around parked cars and dumpsters, until he reached the side street where his car was parked. Once in the car, he blasted the AC to cool him off as he drove around the block and parked in front of the salon.

The salon door dinged as he stepped inside. His heart sank as he recognized the woman at the counter. He slid open his phone and hit an empty reply as he pretended to check the time. Just as she looked up to greet him, Keith diverted to the chair where Claire's fingers sat under a little dryer. "Hey, I've got the check. I'm going to go over and pay for it and arrange shipment." He pulled out a couple of twenties. "Meet you out front in say five minutes?" He hated to do it. She might be in the salon when the team arrived, but trying to pull her out now would definitely make the woman behind the counter pay attention to him. That wasn't in the plan.

"Sure. I'm done here anyway. I'll be right behind you."

For a moment, Keith hesitated. She sounded as if she couldn't wait to get out of there— something that didn't make sense. Was something—nah. *Paranoid.* Surreptitiously, he pressed a button in his pocket, causing his phone to ring. He answered with his left hand and strode from the salon, talking away about how he got the cool motorcycle and praying inwardly that the woman couldn't see his face.

Even as Terry pretended to write down shipping information and pocketed the cashier's check, he watched the street. "I see three agency cars. Frank, Yvette, and it looks like Dean. Argh, I think I saw that silver car go by. Yeah. Dean is whipping around—"

"I wish I could stay and get this done."

"Taking care of her is getting it done. This was brilliant on Mark's part, and here comes Claire. Get her out of here."

---

Claire's hands fidgeted. How could she get information out of him without being obvious? The last time was easy. She'd sent a panicked text message claiming to be in the Dunstan district of Rockland being followed by "thugs" and how did she get out of there? He'd sent a quick text and whatever Alek's tech guy had done to her phone worked. They found them in minutes. The cabin was empty when the team arrived, so someone had been monitoring something. Surely, it wasn't her!

The chill that ran up her spine terrified her. It was one thing to help find the woman who was stealing from Alek. Putting Keith at risk was another thing all together. Then again, the money was good. It had to be good now that she was stuck in it.

Once he found his target and got the money back, she'd tell Keith all about how Alek had found her and asked her to help. He'd been so kind—worried that Keith would get caught in the middle and be accused of aiding a criminal. Of course, once she'd met Alek's men, she knew that crossing him meant death to anyone. Alek had used her, and now she was trapped. However, trapped or not, she refused to turn her cousin over to a creep like Alek Anastas.

She remembered the looks a few of his men gave her and the rumors about his business and shuddered. Claire knew she needed to find out where the woman was before they decided to take their payment from her—it wouldn't be pretty.

"How long do you get off this time?"

"I just got a couple of days. I've got a ton of paperwork to do."

"Did you have a field assignment recently?"

"You know I can't talk about that, Claire."

"How am I ever going to get a job where you do if I don't know what it entails?"

"They're not going to hire you. You know that."

"They will if I know what to do to make them sit up and take notice." She put her hand on his arm. "Don't you get to travel? All those frequent flier miles, right?" She had to remember to stick to the story. "That's gotta be awesome!"

"Forget about it, Claire. It's too dangerous. Your dad would kill me."

"Helping people like that—going to exotic places…" She knew he couldn't resist correcting her.

"Exotic. Ramshackle cabins in the middle of nowhere aren't exactly exotic. They're miserable. Remember, usually the people we're guarding feel trapped, alone, and they take it out on us. You couldn't handle it, Claire. Become a pediatrician. It's what you've always wanted."

"It's too expensive. I'll never get enough money."

"I'll help. Dad would help; Uncle Ted will get another job if he knows you're serious. There are grants, scholarships; you can get student loans. Come on, Claire. Do it."

"Because you don't want me sitting around a dingy cabin in the Rockies protecting some battered wife from her husband?"

He shrugged but didn't answer. Her mind whirled as he pulled into the rental place at the airport. She'd have to do the phone switch thing. It would put him at risk, but she'd just have to refuse to cooperate unless they left him out of it. Besides, he wasn't on that job anymore. It couldn't hurt anything. She'd do it at security.

Claire opened her phone and sent a text message to Jade. PHONE SWITCH AT SECURITY. NEED DIVERSION.

# THIRTEEN

It worked. How, Claire didn't know, but it worked. Her stomach churned at the idea that the toddler had been pushed and cracked its head open, but how else could she explain a gushing head wound at Keith's feet the moment he was supposed to step through the metal detector? It had been brilliant—sick, but brilliant. She wasn't much for prayer, but Claire prayed the kid didn't know that he'd been sacrificed so she could help find Alek's money.

She didn't know if the phone dump had occurred or not. Once she saw the kid and the blood, she'd gone into action. Maybe Keith was right. Maybe it was time to get serious about a career and quit freaking out about the long-term ramifications about student loans high enough to buy a house. Every time she'd gone in to file the papers, she'd seen the numbers, gulped, and chickened out. It was time to stop it and get it done.

Keith returned from the bathroom, his shirt and pants damp and the traces of blood still on the shirt. "Well, I got most of it out. Man, that was gross." He squeezed her shoulders. "You did great, kid. I told you—pediatrician."

"Yeah, I was just thinking the same thing. It's time to get back on the ball."

"Thatta girl."

"So, when does my bike arrive? I still can't believe you bought that thing."

"Hey, sometimes a guy needs to feel frivolous. I don't get time to enjoy that kind of stuff, so I live vicariously through my favorite cousin."

Laughing, Claire punched his arm. "I wasn't always your favorite—well, maybe your favorite pest."

"A fave is a fave, as they say."

"Who says?"

Keith shrugged. "Dunno. Just sounded good." His cell phone rang. "I gotta get this. Be back in a few."

From her vantage point, she could see that something troubled him. He glanced sharply her way, and Claire forced herself to smile before mouthing, "Is something wrong?" Fortunately, he seemed convinced. Shaking his head as he walked away, she knew what he must be discussing. The blood, the hurt kid. One of Anastas' guys must have gotten the phone. Great. Keith's people already knew that someone was tracking him. Man, the people he worked for were good.

Claire always wondered who it was and what he did. Bodyguard was too ambiguous. He'd had a chance at the Secret Service, but as far as she knew, he'd turned them down. Then again, didn't the Secret Service have something to do with money? Counterfeit? Maybe the woman had been counterfeiting? That'd make sense why they'd have her in custody, but not why they were protecting her—unless.

She swallowed. It couldn't be. Alek wasn't a counterfeiter. He dealt in other illegal activities of a less "clean" nature. Then again, who says he hadn't branched out? He could easily be into trafficking *and* counterfeiting, and if this gal had taken off with plates or turned state's evidence or something...

As she watched him slip the SIM card from his phone and toss it in the trash, Claire's mouth went dry. This wasn't good. They couldn't keep track of him without that card. Should she tell Alek or pretend she didn't notice? She'd play it by ear. She could always remember him tossing something later and claim she thought it was a wrapper or something.

By the time they were ready to board the plane, Claire's nerves overcame her—and she knew it showed. Then again, maybe it came off as excitement. She'd run with that. "So, am I going to get you on that bike?"

"Not on your life, and you know it."

"Had to ask." She nearly choked as he picked up his laptop case, carry-on bag, and left his phone sitting on the miserably uncomfortable airport seats. The impulse to point it out was strong, but then she remembered the SIM card. It was a perfect excuse. She could call and tell them he'd left it and they could try to retrieve it. She'd look good instead of incompetent. She glanced at her watch and opted for waiting until she was on the plane. If she left now, it would look suspicious.

---

If Claire's shock hadn't been so genuine, he would have been convinced she was in on the phone tracking. The moment he'd gotten the call, his mind immediately went back to the moment that child's head cracked against the tile at his feet. Surely, it'd been an accident. What creep would cause that kind of pain in a kid? Why he even questioned it, Keith didn't know. Alek Anastas sold people like animals in an auction. Why wouldn't he use one to further his needs?

The idea was preposterous. Claire being in on anything that could hurt him or one of his clients was the most hair-brained idea he'd considered yet. Desperation made him see things in ridiculous lights. Karen told him to ditch the card and phone, so he had, but if they were watching him this closely, there was no way he could get near Erika again. They'd have to find someone else to take over that detail.

The pang of disappointment surprised him. He didn't have illusions about friendships with his clients. His job was to protect them, sometimes against their will—always against their desire. He was happy when a case was over because it meant another life saved, another family protected, another job well done. Nothing satisfied like that knowledge.

Erika wanted to be home so badly that even he could taste it. The idea that he could be attracted to her came and went quickly—perhaps too quickly. It was ludicrous, really. She wasn't very feminine, and Keith had always preferred decidedly feminine women. Her short, spiked hair could have been mistaken as a visual aid for the kind of hairstyle that repulsed him. He didn't like a woman with a foul mouth or a sharp tongue—Erika had both. Furthermore—Keith began to feel as if he had geared up for a tirade—a guy could put up with a lot of things, but lack of respect wasn't one. Erika definitely didn't respect him.

Despite his internal protests, Keith had a sneaking suspicion that he lied to himself. Still, he refused to admit it. Instead, he opted to consider that fleeting feeling of disappointment as due to being unable to finish the assignment. He'd never been pulled from an assignment. In fact, they usually sent *him* in when another agent failed. Withdrawn from duty—tough pill to swallow there. Of course, it upset him—a natural reaction. On and on, his mind tried to justify his unsettled feelings.

A glance at his cousin told him she'd be out for a while. Claire had always been able to sleep anywhere. He stood, stretched his legs, and ambled down the narrow aisle toward the bathroom. He didn't really need the facilities, nor did he relish the feeling of being in a sardine can, but sometimes flight attendants would chat with you if you stood around out there. They, unlike the people in front of you, understood how miserable it was for a tall man with long legs to be folded up like a Jack-in-the-box.

Near the back of the plane, a row of empty seats beckoned him. He pointed to them and silently asked the flight attendant if he could sit. The young man nodded and pulled out a soda can as if to ask if he wanted one. Keith shook his head. Agents weren't allowed to drink anything on flights.

Keith pulled out a virgin cellphone and typed out a simple text, praying the attendant wouldn't notice until it was sent.

BAD NEWS. LOST PHONE. CONTACT AIRPORT LOST AND FOUND? ALL CONTACTS IN IT GONE. AND CAN YOU GET ME A NEW ONE IF THEY DON'T FIND IT? THANKS.

There. Anyone reading wouldn't think a thing of it. Mark knew. That's what mattered.

---

"We missed him. Someone tipped them off. My guess, it was you."

Indignant, Keith's head whipped up ready to protest. "What—"

"I think Servane David recognized you."

"Who?" Keith stared at Mark as if he'd spoken another language. What was with the French and their "Dah-VEED" for David anyway?

"The woman in the salon. I know you did your best, but she could have seen you through the window before you came in."

"Oh." He felt deflated. Every part of him felt like a failure and it showed.

"Keith, stop beating yourself up. You got Claire out of there and safe. You did the right thing."

"I guess."

"Erika demanded to talk to me today."

He couldn't resist laughing. "Oh?"

"She informed me that if I didn't want the biggest lawsuit since Tailhook, I'd better get Corey out of there."

"Great. Who's going?"

"Well, we don't have the manpower to send someone to stay, so Karen is going to go take over until Corey gets back here, and then you'll go in. Meanwhile, we have some tapes for you to review, and Justin in forensics wants to talk to you. He thinks he figured out how you were traced, but he needs to interview you first."

"Interview me? Really? I'm sorry about the phone. I don't see how we could have avoided it, but man…"

"I'm just glad Justin put that program on it. The minute they ran their dump, we knew it. He's amazing." Mark swung his monitor around. "Look here. Watch Claire."

Keith's stomach dropped. Did they seriously think Claire could be a threat? There was absolutely no way. He'd seen her. The stunned expression on her face, the way she hadn't really wanted to go to the salon—if she was trying to get information from him, she would have wanted to go in, wouldn't she? It didn't make sense.

Second by second, frozen frame by frozen frame, they rewatched the scene at security. A hard, cold fury washed over Keith as he saw the woman behind them shove the child with a force that was unmistakable. "What the—"

"It was about your phone. There's no doubt."

"You said to watch Claire. You don't think—"

"No, I don't. But after you saw that, you'd have questioned. Watch."

The child's hand brushed her ankle. In incredibly slow motion, Claire whirled and blinked, looking stunned and uncertain. When the mother didn't grab the child, she went into action, grabbing Kleenex from her purse. The focus and attention she paid to the child and the way she tossed dirty looks at the inattentive mother made it impossible to believe she'd been in on it.

"What was with that woman?"

"I can only assume the child isn't really hers. Look—right there. See it? Does that man look familiar?"

"No way, the TSA guy? How did they know?"

"It's just a cover. He disappears before the regular—see, there."

Sure enough, just as the man turned to hurry the line through the checkpoint, the impostor turned and walked out of the camera's view. "Did you catch him anywhere else?"

"He comes back. Watch"

Sure enough, seconds later, a hand slipped the phone back into the plastic crate that held Keith's things. "I just—how did—wow."

"He's good. If he wasn't a crook, I'd want him. He's not as good as Larry, but then few people are." Mark snapped off the screen and watched as Keith processed the information. "You were adamant that Claire couldn't have done it, and I think the tapes prove that, but I have to ask. Did you doubt her at any time while you were gone—even for a moment."

"I think for a second, after it was over, I remember thinking, 'That was fast. If Claire hadn't been so shocked...'"

"Natural reaction. You're just going through the processing. That's good. I'd be more concerned if you said no."

Keith nodded. "Denial is powerful stuff. You're right. If I hadn't questioned, it'd be bad."

"You've been feeling guilty." It wasn't a question.

"Yeah. She's family. You don't doubt family."

"Don't make me lose all faith in you, Keith. You doubt everyone. To keep the client alive, you doubt everyone. Me,

Karen, Corey, even Justin, Jill, Anthony, and Larry. You doubt anyone and everyone. It keeps people alive."

"Yeah. I don't have to like that part."

"No, but you do it because it's instinctive. I bet you doubted me the minute that second call came through." Keith didn't have to answer. The truth of it was written across every feature. "That's good. I can sleep at night because I know you'll do your job. That's why you're going back in. Saturday."

"Three-week anniversary. Should I bring flowers and chocolate?"

"Take a chick flick. I'll find out from Karen what Erika wants to see."

"There's no electricity, Mark."

"Take a portable DVD." At the disgusted face Keith made, Mark howled. "Yeah, you'll have to sit a little closer than you like, but watch the stupid movie with her. She'll relax with you again."

"Whatever."

"How are you going to win back her trust? We can't afford to be exposed. I swear, the directors of every agency in Washington would be down on us so fast.…"

"I'll be honest but show loyalty to the agency. I won't trash Corey, but I won't condone her garbage either. I think it's the best way to ensure she knows I'm still me. I think that's a big part of the big picture. She trusted Karen and she trusted me. When we brought in Corey, we violated her trust by bringing in someone who, in her mind, she couldn't trust."

"Makes sense. I don't know, though. Corey did some serious damage."

"I'm just going in and being who I was and treating her the way I did before—like none of this happened. I think it's the best way to put it all behind us."

"I'm trusting you, Auger. Get out there and do some damage control—even if it means you have to watch Kiss and Make Up until that stupid battery dies. Take spares, just fix this."

"I want another bonus—one I can keep."

Mark laughed and rose to shake his best agent's hand. "You keep us out of the papers and the courts, and I'll see that one happens."

"Don't tell Erika about that."

Mark never would, and both men knew it, but Mark had to ask. "Why not?"

"She'd insist on taking half."

# Fourteen

Erika paced the living room despite her exhaustion. She'd discovered, about eighteen hours after Keith left, that pacing irritated Corey. So, when she was up and awake, she paced. The rattle of the chain, the occasional thud as she turned the corner, and the shuffle of her shoes across the floor would normally have driven her to the brink of insanity and back, but the stress visible on her "guard's" face made every irritating noise worth it.

Corey had tried everything, but Erika couldn't help gloating at failure after failure. A shortened chain meant more frequent thumps as she did an about-face. The woman demanded that Erika clean the bathroom, but she refused. If the person "the Agency" sent to guard their abductee wanted a clean toilet seat upon which to dole out the rest of her excrement, then she could clean it herself.

Erika ate her meals walking, her snacks walking, and even paced in the shower just to keep the chain rattling. Corey retaliated by making her wear the infernal thing twenty-four-seven. Once it became a battle of wills, Erika determined that she would win—at any cost.

When Corey had blasted her once again, pulling her gun and demanding that she sit, Erika had held out her hand for the phone. It became an instant, utterly satisfying, memory. Corey blanched, but dialed. Erika hadn't actually expected to speak to anyone, but Keith's "Mark" had come on the line and listened courteously as she'd bawled him out. Instant catharsis. And now, in just an hour or two, Corey would be gone, and Erika planned to collapse on the couch without moving for any reason—aside from sleep and using the bathroom—for days if necessary. If they didn't want her having blood sugar issues, they could bring her food. She wouldn't budge.

"Your calves are going to be bigger than an elephant's."
"But they'll be strong." Erika refused to take the bait.
"Strong and huge."
"And your problem is?"
"Look, if you want to look like a freak, that's your business." Corey's voice sounded positively peevish.

The satisfaction in realizing she'd caused it nearly sent Erika into visible ecstasies. "Sure is."

"Look, when Karen gets here and practically shoves you out there to get shot, just remember that the stupid things you do puts more than you in danger. These people are working hard to keep your sorry backside alive. Show them the courtesy of not doing anything that'll force them to take a bullet or twenty for you."

"You've told me half a dozen times that I had the best man in America protecting me. Well, you sent him away, so does that make you the stupidest woman in America or just the most arrogant?"

"Listen, you—"

"No, listen both of you! I could hear you for the past quarter mile! How on earth do you expect to protect her if you're shouting like a crazy woman? Get your stuff together. It's almost dark. You gotta get out of here the minute that sun is down."

Both cabin-bound women stared at Karen in the doorway. Then, as if relief hadn't arrived, Erika kept pacing. Karen took one look at her and asked, "Has she tried to escape or something?"

"Um, she's here under duress. She's supposed to be chained."

"You don't have a gun?" Karen seemed to deliberately tack patience onto each word.

"I have one." There was that peevish tone again.

"Then get that shackle off her. Man, Corey, where're your brains?" Before the disgruntled woman could answer, Karen added, "Nah, don't bother. I really don't want to know."

As much as she didn't want to do it, Erika kept pacing. The second she saw Corey's furious expression, she sighed in relief. It wasn't worth the exertion if she didn't irritate Corey in the process. "Do you see this? She's just trying to annoy me!"

"If you ignored her, she'd quit. I bet she stops the minute you step out that door."

"Probably," the woman muttered, giving Erika even more personal satisfaction. It was worth every minute of self-inflicted torture. Every second, really.

As predicted, the minute Corey passed through the door Erika plopped onto the couch and put her feet up. Glancing at Karen, she stretched. "What took you so long?"

"I got here the minute it was safe. Oh, and we're leaving."

"Where are we going?"

"You're going to park your car in the garage at Helen Franklin's and then we're taking off again."

"Where to?"

"What matters," Karen continued with an exaggerated roll of her eyes, "is that you'll be away from here. They don't expect us to move you, there's been no threat, so it's perfect." After downing a glass of water, Karen crossed the room and sank into "Keith's" chair. "We're close, Erika. I wouldn't be surprised if it was less than a week."

---

Keith felt ridiculous. Why should he be nervous? The helicopter was less than an hour out. The only disadvantage to the move was that it meant they now had electricity, which meant she could torture him with the movie for days if she wanted to—and she'd want to. That thought made him smile. No one could say protecting Erika Polowski was dull. Nope. No one.

The cottage—you really couldn't call it a cabin—had been left spotless by the last occupants—a great relief after the previous cabin. In fact, it looked as if they'd stepped into someone's home rather than a safe house stuck in the coastal woods of Oregon. The décor, style, everything seemed to indicate that Martha Stewart planned to stop in and critique or something. Comfortable furniture filled the living spaces; personal touches to bedrooms such as school awards and posters hinted at a real family home. Either it truly belonged to someone in the Agency, or the house was a masterpiece of diversionary proportions. Regardless, it impressed Keith.

The cliffs overhanging the ocean would provide diversion. He'd be able to take her for walks along the cliffs. Erika would like that. The dossier said she'd never been to either coast; at least he could give her a new experience or two. Maybe, once the coast was clear—he snickered at the unintentional pun—they'd be able to take her down to the shoreline and let her walk along the beach. It was a small consolation prize for a month of her life lost, but she still lived. Regardless of their failures, they'd kept her alive. Helen Franklin was alive, and they thought they'd have Anastas and his crew in days.

As it was, they had over half of the most important people under constant surveillance. The minute everyone and everything dropped into place, the nightmare would end, and Erika and Helen could have their lives back. That meant success—two lives saved from the greed and lawlessness of people who used others as a means to their own gain. That's what hurt the most—seeing people as disposable or as slaves to fill the coffers of the insatiable.

As nervousness churned in his gut again, Keith frowned. It made no sense. Then again, this was a second chance to finish the only job he'd been removed from and do it right this time. Anyone would be nervous—wouldn't he? He needed to quit overthinking things. Ever since the trip to Columbus, he had developed the obnoxious habit of uncertainty. Second-guessing everything drove him crazy. Something from that trip still unsettled him, and despite Mark's assurances to the contrary, he knew he'd missed something.

Just as he heard the soft whap, whap of the helicopter blades, his new cell phone buzzed with a text message to announce their arrival. He grinned at the one-word message. CATCH. That had to be Erika's influence.

Duffel in hand, Erika ran from the helicopter just as it rose from the ground and headed farther up the coast. She stopped just short of him and gave him her trademarked—at least he thought it should be—disgusted expression. "I told you to catch."

"Well, that's true but you jumped before I could get out there."

"Excuses, excuses."

Keith jerked his thumb into the house. "Make yourself at home." He grabbed her duffel bag and followed her into the house. "Pick a room—any room."

Her eyes traveled around the house as she entered. "Swanky."

Eyes rolling, Keith pointed to the hallway. "Room service is about to end. Take your pick, or I'm picking for you."

"I'll take this one." She stepped into a pink and purple unicorn-infested nightmare of a little girl's room. "It's sweet."

"You're going to be butchering those things in your sleep."

Erika shrugged, took the bag from him, and tossed it on the be-ruffled bed. "Some people count sheep, I slaughter horses. What's the difference?" His dubious expression prompted the appearance of surrender, but Keith was skeptical—even when she added, "Okay, so I figured out that having the best as your guard-slash-warden is a little better than having a half-crazed psycho."

"Isn't the definition of psycho something akin to completely crazed?"

"Tell me there's food."

Keith rolled his eyes. "There's food. Seriously? You didn't eat before you got in the 'copter?"

"I did, but that was several hours ago. They made a stop, every four miles, all the way up the coast from Mendocino. It's like a very loud, very bad rollercoaster ride."

"They'll continue all the way to Vancouver too. Smart." Impressed, Keith pulled out a couple of kiwi fruit and passed them across the counter. "Karen said you like these."

"Yum! Want one?"

"Um, hairy b— well, I can't say what they look like, but it's gross, so no."

"Grow up. Here, where's the potato peeler?"

After digging through several drawers of various utensils, Keith pulled out what he decided must be the Cadillac of kitchen gadgets. "This?"

"Nice. How'd we score this place?"

"I think Karen is feeling guilty about Corey."

"She should," the visible shudder was unmistakable, "that woman is insane."

"They're sending her for a psych eval and a few other things. She's never done anything like that before." Keith took the green, slimy, slice of fruit and tried to ignore the seeds that looked like little black ants mocking him. "She's really one of the best."

"You can't *all* be 'one of the best,' and Karen says you're *the* best." Erika stifled a snicker as Keith tried to swallow the slice whole. "It's sweet. Chew."

If he closed his eyes and pretended he didn't know what it looked like, Keith had to agree. It was a little like honeydew with a hint of sourness—for which he blamed and complimented the seeds. However, it was difficult to ignore the seeds as he chewed them. "Do the seeds have to look like bugs?"

"Oh, don't be such a baby. Man, what a—"

"I thought you just said I was the best that the Agency has. If I'm the best, I'm not the wuss you want to make me out to be, so stuff it."

Between bites of kiwi and snickers at his expression, Erika gave him a rundown of her week with Corey. "She didn't like pacing."

As he thought about it, that made sense. "Yeah, you're right. She doesn't like that. I think better when I pace, and I think it annoys her."

"Well, I paced for five days straight. My legs are still sore."

"You did what?"

He waited for her to say something that indicated she was teasing, but Erika just shrugged and said, "Look, she was annoying. I wasn't giving her an inch *or* a mile."

"And now you're paying for it."

"Oh," Erika continued as if he hadn't just shown her who really was tortured by the pacing, "and she made it very clear that you'd never be interested in a girl like me. For the record, you like very feminine girlie girls who like to sip sweet tea in large hats and jump at spiders." She winked. "So, don't get any ideas. Corey has determined that we are incompatible."

"Got it."

"I thought about pointing out that you're too smart to get caught up in a drama machine like her. I mean, yeah, I get that I'm not your type. I can take that. I'm not looking to do the whole Stockholm Syndrome thing anyway, but if she thinks a guy with sense is going to fall for—"

"I was attracted to her before the cabin, Erika. When I say she was unrecognizable there, I'm not exaggerating." Whether she didn't believe him or was too disgusted to discuss it further, Keith didn't know, but the subject changed so fast it took him a minute to follow.

"Did you know she kept me chained twenty-four-seven? Were you guys even trained at the same place?"

He had a choice and a hard one. If he defended his co-worker, he risked annoying Erika when he most needed to regain her trust. Then again, displaying too much disloyalty to an agent and the Agency was a great way to imply they'd made a mistake, and that was sure to stick in her mind. After one of the fastest and most nonsensical prayers he'd ever made, Keith tried to walk that very fine line that usually meant straddling a very sharply picketed fence.

"Look, you know I disagree with how Corey acted about some things. She let her emotions interfere with her reason and it made things more difficult than they had to be, but—" Keith shook his head as Erika started to pounce on his words. "On the other hand, she hadn't built a trust with you like I had, and she's a woman. She's not as strong or as fast as I am. Women typically rely more on restraints and locks than men do. It's a simple fact of the job."

"She was rude."

"Unquestionably."

"Arrogant." Erika's eyes dared him to contradict her.

"I'd never deny it."

"And brutal."

"I can't agree with that. You are here, healthy, and uninjured. You weren't as comfortable as you could have been, yes. You would have been more comfortable with a man, yes. You would have been more emotionally comfortable with someone like Karen, without a doubt." He swallowed and waited, allowing his words to sink into her mind. "But Karen, alone in the house, would have had to use the same restraints in nearly the same way."

# Fifteen

With movie in hand, Erika strolled from her pink and purple prison. Why she'd been so obnoxious as to insist on that room, she didn't know, but her pride resisted allowing her to request a change. The look of dread on Keith's face as she waved the movie suddenly made Karen's dismay clear. Keith didn't like action movies. That was odd for a guy, but tough luck. She'd missed it in theaters, thanks to losing three employees at once, and she'd missed the debut on DVD, thanks to whatever she knew or shouldn't know—or something like that.

"I'd say I'm sorry, but I'm not. I've been dying to see this for months."

Keith nodded and took the box, visibly preparing himself for the contents, and then jerked his head up to meet her eyes. "Wha—"

"Okay, so I'm sorry. Sue me. Sheesh."

"Why are you sorry? This was the best movie of the year. I love this."

"You didn't look like you loved it, and Karen seemed bothered..."

He pulled the wrapper from the movie, popped it open, and inserted the disk into the DVD player. "Karen was hoping you'd make me watch *Kiss and Make Up*."

"Oh, ew. Everything that Wendy Panther is in is just nauseating. I bet she grovels. She has to. It's like her trademark or something."

"I think you just passed up Donald on the fun scale."

A sense of satisfaction washed over her as she settled into an overstuffed chair. She'd upstaged the comedic codger. That was something. It wasn't much, but after weeks of mere existence she'd take what she could get.

"So, is the secretary on the good side or the bad?"

"I'm not telling; watch the movie." Keith hardly took his eyes from the screen.

"I'm watching, I just want to know if I'm right."

"You'll find out when the director wants you to."

Erika sent a pillow flying in his direction, but his reflexes—wow. Without taking his eyes from the screen, Keith caught it one-handed, and whirled it back at her. It bounced off her head before she could catch it. "How do you do that?"

All throughout the movie, Erika asked questions, made observations, and proposed hypotheses with abandon. She could see it drove him crazy, but if anything, it spurred her on to greater heights of irritating achievements. His hands balled into fists and gripped the arms of his chair. Her mouth twisted as she watched his jaw clench and his lips tighten.

"Be amused all you want."

"How do you *do* that! That's insane. You never took your face from the screen."

"It's called peripheral vision. Mothers and teachers use it to keep kids in line. The military and law enforcement use it to watch their back, and I use it to ensure that if someone is outside lurking, I'll notice."

"Okay, so what is Jett going to do now?"

"He's going to show you in about thirty-two point seven seconds. Watch."

An explosion ripped across the screen, sending Erika's eyes back to the plot unfolding before her. She had so many questions she wanted to ask, starting with why Corey had let her call Mark in the first place. It made no sense.

At the end of the movie, before the first line of credits rolled, Erika punched the remote, cutting off the noise. "Why did Corey call Mark? I demanded all kinds of things that she ignored. Why did she do that one?"

Keith sat silent for the better part of a minute before he stretched and stood. "Because we're required to. If you ask to speak to someone over us, the only way we can deny it is if we're in the middle of a crisis, and even then, we'd better be able to prove it would put our client at risk."

"Da—"

"Come on, Erika. Really?"

"Fine. *Darn.* Is that better?"

Without answering, he strolled into the kitchen and returned with the garbage can. "So, is it garbage or trash?"

"Okay, okay. You win. How about um…" she thought for a moment. "Oh, forget it. I can't believe we're quibbling over darn vs. da—"

Keith glared.

"Fine. Whatever. Back to the point. I'm ticked. If I'd known that, I would have demanded to call at every meal and bedtime too."

"I'm sure you would have had fun with that, but you could have been taking him from his focus on keeping very real people such as yourself alive. Don't be selfish—even to annoy people who probably deserve it."

"Does that include you?"

"Especially me."

Without another word, he returned the garbage can to the kitchen. Seconds later, the sounds of dishes being loaded into the dishwasher followed. Though she felt she should offer to help, Erika strolled toward the front door and tried to open it. Locked. As she realized there wasn't a way to unlock it, she looked for an alarm panel, but found nothing.

"Behind the silhouette of the little girl. Today's code is 7-2-9-9-3-2."

"You're giving me the code?" Even as she asked, Erika punched the numbers in to see if they'd work.

"They'll change after you go to bed. The windows won't break, the doors will lock or not at the push of a button, and it looks perfectly normal to anyone who doesn't know that's there."

"Why?"

"Because we still have to protect ourselves. Just because you seem willing to try to cooperate, doesn't mean I am not going to do or say something that ticks you off and puts us both in jeopardy."

"I'm still a prisoner, aren't I?" She knew she sounded childish, but it was hard to disguise. Everything had seemed so—so different.

"You are still under the protection of the Agency. This is how protection works. We know how to protect you from those who seek to harm you, from our own procedures, and from yourself."

"It's all so crazy, though."

Keith shrugged and pointed to her room. "Now, do you want to stay in there, or do you want the master suite with bath attached so you won't have to wait for me to let you out in the morning?"

She saw through him, but Erika couldn't help but grasp at the excuse—anything to avoid all night in the pink and purple bubble. "That makes sense. Seems stupid to make you get up just so I can go to the bathroom."

"Take some water bottles and some nuts with you. There's a good TV in there and everything, but keep the shades down. We don't want to light up like a beacon." He passed her a walkie-talkie. "In case you need me. No reason to try to shout across the house."

Twenty minutes later, Erika lay on her back, under the nicest bedding she'd ever encountered, and reviewed everything leading up to that moment—starting with the rude awakening in her bedroom at Helen's.

*He didn't hurt me. Even putting tape over my mouth and rolling me in rope, he was gentle.* She remembered the trek up the mountain, his assurances that they wouldn't hurt her, and the way he'd avoided removing the tape for fear of hurting her. The way he'd warned her before he tackled...

His demeanor though—it didn't fit. He often looked surly or put out. He never acted as if she was a burden, and yet she couldn't discount the visible frustration on his face every time he had to deal with her. She'd thought it was gone, but as she lay remembering, she saw the same scowl and the same tenseness she'd always seen as he waited for her to close her bedroom door.

It didn't fit. None of it did. How could someone be such a contradiction of himself? Her snarky comments never fazed him, and her attempts to remain aloof and independent almost seemed to comfort him somehow. Why was that?

All along she'd been adamant that she wouldn't give in to the whole Stockholm Syndrome thing, but when she realized how much she trusted him and Karen both, it concerned her. Had she lost her sense of identity already?

Erika crawled from beneath the covers and walked to the bathroom as if to her sentencing. She stood before the mirror and awaited the verdict. Was she really giving up already?

---

"You said something once that's been bothering me."

Keith glanced up from his omelet, almost afraid to ask what. "Only one?"

"Well, right now anyway. You once told me that I needed to keep fighting this. Karen said it too, I think."

"You do."

"Why? That's what I don't understand. Why? I laid awake all night thinking about it. I just don't understand why you want me to fight what you think is best for me."

He finished chewing his eggs, the flavor now gone from them as he worked to think of the right thing to say. How did you explain something like that without creating a worse situation than you already had? "Because it's not normal, okay? I broke into your home. I bound you, gagged you, and took you away from everything you know, love, and trust. I'm keeping you captive. This isn't normal. You're supposed to fight what isn't normal. If you don't, then you become vulnerable."

He watched as his words sank in and filtered through Erika's thought processes. As tempted as he was to admit that her complacency put both of them in danger because it allowed him to relax when he needed to be on the top of his game, it just didn't seem wise. That balance of knowledge versus uncertainty kept people safe.

"So, you want me to trust you and resist you at the same time."

"Basically."

Her laughter surprised him. "So, you're saying you're the embodiment of every stereotypical woman? You want two opposing things in one person?"

"Maybe."

Erika glared at him as she shoved her chair away from the table. "I don't get you. You're like this walking paradox or something. You're always frowning, scowling, or looking like this is the most distasteful job in the world, but I can tell you love it. You like being put in danger for someone else. For some sick reason, this is your idea of a good time."

"I like helping people, Erika." He tried to think about a comparison that'd make sense to her. "Okay, you manage a coffee shop. You have customers that come in every day, right?"

"Yeah."

"Don't you like knowing that you made a difference in someone's day? Your diligence made the trek to what might be a very boring job a little brighter because they know someone remembered their favorite coffee combination and asked about their aunt in the hospital."

"How did you know—?"

"We watch, Erika. You know that. We watch."

He observed as Erika processed his words and as he did, Keith prayed. With each assignment, regardless of whether it was a voluntary protection or a forced one, he always prayed that those who didn't know Jesus would see something in his life to pique their interest. For those in enforced protection, he prayed that the nature of his job wouldn't blind them to the reality of their need for the Lord.

Keith had little hope that Erika would show any interest while he knew her, but small seeds, no matter how long they lay dormant under the soil, might germinate with the right conditions. All he could do was pray that those seeds weren't blown away by life's winds.

A wry smile twisted his lips as he imagined what she'd say if Erika could hear his thoughts. She'd accuse him of losing his mind to cabin fever or something equally ridiculous. He couldn't blame her. Blown away by life's winds. *Cheesy.*

"If you like, we can take a walk along the cliffs after dark. We'll have to cross the road, but it shouldn't be too busy. We can't be seen, but at least you can smell the ocean and see the moon on the water. It'll be something different anyway."

"Handcuffs?"

"Nah," he agreed. "Not necessary. I'll have my gun."

"Gee, what a comfort."

Keith almost let it go but couldn't. "You know, I truly do hope you never have to discover exactly what a comfort my gun really is."

# Sixteen

"Well, at least it's a full moon."

She'd been out of sorts all afternoon, but Keith didn't quite know what to do about it. Whatever her problem might be, he'd have to wait for her to spill it. Meanwhile, her comment about the moon unsettled him. *You wanted her to say and do things that kept you on your toes, you idiot. Well, now she has.* Aloud he simply said, "That it is."

He passed her two bottles of water, a package of beef jerky, and a package of nuts. "Want to take an apple or something too?"

"How long will we be gone?"

"You don't leave the house without enough to keep you going if anything happens. Period."

"Wow. You're practically telling me how to escape again."

Laughing, he passed her an apple. "Put it in your pocket. Escape all you want to. It'll keep us from boredom."

"Isn't boredom indicative that we're safe?"

Keith checked his gun and then stuffed it in his holster. "You'd think so, wouldn't you?"

Two miles to the cliffs—a short walk, but he could sense that she needed the exercise. The day would have been better. She could have seen the waves, the birds flying overhead... something. Night was safer. Fewer eyes, harder to see, and easier for him to sense something off in the house when they returned. Mark expected everything to come to a crisis soon. He needed to be on his toes, and fresh air and exercise would help.

"Keith?"

"Hmm?"

"I'm not going to sue you guys."

Of all the things she could have said at that moment, he certainly hadn't expected that. "Well, I know I'd appreciate it if you didn't."

"I want to. I want to make sure that this never happens to anyone again, but I can't."

His heart sank. For days, over a week actually, he'd been certain that she understood that "this" was a good thing even if she didn't like it. "Why not?"

"Well, besides the fact that I have no idea who or what to put on the papers, as much as I don't like it, I have to believe you're doing this for my own good. I don't understand it, and sometimes I still think you've got the wrong girl—"

"Do you know how much I wish I could wake up tomorrow to a text message that says, 'Oops, we got the wrong one. Take Erika home?'"

"How sure are you that I'm the one?"

"If it were possible to be more than one hundred percent sure of something, I'd be more. It isn't possible that we're wrong, Erika. It's *not* possible."

"I don't believe that." She stumbled, but Keith grabbed her arm as if he'd expected her to, and then released her again.

"You don't have to believe it, Erika. If it keeps you sane to doubt, then doubt. Knowing that there's a price on your head isn't easy to live with."

"Is there really a price on my head? What if the one who put the price out there got it wrong? Isn't there some way to convince him that he got it mixed up?"

"Even if he's wrong, he has men all over the country looking for you. We can't just go in there and say, "Look, we know you're a creep and want this woman dead, but you really have the wrong one.'"

"Yeah, I suppose."

He watched the wheels turning, praying she wouldn't press it further.

"On the bright side, at least even if I was the wrong woman, it'd mean the right woman would be safe—for now anyway. Maybe she has children or a husband. Them getting me would be hard on my parents, but I don't have anyone dependent on me." Erika laughed. "Now I just sound morbid."

"Well, I wasn't going to say it...." The sounds of cars told him the road was close. "Okay, Erika. I have to take the gun out now. It's really simple. You stay with me, you don't step out where anyone can see you, and you don't scream."

"Like you'd really shoot me. Come on, Keith. We both know you're not going to hurt me."

"Don't test me, Erika. I'm serious. Don't. I *will* shoot you before I'll let you put us in jeopardy."

"But—"

"Just don't. Maybe we should go back." He hesitated, hand on the gun as he searched her face in the moonlight. The irony of being near the ocean, with a huge full moon shining down on him and an attractive woman, while holding a gun and threatening to use it on her amused him. "I think I'm glad I'm not much of a romantic."

"Yeah, that would have just killed the moment."

---

The steely expression in his eyes, combined with the resolute hold of his jaw, told her he wouldn't budge. Despite his protest, Erika knew that Keith was probably one of those guys who had his own brand of sappy, affectionate displays. He'd probably compliment her on things like her ability to take him down when he wasn't paying attention or that she could hike for miles without talking if necessary. It sounded like a romance made for him—and at that moment, she'd never been more thankful that Corey had been right. He'd never be interested in her. That she was slightly disappointed almost bothered her, but the sight of that gun kept her mind from exploring the reason.

"Come on, I'm not going to run. I just don't believe you'd actually use that thing."

"Well, don't try me, and I won't have to prove you wrong. It's a win-win situation."

"Can we get down to the water?" Changing the subject seemed like the best option, especially now that she could see the lights of a car passing. Vehicles didn't pass often, but they were out there.

"Not near here. About ten miles either way and I think there's some beach, but it's not smart to walk that far in the dark."

"So," she peeked out from the trees. "There're no cars. Can we go?"

He listened and shook his head. "Semi coming. We'll let him pass first."

"How can you hear that? I don't—" Just as she started to insist he was crazy, the distinctive sound of an approaching truck reached her ears.

"I have excellent hearing—particularly when it's something I don't want to hear."

The dash across the road? Anti-climactic. She'd expected something more exciting than a glance, a listen, and a brisk walk across the road and over the guardrail. They scrambled down a few feet to the ledge and made themselves comfortable. Once settled, Erika sighed.

"When this is all over, I'm taking my vacation and coming back here. This—" her arm swept over the view before them. "Totally amazing."

How long they sat there—neither of them talking but both listening to the sounds around them—only Keith knew. He had his phone and his watch, but Erika didn't even ask. Each second that ticked past could have been a century for all she cared. The waves below crashed loudly against the rocks, but the sound soothed. She loved the scent of the salt, the spray that occasionally sent a light mist up toward them, and even the occasional car that whizzed by on the way to who knew where.

She heard the buzz of his cell phone before he could reach in his pocket and pull it out. "If they're calling to say we're free to leave, I don't wa—"

Before she could finish, he jerked her up, whispering into her ear. "Shh. Follow me, don't talk, and try not to make any noise."

Though she knew fear must have washed over her face as well as her heart, Erika nodded, swallowed hard, and reached for his hand. If they had to be quiet, she wanted him close. The minute his wrapped around hers, he gave it a squeeze before he pulled her up behind the guardrail. "Ugh. There's another semi coming. *Run!*"

She wanted to ask why they didn't wait, but she couldn't. His feet pounded across Highway 101, nearly pulling her through the air behind him. She stumbled, but as if able to keep her afloat by his sheer willpower, he jerked her up behind him and then flattened them both against a tree.

"Shh. We have to keep moving but let the semi pass. If a car comes, we become one with a tree, got that?" His whisper in her ear sounded stern—almost fierce.

Despite her bravado, Erika trembled. The idea that they were vulnerable, out in the woods, unprotected and with no way to escape, terrified her. "You won't leave me behind, will you?"

"They're going to get him, Erika. Karen, David—the team is all ready to close in. Just follow me and keep quiet."

He dragged her through the woods of the Siuslaw National Forest, and away from the wonderful cottage. She didn't want to go back to a place like that second—or even the first cabin. No, Erika liked having TV reception and a good kitchen to cook in if she wanted, thank-you-very-much. She hadn't even had a chance to do it.

Sounds behind them seemed to squeeze an involuntary whimper from her. Keith's hand pulled her closer and then released hers while he wrapped an arm around her shoulder. "It's okay, Erika. I've got you; we've got your back; this is almost over."

"Over? As in, I get to go home over?"

Under cover of so many trees, the moonlight hid the smile she knew he wore, but his words said it all. "As in, you've got your life back over."

"How long?"

"An hour? Two. I just have to keep you as far away as possible in case there's anyone around the perimeter watching for escape."

She started to squeal--highly out of character for her. Erika considered it understandable under the circumstances, but Keith clamped his hand over her mouth. "Shh. We're not out of the woods yet." The merest hint of a chuckle rumbled in his chest before he added, "So to speak."

They walked for an hour, stopping every few feet to listen and for Keith to scan the terrain with his infrared binoculars—how had she not noticed them?— before they continued for the next yard or two. Part of her wondered if it weren't an act—some kind of pretext to make her think things were worse than they really were so she wouldn't go public with her story.

Then he froze. She felt the tension fill him so quickly that she feared his nerves would snap. He jerked her against a tree trunk and held her close while he listened. Taking a deep breath, he whispered. "You have to do exactly what I say. Do you understand?"

Terrified, Erika just nodded, her eyes answering, though she knew he couldn't see them. "Good. Stay here. Count to twenty. Then, dart from tree to tree in a straight line. Can you do that?"

She shook her head. The fear mounted until she felt like a little girl again. "No, please—"

He peered around the tree with his binoculars and growled in frustration. "Erika, I really need you to do this. We're sitting ducks here. If you go, he'll follow, and I can take him down from behind." Each word was the merest whisper in her ear. How a man with such a deep voice could speak so silently, she'd never understand.

"I—"

"I knew you could do it. Pretend Corey just told you that you couldn't."

His words infuriated her. If he had to use Corey to get some backbone into her, then she must really sound pathetic. Her feet crunched the leaves as she dashed from tree to tree. She hadn't spoken to God since she was tiny, but Erika prayed with every step. Terror filled her heart as she forced herself to keep going, even as she heard footsteps following—gaining on her.

Self-preservation stepped in and overtook her. She began zig-zagging, hoping as she did, that it'd make aiming at her difficult. Why hadn't the guy shot yet? Could it be one of Keith's co-workers? What if he took down a good guy!

Suddenly, she realized she didn't hear footsteps anymore. She paused, listening, and then started to run again, but a hand clamped over her mouth and jerked her. "Shh. I got him."

She whirled, eyes staring up into Keith's face, stunned. How had he shot anyone? She didn't hear a thing. "How—?"

"He's zipped about thirty yards back. The second you took off, he took off after you, so I got him fast. Just had to get you then."

"So," she sighed, and then began to speak in a normal tone, "you—"

His hand covered her mouth again. "Shh. We don't know who all are out here. We keep moving until I get the call."

With each mile that they traversed, Erika thought she'd go crazy. Twice, he flattened her against a tree, his hand over her mouth, and his body rigid with tension. Each time, he'd slowly relaxed, took a deep breath, and apologized. "Sorry, I'm jumpy."

"Hey, if it's keeping us safe...."

The call came just as Erika was ready to beg to stop for a snack. The adrenaline rush, combined with too long since dinner, made her dizzy. She listened to his side of the conversation, and then froze when a sound—one that didn't fit—broke through her consciousness. Erika tugged his sleeve, but he ignored her until she jerked the phone away and covered her lips with her finger.

Keith nodded, disconnected the call, and pulled her close behind him, scanning the trees again with his binoculars. Once he found his target, he pulled her around the tree and whispered, "Can you manage one more time? I think I can call out to you this time, so you won't have to run as much."

It took every ounce of strength she had left, but Erika nodded. It was almost over. She could do this. She could go home if she could just do this. "Tell me when to go."

The crunch of boots coming their way nearly drove her insane. Seconds passed as he waited, and then she ran when his finger pointed in the direction she should go. The heavy footfalls of a larger, heavier-shoed man sounded ominous to her, but then silence came. She kept going for a few yards, and then dared to glance over her shoulder. Nothing.

As her neck craned to see what could have happened, she ran into a tree, stunning her. How stupid could she be? Disoriented, she stood, trying to get her bearings, and then watched agape as Keith fought a man. Where the gun was, she didn't know, but from the way he fought, she didn't think he'd need it. For a moment, she changed her mind and started to run again, but fury drove her back toward the fighting men. Keith saw her and ordered her to go, sending the other man scurrying in her direction, but Keith tackled him again, sending another fist into the man's face.

"Where's your gun?"

"He knocked it out of my hand, now get out of here!"

"Where were you?" Seeing him ready to refuse to tell her, she shook her head. "I'm going to look either way, so you'd better just tell me."

"At the base of that tree, now get it and go!"

It took several frenzied seconds of scrambling to find the gun, aim it at the man who now straddled Keith, and fire—nothing happened. "The safety," he choked out.

Erika fumbled with it, trying to feel for anything that might be a "safety" and then found a little button above the trigger. Feeling quite smug, she released the safety and promptly squeezed the trigger.

Wooziness overtook her. Erika's last conscious thought barely had time to formulate. *I can't believe I just shot myself at a time like this.*

# Seventeen

A haze coated the room and voices sounded garbled as Erika fought unconsciousness. When an unfamiliar face loomed over her, calling her name in what seemed like exaggerated enunciation, she screamed and went ballistic. With adrenaline coursing through her veins, Erika tried to fling herself from the bed and escape the room full of strange faces.

"It's okay, Erika, just calm down. We don't want to have to sedate you—"

Another voice called for Keith, and hearing the name made her pause. "You have Keith too?"

Her eyes tried to make out the man in the doorway, but until she heard his voice, much less garbled than any of the others, she wasn't sure. "Erika, relax. The tranq isn't out of your system yet."

"The *what!*"

He snickered as he motioned for the others to leave the room. "You shot yourself with my gun, remember?"

"Tranquilizer gun? Seriously?" Before he could answer, she shook her head as if it would actually clear it. "Wait, no, that's not possible. They don't use tranquilizer guns on people. I did a whole paper on that in high school."

"Well, that was a few years ago, Erika."

"No, no," she sat up again as if determined to prove him wrong. "I was arguing with Jerry at work a couple of weeks ago. He didn't believe me, so I looked it up on Google. It's too easy to overdose and kill people."

"Well, let's just say that we have a specially formulated tranquilizer."

She shook her head. "Either way, you have to know how much to give a person—you have to know their weight and everything, or it's too much."

"We know all that about you, Erika. That's who the gun was for, remember? For you?"

"But you shot that guy—the one following us."

Keith sat next to her and offered her a cola. "Drink. Yeah, I had to shoot him with it. He'd have killed us. I just had to hope I didn't overdose him."

"Respiratory failure."

"Yep. You did your homework. But, normally I'd have used a Glock, so this way, he still had a better shot—no pun intended," Keith joked, "—than if I just used my regular weapon of choice."

"What about the guy you were fighting?"

"He's in custody. We got them, Erika. You can go home as soon as the drugs are out of your system. They're making the arrangements now."

"It's over?" The words seemed too impossible to believe. Part of her had become convinced that she'd be in hiding for the rest of her life for something she didn't understand or remember. None of it made sense, but the relief did. She could go home. No more locks, shackles, keys, or guns. No more Corey, no more, Karen, no more Keith.

For a brief moment, she felt a pang at the thought of no more banter with Keith, but it didn't last. She pushed herself from the bed and glanced around the room. "Where's my bag? I'm ready to go."

---

*Fiji—*

"Helen, Helen, wake up."

As a younger woman, Helen Franklin had been attractive. Her features, unique enough to be considered exotic, were striking and appealing, but every year after thirty-five added angles and harsh lines that stripped the beauty and changed her into something almost masculine-looking. In her fight against aging, she slept with ear plugs, eye mask, and face cream. She also had a facial routine, morning and night, that rivaled day spas. As a result, her sleep was usually deep and not easily interrupted—not exactly helpful when you might need to leave in a moment's notice.

"If you tell me we're in danger and leaving again, I'll just die and get this over with. I'm done."

"No, it's over. They got him."

"Alek? What about his men?" She sat up, pulling the earplugs from her ears. "That's better. What about Erika? Is she still safe?"

Jill nodded. "Yep, they went after her at one of the cottages, and we were waiting."

"Good. So, she can go home?"

"Yep. You both can."

Helen nodded as her mind raced in a dozen directions. Alek's men failed, but at least he was out of the picture. She'd have him removed in a transport "accident." Meanwhile, she needed to be sure Erika didn't know about her connection to any of it. "Erika still doesn't know this has anything to do with me, right? I can't imagine anyone is left who could hurt her if she does, but it still makes me nervous."

"That's why you hired us. We kept her completely in the dark. She's still convinced we have the wrong Erika Polowski."

"Good. Maybe that'll protect her—as long as there aren't any rogue men left from Alek's syndicate."

"We've got them. It was such a big sweep that there's no way anyone would risk it."

With heart pounding, Helen forced her tone to sound frightened rather than frustrated. "Well, he's got a few who are vindictive enough to be ticked at losing out on their money. It's all about money in that racket. That's why I tried to get in—to take them down. Almost got me killed." Her shudder was perfect. Maybe it was time to consider a career in acting instead of human trafficking—nah. The money was in people, and she wasn't about to let go of the money for any reason.

"You can't go home, though, Helen. If you come home any more than a few weeks early, it might make her suspicious and if she connects you…"

"Yeah, well, I have business in Brisbane anyway. I've been gone long enough to raise eyebrows, and that's dangerous in my line of work."

Anthony popped his head in the doorway. "Okay, I've got our things—She isn't even dressed yet? Let's go people! I have a birthday to make up for as it is. The more days that pass, the worse of a father I am!"

Helen waved him off saying, "I'll have tickets to Disney World waiting for you when you get home. Just give me time to get dressed and make the call."

As Jill and Anthony left the room, Helen overheard Anthony whisper, "How is it that someone with her kind of money lives in a suburban neighborhood with three bedrooms, two baths, and shoddy landscaping?"

How indeed, you idiot, she thought to herself. How indeed.

---

Mark scanned the reports before him. The Hard as Nails franchise had locks on every door—shut down in the wake of the arrests. The FBI had Anastas in custody, and the rest of his merry band of assassins occupied a cell or morgue slab—without a single bullet and only one tranq fired. Well, two, if you included Erika's self-inflicted one. He snickered at the memory of Keith's call.

Best of all, however, they'd managed to intercept a shipment of girls—some as young as eleven—before they left Columbus for who knew where or what fate. The thought churned Mark's stomach. Yes, someone would step up and take over the management of Alek's so-called business, but it was a step in the right direction—one they hadn't hoped to make. It felt good.

His team would convene in just hours. Keith had already landed in Rockland, Karen was due any minute, and Jill and Anthony were on their way. He had new assignments for everyone, but first, bonuses. Helen Franklin had been generous—very generous. With Erika and Helen back in their own homes and resuming their lives, he could close the books on that case—just as soon as the files were complete after debriefing. It was a good day in the history of the Agency.

They'd chosen the name of their business carefully. It needed to be simple, memorable, and ambiguous enough to make people think of a government agency rather than a private business. Located in any other city, the name would have meant nothing, but considering that Mark's cousin ran the most prestigious wedding coordination agency in the greater Rockland area, with the simple name, "the Agency," it had been just one of those coincidences he couldn't resist.

A knock sent his fingers flying across the computer keyboard as he called for whomever it was to enter. "Hey, Keith. I'm just about ready to print out your report for you. How is Erika?"

"Good. I took a cab to the coffee shop before coming here. You'd never know she took a month-long leave of absence."

"Excellent. And how is Claire doing? She like the bike?"

"Yep. Loves it. She's asked me to come over for dinner tonight. Says she has something to talk to me about."

"Well, good. I'm going to go check on a few things. You just read over that, make any changes, and I'll be back in a bit."

Mark left the room and strolled down the hall, past the Internet division of Mayflower Trust and into the elevator. Once outside, he flipped open his phone and dialed the number for his latest client. "Are you sure it must be now? Everything looks calm for at least a week."

The voice on the other end sounded quite decided. They'd be ready to be whisked away to safety at eight o'clock. With a family of five to protect, Mark needed his top three people on the case, and that left him shorthanded—again. They'd received three notices of threats for assessment, two requests for aid, and somewhere between four and nine emails, most of which would turn out to be bogus, but they must be investigated. As it was, Helen's file might be closed within hours, but dozens of spiral cases had been flooding their office from the Anastas Syndicate. It'd be months, possibly years before they'd be completely free of the revolting business.

He needed to hire more people. Always a problem. The best candidates were ex-law enforcement, ex-military, or the saner members of militia groups. Training someone from scratch meant time, money, and personnel that he couldn't afford. His mind went to Claire Auger. Young, healthy, intelligent, and there was enough evidence to assume she'd been recruited by Anastas—probably under the guise of "helping" her cousin—to prove she had the brains to keep from getting caught, Claire had potential. Keith could train her. That'd be good—on the job even—it might work.

He retraced his steps, waved at the receptionist of Mayflower Trust as he reentered the building, took the elevator to the fourth floor, and strolled back into his office. Keith started to speak, but something about Mark stopped him. Good. That's exactly what he needed—uncertainty. With it, he could control just about anything.

"I need you to talk to Claire about joining us."

---

"Okay, so I've got something to tell you, and I can't do it without you getting mad, so I want you to promise not to yell at me until I'm done, okay?" Claire swallowed hard as she waited for Keith to agree. He would be angry, she knew that, but setting him up like that usually meant he'd be quiet about it.

"What's up, kiddo? If you don't want to do the pediatrician thing—"

"That qualifies as yelling."

Keith stared at her, visibly stunned. "Trying to reassure you is yelling."

"Speaking is yelling. Just listen. About a month ago, I was talking with this guy I met at a coffee shop over on 34th." Claire wondered if he'd blinked too quickly or not, but then brushed it off as her overly active imagination. "Anyway, he took me out to dinner—to a cool club I've never been able to afford to go to—and then somehow you came up and he knew you."

"What was his name?"

"Alek Anastas." She waited. This was where he'd start yelling. She couldn't blame him. She knew she'd been stupid, but she'd meant well. Shouldn't that count for something? She waited for him to let her have it with both barrels, but instead, his eyes darted around them and then he grabbed her arm and literally pulled her into the garage.

"Do you have a spare helmet for that thing?"

"Yeah, I thought maybe—"

"Good, let's get it into the back yard. I'll get the gate."

"What are you talking about? Didn't you hear me?" Claire tried to protest, but he was already pushing the Harley through the side door of the garage.

"Let's go."

"You're going to ride it?"

He pulled the gate open. "Get it into the alley. If you were leaving, what would you not leave behind?"

"I—"

"Don't argue, tell me. Now."

"I'd take purse, backpack with makeup and hair stuff, and a change of clothes or something. I always leave a note or call..."

"Call your parents and tell them you're going to..." She watched ideas flicker through his mind and be rejected as each surfaced. Finally, he nodded. "Tell them you're going to Stanford for a tour."

"You're telling me to lie." Claire knew her jaw was hanging open in a way that was particularly unattractive on her, but this was her cousin and she was too stunned to care.

"Do it, squirt."

While he dashed into the house, Claire took a few deep breaths, and then dialed her father's phone. "Hey, guess what! I just got a call from Stanford and they've invited me to come for a tour! Keith has been pushing me to reconsider med school, so I sent out stuff last week and they already called!"

For the next three minutes, she went over her bogus itinerary, promised to give her father her hotel and room number as soon as she got it, and thanked him when he assured her that he'd deposit money into her account so she could really enjoy the trip. "Thanks, Dad. I know I'll be busy, but I'll try to check in often. I might be gone for at

137

least a week. I can't stand the idea of being there without sitting in on a few classes and checking out the sororities and stuff."

She was still chatting as Keith returned, making slicing motions across his neck. Once she disconnected, she stared at the bag. "You got it all in there?"

"You're good. Okay, let's go. Mayflower Trust."

"Not the airport?"

"Nope. Mark wants to talk to you about joining the Agency."

Claire's heart nearly stopped beating. "And you're taking me there even after I just told you I knew Alek Anastas? You know what that means, right?"

"I know."

"And you're still taking me to Mark." She swallowed as she started the motorcycle. "I'm not going to die or anything, right?"

"Look, if you were talking to Alek, Mark knows. It's fine. We've gotta get you out of here though. Go!"

# Eighteen

Keith rubbed his temple, watching out into the inky blackness of the desert, and tried to relax. His head had been pounding for hours. Protection was always hard—always. Protection with kids was ten times worse than involuntary protection. Maybe a hundred. Children didn't understand the concepts of quiet, of staying inside, why they couldn't go to school or soccer practice, or why they couldn't play with their friends. Children whined, talked incessantly, and reacted with tantrums and fear.

A tug at his sleeve told him one of the kids was up again. He glanced down and reminded himself to smile. "Hey, Jordan. What are you doing up?"

"Can't sleep. What are you doing?"

"Watching." He shook his infrared binoculars.

"How can you see out there? It's dark."

He handed the boy the binoculars. "Look over there... that way." Keith pointed to some brush in the distance. "See behind that creosote?"

"A rabbit?"

"Yep."

"You're protecting us from rabbits?"

It was always a delicate balance, trying to decide how much to tell a kid. "Well, if that was something dangerous, I could see it. That's what I was trying to show you."

"Why do we have to be here?"

"You'll have to ask your father that, Jordan. My job is to protect you."

"Dad said I had to ask you."

Keith hated it when parents did that. He understood the reasoning. It was too easy to give too much information, and the agents knew what was and what wasn't too much, but leaving it all to him meant that he had to make judgment calls for their children—not his responsibility.

"Well, your father found out that he was working for someone who was breaking the law. So, we're protecting all of you until he gets the proof he needs. Then he'll turn it over to the police and they'll arrest his boss. Then you guys can go home."

"But why do we have to come? He's the one who knows stuff. I don't know anything. Katie doesn't know anything. Mom and the baby don't. It's just him."

The child's tone was a familiar one—resentment. This father was another workaholic. Kids never understood why their parents chose work over time spent with them, and parents never understood that all the money earned meant nothing to the kids who just wanted their parents' time. "One way to hurt someone is to threaten the people they love. We just make it so they can't even do that."

"Dad wouldn't care. As long as he could get to the office on time, he wouldn't care."

This was something he could truthfully refute in a way the child could understand. "Jordan, I don't know your father and what he's like, but I know this. Men do not spend the kind of money he's spending—money I know he really can't afford—to keep their families safe if they don't care. They just don't do it."

"My dad has a lot of money."

"Listen." Keith waited until the boy's surly eyes met his gaze. "We're expensive. Paying me to guard and protect your family is very expensive. It costs a lot more money than you could ever imagine. Your father is not only paying that money, out of his own pocket, he is also turning his boss into the police. That means he won't have a job. All that work he's been doing that kept him away from home? That means that you will still have enough to live on now. If he hadn't done that, you would be unsafe right now and he'd be worried about how to take care of you."

The boy listened. How long the words would stay in the child's mind and soothe the heart, he didn't know, but he had to try. At last, the child nodded. "He doesn't like to spend money, but if you're so expensive, I guess that means something."

"My dad didn't like to spend money either, Jordan. But it wasn't because he loved it more than me; it was because he loved me and wanted to make sure my future was secure. It's how some dads say, 'I love you.'"

The boy shuffled toward the bedroom and then returned. "Miss Claire is scared. You should talk to her. You'll make her feel better."

"Why do you say that?"

"Because you made me feel better." Jordan's voice seemed to scream, "duh."

"I meant, why do you think she's scared?"

"She just is."

Without another word, Jordan went back to his air mattress in the other room. Keith made a sweep of the house, checking the outside from every window, and then crept over to Claire's pallet on the floor. "You asleep?"

She stirred, and then sat up, glancing around as if waiting for instructions. "No."

"Come on. Come talk to me."

Back in the front room of the small stucco house, Keith pointed to the lumpy recliner and insisted she sit. "You still need rest."

"I'm not sleepy."

"What's wrong, Claire?"

"Nothing." Something in her tone seemed to indicate how unconvincing her words were. "I'm just nervous. What if Alek's people find me here? It could put these people in real jeopardy."

"This is the safest place for you, and here you get a chance for some on the job training. Most people don't get that until they're ready for the field."

"Why did Mark give me a chance like this? I put you at risk."

"You were stuck, Claire. He fooled you. We understand that. You also hid the fact that I tossed my card and my phone until we were safe on the plane. That was quick thinking and smart."

"I would have told him to forget it if I thought he'd just take it out on me."

"I know, squirt. I know. We blew it there. It never occurred to me that he'd court my family. We still don't know how he knew I was on the case."

She shrugged. "He never said anything that would make sense. It was all so fast—"

"Don't worry about it. Really. Right now, learn the job by watching and asking questions."

"Do you think any of his guys would really come after me?"

"Mark doesn't."

Claire's eyes snapped up to search his. "You don't agree?"

"I don't know. Mark is usually right, but he's still human. Alek Anastas had quite an empire. He shipped girls all over the country. If any of his contacts thinks you have any information that could be damaging, no matter how wrong they are, they'll do everything they can to take you out of the equation."

"Columbus was so hard. When you told me to go into Hard as Nails, I almost choked."

"Servane David recognized me."

"Well, you got her. That woman is cruel. I overheard her on the phone once. That's how I found out Alek's business."

"Did he know?"

"I'm alive, aren't I? I hung up and then called back and said we got disconnected."

Keith nodded appreciatively. "Smart move—calling back, that is. Very good. You have good instincts."

"You said they'd never hire me."

He shrugged and passed her the binoculars. "Let me know what you see out there." Once she was in position, he kept talking, anything to relax her. "I suppose it was wishful thinking. I didn't want you to know what I did."

"But I did, really. I mean, we all know you're a bodyguard. That's what we're doing now, right?"

"Kid, it's not always like this. My last case was an abduction."

"You had to find someone who was kidnapped?" Admiration filled her voice. "Did you find him—her?"

Part of him resisted. He didn't need to tell her yet, did he? What was the point? If he had his way, she'd be heading to Stanford as soon as this assignment ended. One look at the concentration Claire showed as she scanned the shrubby terrain told him she'd never do it now. This was already in her blood.

"Claire, look at me." He nearly choked at the pride and earnestness in her eyes. The minute he told her the truth, she'd lose all respect for him, but maybe it'd be worth it. Maybe she'd realize why he didn't want her to join the Agency. "I was the abductor."

"What!" Shock registered and then disbelief. "Why?"

"It was the Anastas case. The girl didn't know she was endangered, so we had to remove her against her will."

"Can you do that? Legally, I mean?"

"No. It isn't legal."

He watched her face, each emotion, each thought, flickering across her features as she processed his words. "I don't understand. How can you kidnap someone and get away with it?"

"They eventually see the need, even as much as they hate it, and we do everything we can to ensure their lives are disrupted as little as possible. We make arrangements with employers, pay bills, keep account activity normal, everything. They reenter their lives as if they took off on a spontaneous vacation, usually only for a week or two."

"How often do you do the involuntary protective things?"

Keith swallowed hard. He'd been wrong. Already, Claire was choosing words that sounded more palatable than kidnap, abduction, and hostage. "I've just transferred to that division. I've only done two. Karen has done dozens."

"Wow. Dozens?"

"A lot of our clients don't know they're in danger. If we try to tell them, they often don't believe us, or we actually put them in more danger. So, we have to do what's best regardless of what they want."

"How do you—?"

He shook his head. "Not here. Not now. We can take a walk tomorrow." Keith let his eyes roam back to the room where most of the family slept.

"Right. How do you find clients—or rather, how do they find you?"

"Mark has connections in all of the government agencies, in political circles, and even among organized crime. People can contact him in a variety of ways and then he puts together a package that suits their situation."

"How do you get paid?"

"Well," Keith began, trying to decide how much information was enough while still doing his job, "most are like John Frielich. He finds out something he knows he shouldn't know, he goes to the FBI but doesn't have the evidence they need to take him seriously, he's scared, so they contact us. Mark gives the okay, he calls, and they meet. Based on that, we're here."

"What about things like the abduction?"

"Well, the last one was part of a bigger protection detail. The girl didn't know she was in danger, but that's because Anastas knew the house but not what the person who owned it looked like. He based his hit call on the information he got on the resident of the house rather than the owner."

"How'd he know about the house? Why wouldn't he know the owner and then find the house?"

Keith leaned his forearms on his knees, his hands clenched together. "That's how you think it'd work, isn't it? It rarely does. People start with bits of information from somewhere—this time from an address. Rather than searching house records to see who owned it and going after that person, he went after the person residing there." Keith pushed back as if the memory was distasteful. "On the one hand, it makes sense. The house could have been a rental or anything, but once he found out about the woman, he should have looked into the owner to make sure he wasn't barking up the wrong tree."

"So, who paid you if she didn't ask for help?"

"The owner. Somehow, she got information about Anastas' syndicate and she knew about the Agency."

"So, she paid for someone to guard her *and* the girl?"

"Yep. Nice when it works out that way. My first abduction was an old guy that didn't know he was in danger. Mark just learned about it in passing and sent us in."

"So, you worked for free?" Claire's incredulity was charmingly naïve.

"Something like that. Don't worry, at Mark's prices, we can afford to protect people regardless of their payment ability."

"Will I get to help with those?"

"Normally," Keith admitted, "no. Me being your cousin means possibly. It makes it easy to train you when you're there, but it's very different than this."

"How so?"

"I'll tell you tomorrow. Go to sleep."

---

"You have to use locks and guns and stuff!" Claire wasn't sure she believed him. It made no sense to her, but Keith's face was free of any hint of teasing. He meant it.

"Okay, put it this way. You wake up in the middle of the night, and some strange man tapes your mouth, ties you up, and carries you out of your home. You drive for a long time, maybe fly somewhere, and then end up in a remote place—sometimes alone with the guy. What happens if he doesn't chain your ankle to the floor or hold a gun on you?"

"I run the first minute he goes to the bathroom."

"Assuming he goes."

"What do you mean?" Claire frowned at the scenarios that ran through her mind. Surely, he didn't mean—

"Well, in one place, Anthony couldn't go outside, and it was a one room place."

"Tell me it was a man."

He shook his head. "Nope. Kelly had to hold up blankets and sing to give everyone privacy. I hear it was hilarious."

"That's gross." The job didn't seem as exciting and glamorous anymore. Seriously? No bathroom? Disgusting. "How often does that kind of thing happen?"

"Not often. The abductions are relatively uncommon—primarily because they're usually pro bono. It's harder to hear of them when people aren't asking for help, y'know?"

"I guess. Still, this is pretty boring stuff. We just sit here and watch for something to happen." She hated to hear his laughter, but Claire had to admit to herself that she probably did sound very foolish.

"Well, usually, we like boring. It means people live."

"Have you ever had to run?"

"On almost every case, we have to run. About half or a little more are just drills, but you just don't know it is until it's over."

Drills sounded both exciting and juvenile. The word reminded her of grade school and tornado and fire drills. "So, we'll get a call to evacuate? Why? I mean, if no one knows we're here, why move and expose ourselves?"

"Because moving before they think you know they are there means that you surprise them. Moving keeps you from being a stationary target. If we go before we're found, it cuts the danger by a factor of ten or more."

"When do you think they'll call? We've been here four days already."

Keith jumped and caught a lizard before it scurried out of reach. "We never know. I've gotten the call an hour after settling and the day we expected to go home. Mark keeps it varied, but we're usually in place for a minimum of three to five days."

Claire glanced back at the house where she knew John Frielich clicked away on his laptop, hacking into accounting databases and downloading the files needed to prove his boss guilty of criminal activity. "How long will this take?"

Even as she asked, she knew he wasn't likely to tell her. She could see the hesitation in his eyes and almost begged, but she resisted. If he shouldn't tell her, she needed to learn to accept that. Keith stroked the head of the lizard, offered it to her, and then let it go when she shook her head.

"Every hour it takes him means two more he'll have to work to finish. Every minute he spends trying to retrieve the necessary information means that much time his boss has to have someone putting safeguards in place to protect it."

"Is John that good with a computer?"

Keith shook his head. "He's better than most, sure, but Mark is getting us a hacker. My guess is we'll get the call to move and the hacker will be at the new location."

Claire's eyes widened. "Then the drill will be soon."

"Why do you say that?"

Sometimes she couldn't tell if his questions were intended to make her think or if he just really thought she was that stupid. "Because, you said that every hour John works means two more he'll have to work to finish. Mark is going to want that hacker on the job fast."

"Exactly."

# Nineteen

Once again, Erika stood at the corner of her bed, reliving the night she'd awakened to find her mouth taped and Keith wrapping her body in rope. She tried to resurrect the indignant protest and the fear she'd felt, but with her knowledge in retrospect, she couldn't do it. Keith hadn't been the terrifying man she'd assumed, and they hadn't done unspeakable things to her. The memory of the heroin injection still riled her but not as deeply as it had at the time.

For days she'd relived each moment, trying to discover the cause of her reluctance to blame Keith, Karen, and even Corey for the enforced interruption to her life. She'd been kidnapped, for crying out loud! Why wasn't she ready to move mountains to have them arrested? Why was she, instead of holding media conferences to demand that that kind of thing be stopped, justifying their behavior and wondering if they were okay? Was Corey getting the medical attention she obviously needed? Did Karen have post-traumatic stress syndrome or anything like that? Was Keith protecting someone else now? Was it voluntary? Did he scowl all the time?

She'd found the return to work easy. Despite her doubts, she'd walked into the coffee shop, sat down at the desk, looked over the scheduling, checked inventory, placed a few orders, and been on the floor ready to greet the customers the moment the doors opened. It was as if she had never left. The second day back, she could have sworn she saw Keith walk past, but of course, it couldn't be him.

They'd kept their word. Her car waited for her at the airport, her bills were paid, her bank account reflected spending all over the country, and yet not a dime was missing. There were no unusual deposits to make up for things, but after a while, she found that the deposits from the last six months had been altered. How did they change things like that?

Her house phone rang, making her squeal like a girlie girl. "Hey, Helen, what's up?"

"Just making sure you're all right? I called a couple of times, but you were never home."

"I was busy, but everything's good. Sorry about not calling you back. I'll have to check the answering machine."

"I'll have them add voice mail to the phone. There's no reason you should have to fight those stupid machines. I should have done it years ago." Helen sounded annoyed.

"Hey, Helen, I'm really sorry. I would have called if I'd gotten a message."

"Yeah, I know. I just thought I might be coming back early and had left a few messages about it."

"Early?" Warning bells, from where she couldn't imagine, buzzed in Erika's mind.

"Yeah. I was thinking about making some renovations, so I thought I'd wrap stuff up early this year, but I can't. I was just calling to tell you that you didn't have to worry about moving out early after all."

"Oh." Her nerves settled once again. The past weeks seemed to have made her skittish over the most ridiculous things. "Well, if you decide to do it, I can be out in just a couple of days. I've gotten good at living here as if it was mine while not taking over the space."

"Well, I just don't see how it'll work. I was afraid you were ticked off at my messages and ignoring me. I should have known better. You've never played those kinds of games before."

"Nah. Just didn't get them. Sorry, though. That must have been really annoying."

Helen rambled about kitchen renovation plans, a new deck around the swimming pool, and asked what Erika thought of radiant heat in the master bath. The questions made no sense. Why should Erika care? It was Helen's house. Ever since she'd taken the housesitting job, Helen had made it very clear; she was an employee and had no rights regarding the house. If something broke, get it fixed.

"Look, Helen, I'm on my way out with some friends, so if that's all..."

"Um, yeah. Sure. I'll be in touch. I might have a few guys come out to give me some estimates, so I'll have to touch base to see when you'll be around to let them in."

Great. Just what she needed. "That's fine. I'll email you my work schedule for whatever week you want to plan for. Talk to you later. Bye."

Erika reached into her drawer for her favorite lounge pants and hesitated. She'd said she was going out, but she hadn't actually planned to go. Suddenly, it seemed almost imperative that she leave as she'd claimed. Some of the girls from her college dorm had planned a get together at Club Retro, but she hadn't planned to go. With lounge pants in one hand and her best fitting skinny jeans in the other, Erika deliberated.

Disgusted with herself, she tossed the lounge pants on the bed and unzipped her uniform pants. "I blame you, Keith Auger. It's your fault. I wouldn't be going if you hadn't—" She paused, mid-thought. Keith Auger. Was that really his name? Surely it couldn't be. Her eyes glanced at her laptop, but the clock next to it told her if she expected to make it on time, she'd better hurry.

---

The cell phone slid shut, as Helen played with it, lost in thought. She scribbled a note to have voice mail installed, but her mind was lost in calculating exactly how early she could return without her call seeming out of place. Erika was so gullible. Several messages on an answering machine—all mysteriously lost. Come on, what kind of idiot did she have living in her house, anyway?

Maybe the girl could live. As gullible as she'd been, Erika was the perfect house sitter. She worked hard, was reliable and dependable, and didn't throw parties. Yet irrational anger had welled up in Helen when Erika hadn't mentioned being away from home. After all, the point of the job was to be at the house, not take off for a month, but then, it wasn't as if the girl had a choice. Still, she could have lied about it. The way she'd spoken, it sounded as if she'd never been any farther away than the coffee shop.

Helen had hired her because of her degree. Anyone crazy enough to get a degree in anthropology seemed intelligent enough to make sound decisions, but enough of a rebel not to let neighbors walk all over her. Once the girl had saved enough to pay for grad school, she'd probably quit and buy her own place.

*Well, maybe not...* The moment that thought entered her mind, Helen sighed. She'd lose Erika all right, but not when she returned to grad school. Erika would be dead inside of a month. Then came the hassle of finding someone new. "Ugh, I hate it when things get complicated."

She dug through her USB drives and found the red one. Color coordination might make her look like an OCD freak, but it sure saved on hassles when it came time to look for things. She plugged it into her laptop and pulled up her files on "hospice care." The irony of it always amused her. Timing was everything. She needed to pick someone patient but good. Even twenty-four hours could make a hit look like it was coming from the wrong direction, and Mark Cho would catch an anomaly like that faster than she could cover it. She needed him in her court. She needed to be the victim. Without that, her business would crumble.

Ainsley. Ted Ainsley was the right guy. He'd never muffed a job yet, and he had the patience. Helen frowned as she hovered over his email address. Ted hated jobs involving women or children. He often didn't accept them, but she really needed him to agree. Maybe if she offered enough money....

Another name caught her attention. Ben. Helen didn't know his last name. All payments went to an account in the name of Coralie Westbury. There were only two Coralie Westburys that she considered reasonable options. One was a patient on a mental ward; the other was a city council member in a town in Illinois. Either way, it was weird. But Ben had one thing in his favor. He had no conscience. Infant, old lady, or puppies, if she wanted them gone, they died. He was patient in everything except payment. That might create an issue, but she'd work with it.

"Well, Erika. It's been nice knowing you. I hope you're having fun with your friends. Your last couple of weeks might as well be good ones."

---

Despite Claire's confidence, the next day proved to be just as long a wait as the last. While John Frielich worked nearly all day, trying to gather what information he could, Claire tried to keep the children from screeching and keeping Keith from sleep. Brian, who had arrived during the night to replace Liz, shrugged as she tossed him apologetic glances every time the decibel level jumped dramatically. Katie Frielich was a screecher. That fact alone nearly prompted Claire to vow she'd never have children.

As each hour passed, her fidgeting grew worse until even Jordan noticed and commented. "Do you miss cigarettes?"

"Cig—no! I don't smoke. Never have. It's a nasty habit."

"My mom used to smoke, and she got all jumpy like you when she was quitting. That's all."

"I'm just new at this. I have to learn to be patient and enjoy the quiet."

"Well, I don't have to like it, and I don't. It's stupid. If he wasn't such a freak about work, he wouldn't have gotten us into this."

Even as the boy spoke, Claire saw the droop in John's shoulders. "Hush. Your father is a hero. He's going to help put a stop to criminals. Without him, people would get away with hurting lots of people. You should be proud."

"We're hiding out because of him," the boy insisted, not even attempting to keep his voice quiet. "Mom and Katie are scared; we're all stuck in this stupid little house in the middle of nowhere, and for what? Stupid computer stuff."

At a loss for words, Claire struggled to speak, but couldn't. She'd never heard such venom spewed toward

152

anyone in family from such a small person. Just as she started to assure him he'd think differently as an adult, Keith's voice from the corner interrupted. "Jordan, do you know any kids at school who don't have a lot of money?"

"Yeah. There's some."

"What would you do if one of those kids hung their only jacket up on the hook in the classroom and another kid, a very wealthy one, took it knowing that it was the only thing keeping the kid warm?"

"I'd tell the teacher."

"What if that meant you had to stay after school and tell the story to the principal. Wouldn't your parents be mad that they had to wait?"

"No. They'd be proud of me because I—" He flushed. "Oh."

"That's right, Jordan. It's an inconvenience, but your father is protecting innocent people from losing their money. He's doing a very good thing that he couldn't have done—he couldn't have helped anyone—if he hadn't been such a dedicated employee while trying to provide for his family. Remember what we talked about?"

The boy nodded, but still looked surly. Brian tossed his magazine and stood. "Want to take a walk with me? Maybe we'll find a lizard or something."

Claire's eyes followed them out the door, across the short dirt drive, and into the scrubby brush that seemed to stretch endlessly. Her mind felt numbed by hours of inactivity, her body visibly twitching as if demanding action of some kind. Keith's voice startled her again. "Do push-ups, wall push-ups, squats, stretches, or something. You have to keep fit, so you might as well take advantage of the time you have."

"Shut up and go to sleep."

"I'll sleep. I know what I'm doing. Just move. You don't have to sit there and stare at the door or the phone."

So, whenever she was awake, she played tea party with Katie, helped Jordan with his thousand-piece puzzle, and gave herself the best workout she could within the "four walls" of a thirteen hundred square foot house in the middle of nowhere. Melissa Frielich held herself aloof, and no matter how much she tried, Claire couldn't get the woman to relax and chat. John, she ignored.

Day turned into night so slowly that she hardly noticed until Keith demanded that she try to sleep. As much as she thought it'd help, it didn't. Every sound jarred her awake. Each snore, shuffle, howl of a nearby coyote, each gentle click of the lock in the door as Keith did a survey around the perimeter woke her from her fitful sleep. He'd promised that she'd adjust, but Claire didn't think so.

By day three, all her theories seemed shattered. As she picked at scrambled eggs, again, she grumbled that every logical thing seemed overlooked by Mark and his team. "We're wasting precious time here while they twiddle their thumbs. They have a hacker; we need him. Why are we just sitting here?"

Brian's voice, clipped and short as always, answered her before Keith could say a word. "Logic equals death."

"What do you mean?"

"He means," Keith interrupted, sending a warning look at their colleague, "that if it is clearly logical, then it's exactly what we're expected to do. We have to think outside that box but not so much that our unexpected is expected too."

"Deliberate randomness?" It made perfect sense but didn't at the same time.

"Exactly." Brian nearly beamed as if she'd answered the million-dollar question rather than asked one.

"We've been here five days! All that time, the hacker—"

"Worked." At her stunned expression, Brian rolled his eyes. "You thought otherwise? Come on."

"Back down, Brian. She's working it out just like we both did."

"Sorry."

"No, you're not, but thanks anyway." Claire shot her cousin a grateful look and went to scrape the rest of her eggs into the garbage disposal. She couldn't eat another egg—

At the buzz of Brian's phone, Keith turned. One look at Brian's face was all he needed. While Claire rushed to read the one-word message on the screen, "Go," Keith began throwing everything not in bags into them. "Children in the van with Melissa, John in the Jeep. Claire, you'll go with Brian, I will take John, you two take the rest."

The Frielichs all stared at the three "Agency" workers, terrified. "I want to go with my family." John tried to sound assertive, but fear shook his hands and left the faintest tremor in his voice.

"Remember, this may be a drill. We have to take it seriously, but let's go. You'll go exactly as I've said. We have a contract. Go."

Children whimpered, Jordan protesting as Brian swept his puzzle into the box without regard for the work he'd put into it. Claire dumped canned goods into boxes and piled the bread and chips on top. The refrigerated goods went into the oversized ice chest, and into the van. She barely had time to grab toothbrushes from the medicine cabinet before Brian pushed her out the door. "You're taking too long."

"But—"

"Get in the van now."

A glance at Keith reassured her. Her cousin nodded and pointed at the van's passenger's seat as he climbed into the Jeep, seemingly alone. John, already hidden in the back seat, must be kept from view at all costs. Now that the excitement had arrived, even with adrenaline pumping and her eagerness to see the job finished, Claire's heart filled with dread. She now understood what the men meant. Moving meant danger. As Brian drove down the driveway and turned left onto the dirt road that led to the highway, she shook with nervousness, feeling ridiculously exposed. The only thing that kept her from crying was knowing Keith followed right behind them.

And then Keith turned right.

# Twenty

"What is he doing? Where is he going? Brian!"

Her verbosity-challenged escort ignored her and bumped over the road as if her banshee-like screams didn't threaten to cause permanent hearing loss. When the children began to sniffle, he sent her a warning look and said, "Stuff it."

"But why is he going that way! What—"

"Because it's smart. Now quit freaking everyone out."

She hadn't heard him speak so many words at one time, but regardless, Claire was livid. Keith hadn't even hinted that he wasn't following them. What if the guy's— she couldn't remember John's boss's name anymore—goons found him? He'd be all alone. They'd be dead! She started to remind Brian of the danger of being alone with the target when the man clamped is hand around her wrist. "Don't. Just don't."

"Brian, are we safe?" Melissa Frielich sounded nearly as panicked as Claire felt.

"Ma'am, we're professionals—well, Keith and I are— and we won't do anything to jeopardize you or your family. Claire is a rookie in training and isn't used to sleep deprivation."

"Jeopardize? Deprivation? Rookie? What is this, expand your vocabulary day?"

Brian didn't respond, but the look on his face clearly said, "If you consider those words an expansion of anyone's vocabulary, you're more pathetic than I assumed." She ignored the exasperated expression on his face and turned to do her job. She could reassure this family even if she did think everyone around her was half-crazed and ridiculous.

"We're fine. I'm just used to having a clearly defined work plan. Sorry for freaking out on you like that."

Katie's whimpers grew to decided wails. The baby, clearly angling for a career in singing barbershop style, sent up his own screech. Yeah, he'd be a tenor. Their driver, still visibly irritated with her, sent eloquent glances her way, but Claire chose to ignore them. If the guy couldn't "use his words," she wasn't going to "listen."

Once on the highway, they whizzed down the barren road, seeing few cars and even fewer signs of civilization. The road wound and curved, occasionally through towns that looked as barren and dead as the vegetation around them, until they came to another highway. Just as they neared some semblance of civilization, Jordan insisted he needed to use the bathroom.

Without blinking twice, Brian reached into the console, pulled out a zip-lock bag, and handed it to her. "Pass it back."

She tried not to shudder as she turned to hand it to Melissa, and then winced as she heard him whisper, "But Mom, I need to go number two!"

"Um, he needs—"

"To use the bag. We can't stop. If you need to go back to help him, crawl under or around—not over—the seat."

Claire stared at him as if he were as much of a lunatic as she'd imagined, but kept her mouth shut. Even that drove her to distraction. He gloated over there under those ridiculous sunglasses; she could almost see it in the way he held his chin. As they pulled onto an interstate, Jordan began crying about the indignities he was forced to endure, and Claire cracked a window.

"What do I do with the bag?"

Brian dug through the console again, pulling out a plastic sack from a grocery store she couldn't identify and handed it to Claire. "Zip it and put it in here. We'll dump it when we stop for gas."

"How long—"

He interrupted Melissa mid-sentence. "We'll be driving all night."

"I can't keep the baby cooped up in that car seat that long! He'll be screaming again if we don't let him out soon."

"Then he screams. Give him a cup, something to eat, whatever, but we don't stop until we need gas. Even then, you don't get out of the van. Period."

"But—"

"Just wait." Brian's voice screamed a warning even though it was almost inaudible in the back seat. "Claire, write down why she isn't getting out and pass it back."

"Why—"

"Are you really that stupid? Why did Keith do what he had to with his last case?"

She didn't want to do it. It seemed cruel to throw up reminders of how dangerous their trip was, but Claire didn't have the inner strength to resist Brian's stronger personality. She pulled out a notepad from her purse, her favorite orange pen, and wrote, *If you get out, you're exposed. Exposure= dead. It's going to be okay, but you have to do what Brian says.*

By the muffled "humph" from Brian's side of the car, she imagined that he wasn't pleased with the content, but he nodded and watched Melissa in the rearview mirror. Claire watched both. Melissa's eyes grew wide and fearful again— exactly what Claire had been working to remove for the past few days—and Brian looked satisfied.

Maybe this job wasn't such a good idea after all. Brian seemed to get some kind of sadistic pleasure in freaking out his clients, and even Keith had left her alone without warning. They had to weigh every action on the grounds of necessity versus danger. Danger nearly always won. *I just forced a kid to poop in a plastic bag, for heaven's sake.*

Disillusioned, she reconsidered her recent career choice. It had sounded so exciting—almost like *living* an action movie—to protect people. She'd imagined herself holed up in a rustic cabin somewhere, water spilling over rocks in a stream nearby, and a terrified woman, hiding from her abusive husband, cowering in the corner as Claire swept the area and took him down. She thought there'd be dull days when solitaire was more mind numbing than a reasonable pastime, but still, she expected a certain kind of romance to come with waiting for the approach of the enemy.

"Do you like your job?" Why she thought she'd get Mr. Silence to open up to her, Claire couldn't imagine. The second she asked, she felt like a fool.

"Yes."

"If someone offered you another one making the same amount of money or more, would you take it?"

"No."

Well, he answered anyway. Since he didn't seem prone to elaboration, she could work with asking yes or no questions. "Does it ever get tedious?"

"Yes."

"Are you ever afraid?"

"No." This time, he looked her way and after he answered, he mouthed, "yes."

Interesting. Tell the people you're not scared, but you are. If you wanted them to be scared, shouldn't you show that you are too? Similar questions bombarded her mind, but Claire ignored them and kept going. "Who is the best agent you know?"

"Keith."

Pride welled up in her heart in a way that reminded her of mothers and kids with scribbles on paper. Nauseating, but cool at the same time. Keith. She knew he was amazing—almost like it was the meaning of his name or something—but for someone else to admit it. Her eyes narrowed, and Claire whipped her head to read his expression. Was he saying what he thought the family needed to hear?

"You're catching on. No, Keith is the best. Hands down. Karen's a close second, though."

"Where are you?"

"You don't evaluate yourself. You listen to others' evaluations and learn from them."

She thought about that before asking, "Best part of the job."

"Saying goodbye."

"Gee, you're pleasant." Keeping her disgust hidden—impossible.

"Think about it."

He was worse than her mother during homework sessions. Every question had been answered by another question or an admonition to figure it out on her own. What was there to think about? His favorite part was getting away from the people. Something niggled at the back of her mind, but she was still too agitated and nervous to think it through. Her brain refused to cooperate.

Jordan did it for her. "He likes saying goodbye because the good guys win. If the bad guys win, there's no one to say goodbye to. They're dead."

---

"Sorry about the road."

"Never mind that. Is this a drill?"

"We don't know, John. Sorry. They don't tell us because lives are at stake. We can't ever assume anything but threat."

"My family is safe, though, right?" John's voice shook with the jostling of the Jeep over the washboard masquerading as a road.

"Brian is one of the best. He's going to get them to the next place safely."

"I thought you said you didn't know what the next place was until you were on the road."

"They'll text instructions at irregular intervals—just enough time usually to make a change in direction. Mark knows what he's doing. You've got to trust him."

The shake in John's voice seemed to have less to do with the road and more to do with his mental state. "It's hard when you can't see them."

"Claire is there—"

"No offense, she's a nice girl and I know she's your cousin or sister or niece or something, but she doesn't know what she's doing."

"She has good instincts when she's put on the spot. She saved our lives recently and without any training. Give her a break."

"Are they behind us or ahead of us?"

Keith took a deep breath. John would not be happy about this—much like Claire was probably fuming. "They're headed in another direction."

"What! I specifically stated that I wanted us kept together."

"And you signed papers giving us the right to rescind that request if it meant protecting your family."

The blanket behind the driver's seat shifted, but before Keith could remind him to stay down, John's voice, still muffled and sounding very weary, asked the question Keith dreaded. "What changed?"

"I'm really sorry, John. They don't tell us. While we're under threat, whether real or drill, we don't get communications like that. We just follow orders, so people stay alive."

"How long have you been doing this?"

"Five years—three months in this branch."

"Do you like it?"

"Love it." Keith always felt so callous saying that. Everyone asked. Everyone. However, saying he loved hiding people, making decisions that terrified them, and living on a dangerous edge just sounded a little insane.

"Be truthful with me, Keith. How many people have you lost?"

"Me personally?"

"Yeah."

"None." It felt good to be able to say that. He'd come close a few times, and he'd been backup that arrived too late on a watch, but the fault, so far anyway, hadn't been his.

"And the Agency?"

"We have a much higher success rate than the US Marshalls, FBI, CIA, NSA combined."

"That doesn't tell me much."

"Well, I'm not allowed to give specific numbers, but I can tell you that Mark has promised to close the doors if we ever reach ten percent. We're nowhere close."

"That makes me feel a lot better."

The miles seemed to crawl by, and twice John asked to crawl out from beneath the blanket, but Keith insisted that he remain there. "It's about your safety. They'd be looking for a car with at least two people."

John finally fell asleep—most likely due to the oppressive heat under the blanket—and Keith drove. The intermittent directions made less sense than usual; until, hours later, he realized where he was going. As he drove, he thought of Claire, wondering if she was freaking out over being separated. She'd expect to meet him when she arrived at the next house. Yeah, that wouldn't happen.

So far, she'd forgotten, most of the time anyway, that she was as much a client as an agent. From what Mark had discovered, the few remaining members of Anastas' syndicate had been approached by another trafficker and were now looking for him and for Claire. In Keith's opinion, the Columbus trip had bungled everything. It was almost a miracle that he, Erika, and Claire were still alive.

As he reached the turnoff, Keith prepared for John to wake up again. This wasn't going to be pleasant. Sure enough, the moment the Jeep bounced along the dirt road leading to their destination, John's voice, sounding confused and lost, muttered from under the blanket, "Do they really look for the worst roads in the country and then send us there?"

"Actually, that's not a bad idea, but no, they don't."

"Can I come out yet?"

Keith glanced around him, trying to see how long it'd be before it was just too late, and then said no. "Sorry, it's best to wait until we get there. I'm going to pull up really close to the door and you run inside."

"It'll be unlocked?"

"Yes."

Keith's phone buzzed just as a helicopter rose from the ground a quarter mile away. A text flashed. ALL CLEAR. MIKE IS INSIDE.

The Jeep pulled up in front of the house, and John opened the door, flinging back the blanket. He blinked twice and gave Keith an odd look. "We're back here again?"

"Get inside!" Keith peeled away from the house, letting the door slam shut on its own, and hid the Jeep inside the detached garage.

As he walked back to the house they'd left well over twelve hours earlier, Keith prayed that John and Mike got the info they needed quickly so they could all leave. A shout followed by the sound of breaking glass sent him flying over the last yards to the front door. He pulled out his gun as he kicked open the door, "Let him go."

The man, Mike, hesitated a second too long, and Keith fired four darts into him. Gasping and choking, John tried to speak, but Keith ignored him. With zip ties, he bound the man's hands and feet, and then pulled his phone from his pocket. "Karen, get back here. Now."

# Twenty-One

"What were you thinking, Karen? You left him in there alone! What if he'd gotten a knife—?"

"We cleared the house of anything that could be used as a weapon."

"Except his hands!" Keith glared at the woman as he refilled John's water glass.

"You were here. There was no danger."

Words that usually made him wince nearly erupted from him as he exploded with frustration. "Oh, come on! What if I'd made an outside sweep first? What if John hadn't broken that lamp! What if—"

Karen's calm demeanor infuriated him further, but he clamped his mouth shut as she shook her head and said, "Look, Keith. You wouldn't do that because your instincts are good. Check out the guy. That's the first rule. You did it. He's fine. Everything's okay. And we got him."

"Did you get Mark's okay on this?"

"This was Mark's plan, Keith. Not mine."

Keith glanced at John as he coughed again, holding his throat and then sipping more water in hopes of soothing the damaged airways. "Mark decided it was a good idea to toss John in here with a stranger and no protection? Where is Jill? I thought Jill was coming."

"Mark tested him. He failed."

"Testing how?" Keith glared at the man on the couch. Mike lay there—still sleeping off the effects of the tranquilizer. "I think I gave him too much."

"Well, he's fine. That's what counts. Mark knew he was a plant; he just didn't know if it was from Anastas' successor or if he was after John. Now we know."

"We know nothing, Karen. The man attacked the first person to come in. If I'd taken a bit longer, he could have had John out long enough to attack me when I got in. This whole thing is a nightmare. I can't believe you guys pulled this." Keith slammed his fist onto the counter, rattling the empty plastic serving bowl that, just half a day earlier, had held fruit.

He didn't wait for Karen's response. With adrenaline still pumping, he stormed out of the house, into the garage, and slammed the door shut behind him. Sliding open his phone, he called his boss. This was unacceptable. "Mark. What is going on?"

"I think he's with Anastas—or was. I don't think he was after John."

"Why do you say that?" Mark's words made sense, but Keith wasn't willing to make any assumptions. He'd already endangered one person.

"If he was after John, he would have waited to take you down first. He couldn't risk you coming in like you did. He took out backup and was prepared to take you next. Now, you have to get John out of there."

"Wha—" Realization hit. "Oh man, I lost focus. Bye."

When Keith backed the Jeep out of the garage, he found the helicopter rising from the ground, and his phone buzzed. HOUSE CLEAR.

"Great," he muttered as he took off down the road in the direction he'd just come. They had John. Great. He was a decoy. The only thing worse than protecting someone— hidden from everything and everyone—was being a sitting target.

Target. The word tumbled in his mind as he bounced over ruts that seemed determined to destroy his suspension or break the axle. How many would come? Cars? 'Copter? Did Mike have a phone on him?

Foolishly, Keith rammed on the brakes, spinning the vehicle and creating a cloud of dust that could be seen for miles. He fumbled for his phone, and hesitated. Text or voice. Text had less chance of being traced, but voice was sometimes faster if you didn't get the question right.

Text. He'd risk it. As his mind reviewed the situation, he considered his words carefully. DID TARGET HAVE ACCESS TO A PHONE? Was it enough? Frustrated, he hit send and waited. If it wasn't enough, he'd call.

The reply wasn't satisfactory. ASSUMING NO MOLE ACCESS, NO.

The mole. He'd assumed that Claire was the mole, albeit an unintentional one. If she wasn't, and someone else was, a phone could have been planted. His phone buzzed with a message from Karen. GET OUT OF THERE.

Keith powered off his phone, backed up, and turned around. The Jeep, despite its design, fishtailed several times as he whipped around corners and flew over the rutted road. He drove into the garage, closed the door, and reached under the seat. His Glock was strapped to the undercarriage. He couldn't risk a tranquilizer this time. Not this time.

With the gun out and ready, he ran for the house. Nothing indicated anyone had arrived. The tire tracks, 'copter markings, footprints. There was too much to be sure, but he did take a cleansing breath as instinct took over; the house would be empty. Even so, he took every precaution as he opened the door, crossed to the other side, listened, and then swept the house. Empty.

He had to work quickly. As much as Keith wanted to call and see how long Mike had been alone, he couldn't risk it. His disregard for orders already put him at risk for being fired. If he failed, there was no doubt. He'd be out. Regardless, he had to do it. His job required that he make rogue decisions if the situation warranted it, but if he botched it, the Agency couldn't support him.

Just as he decided to give up and leave, he found it. A basic pre-paid cell phone, sprayed a bland tan, had been velcroed to the back of the ancient fiberglass drapes, up near the hooks. If you weren't looking for it, you'd never find it. As it was, even with his thorough search, he nearly missed it.

He nearly grabbed it without thinking, but training kicked in before he blew it. Using the hem of the drapes, he pulled the phone from the fabric and gingerly flipped the phone open. There was only one message. HERE. WILL NOTIFY WHEN CLEAR.

Great. Was there a code? It didn't seem like it. After all, he'd promised to "notify." Banking on the improbability, he glanced around, looking for anything that might work to punch buttons. The chance that he'd avoid destroying fingerprints was slim to none, but he had to risk it. At last, he found a crayon half under the couch. That'd work.

Nerves nearly overtook him as he tried to come up with a plausible notification. It'd been so long already. He couldn't wait much longer without looking suspect. Desperate, and then ashamed that it took desperation to send him to it, he prayed, begging God for the wisdom to know exactly what to do. He reread the text message. Clear. The guy used clear. Either he was a professional with possible military training, or he was a wannabe. Either way, it was best to go that route... wasn't it?

Taking a deep breath and shooting up another prayer, he took the crayon and punched his reply. CLEAR. REQUIRE EXTRACTION. N 39.339069 AND W -120.535208.

He had to protect the phone and make sure it could be found if he failed. That thought alone made his mouth go dry. It was always a possibility. When you protect people for a living, you know your life is in constant jeopardy. It's an odd combination of "the job" and slight insanity. No matter how often he faced danger, Keith never became immune to it.

In the bathroom, under the sink, a plastic wrapper over the toilet paper gave him the protection he wanted. He tore the remaining rolls from the packaging, tucked the phone in the corner, and rolled it completely into the plastic. A glance at his watch told him to hurry. He didn't know how far out Mike's backup was, but he had to get the phone to safety and then call Karen.

His first instinct was to cross the road and jog down a ways, but he resisted. Instead, he found a snake hole near the garage, stuffed the phone inside it, covered it with a rock, and snapped a picture of it, of the garage from where he stood, and then another one from the garage. With those three for reference, he took a branch from a creosote, pounded the sand with it to remove his footprints, and then tossed it back inside the bush.

Once the pictures were sent, he called Karen. "Okay, from the northeast corner of the garage, walk straight to the second creosote and Mike's cell will be in the hole there. Be careful. It's possible I used a snake hole with a live one in it."

"Keith, why are you calling me?" Karen's voice sounded stunned.

"Because I know you're not the mole. I've got to get off and be ready."

"Is it Mark?"

Keith's eyes closed as he absorbed the question he'd tried not to ask himself. "I hope not, Karen. I really hope not."

---

It was nearly dawn and Keith still waited—waited for a rescue team that might never arrive. His mind replayed various scenarios, trying to make the best decision, until he thought he'd go crazy from lack of sleep and indecision. Staying meant possibly taking out whoever was out to get him. That, clearly, was important. However, every minute that passed was one minute further from discovering if Mike's cohort had left any traces of anything on that phone. The longer he waited, the more likely the mole would spook and run. Sure, they'd discover who it was, but the chances of capturing him became next to impossible.

At last, he decided. Ten o'clock was the cutoff. If no one came by then, he'd leave. Much later than that, and he'd be unable to drive long enough to be able to get a room and sleep. He needed to ditch the Jeep, but the replacement vehicle forty minutes away wouldn't be safe. Not now. There might not be enough time, but he had to see if Karen could provide something.

"Hey, need a replacement. Something loud and flashy. Kernville."

"Can do. I'll send an address where to park the Jeep. Take the car in the driveway to the park and swap out there. Yellow mustang or Red Jag?"

"Mustang."

"John figured out that he was in danger. He's now appreciative that we separated him from his family."

Keith smiled to himself. This was good. "How'd he come to that conclusion?"

"He said that we wouldn't have used the discretionary clause for a drill."

"Is he any closer?"

"Well, we could use that hacker." She sounded tired. That wasn't good.

"And have you heard from Claire and Brian?"

"I think Brian is ready to kill Claire, but don't worry."

"Why not?" He could almost guess the answer.

"The feeling is mutual."

"Okay, I'm getting off here. I see dust in the air. Probably just a motorcyclist, but you never know."

"Tranq anyone who comes near the house and run. Got it? Don't risk anything. If they pause near the house, you tranq them and go."

"Yes ma'am." He started to hang up, but her voice stopped him.

"And Keith?"

"Yeah?"

"If you get yourself killed, I am not coming to your funeral. Got it?"

Keith laughed as his finger hovered over the power button. "Got it."

# TWENTY-TWO

John tapped away on his computer, seemingly oblivious to the battle of wills taking place around him. Mike refused to speak, which drove Keith crazy. However, no one but Karen knew it. As the morning passed, they watched him, each waiting for some kind of indication as to what move to make. The phone had revealed only Mike's prints—something that didn't surprise any of them.

After three days of observation, it was clear. Mike was an amateur at best. He either owed someone something, or he had tried to break into a business he wasn't suited for; regardless, his reticence actually to kill someone had likely saved John's life. As distasteful as it was, Keith had to play on that knowledge. His eyes sent Karen a warning signal, and then he began his game.

"That's it. If he won't talk voluntarily, we'll have to make him talk."

"What are you talking about?" Karen played her part well. She gave Keith a look that clearly said, "Are you nuts?" and shook her head. "You can't do that, and you know it."

"Sure, I can. If we were government, no way. But, since we're not, I'm not playing this game anymore. He came after me, and I want to know why."

"Mark'll be ticked," she warned. Karen gave a brilliant performance. Keith could almost see the uncertainty oozing from her.

"Let him. We're stuck here waiting to find out what happens when this guy doesn't return. The guys who came for him are dead, so we make him talk."

"Dead! No one told me anything about them being dead!"

"Well, you didn't need to know, did you?" Keith swallowed the rest of his coffee in one gulp and slammed the cup on the counter. "Okay, let's get this over with. It's simple; I'll start with a simple punch. You'll get thirty seconds between punches to reconsider. It'll give my fists a break too." He flexed his muscles for effect. "Got a favorite side?"

"You're sick."

For a moment, he hesitated. The idea of pummeling anyone for any reason revolted him. No, he was more of a "turn 'em over to law enforcement" type. However, if this was what it took, he'd do it. His fist slammed into Mike's cheek. "Clock it, Karen. I might count too fast if I do it myself."

Despite his inner turmoil—prayers flying heavenward faster than he could mentally articulate them—and the throbbing he could feel starting in his hand already, Keith managed an air of being unbothered by the punch. As he waited, his hands resting on his hips, Karen called out the time in decreasing five-second intervals. "Fifteen."

"Man, this drags."

"Ten."

At five, Keith wriggled his fingers, balled up his fist, and flexed for effect. He hoped for a last second capitulation, but it didn't come. Karen announced, almost as if bored, "Time."

Keith's fist hit Mike's jaw this time. Anyone watching would assume that he held nothing back, but he'd given the swing no more than half-force. The back of Keith's mouth tasted like bile. *Lord, please...* If it didn't mean possible danger for his cousin, he probably would have been willing to risk someone else coming for him, but Claire was another story. "Clock it."

At twenty, Mike began to perspire. At fifteen, he whimpered. By ten he looked ready to pass out from sheer fear, and at five he shook his head. "Don't. Really. No one is worth it." The man looked around Keith and shuddered. "This guy is a freak."

"Yeah, whatever." Karen didn't sound nearly as sympathetic as Mike obviously hoped.

"Start talkin', Mikey. You've got thirty seconds to convince me that I don't need to take another swing." Out of the corner of his eye, Keith saw Karen stifle a snicker and hesitated. Did he need to cover for her, or did Mike miss the assault on his overly dramatic threat. Yeah, it was cheesy, but from where he was standing, it looked like it had worked.

"I don't know much. I was supposed to get in there, take you out, and then go to the next one."

"Who is the next one?"

"Erika somethingski."

"Who sent you?"

"I owed a guy. He said I could pay him off this way or work it off—" Mike swallowed. "The guy's a creep, okay? Don't ever get in business with a creep. They'll totally—"

"Got it. Who's the guy?"

"I don't know his name. These people don't just hand out their business cards if you know what I mean."

"Where?" Keith was unaware at how his entire body tensed as he asked.

"Columbus."

Keith and Karen's eyes met briefly, until Keith dug his hands into his pocket for his keys. "Trade. I can't take that thing to the airport."

With Karen's keys in hand, Keith grabbed his duffel, tossed his toothbrush in it, and waved goodbye to John. "Get those documents fast."

"Almost there. I'm just working on offshore account numbers now and I'll be done."

"Good. Karen, have Claire go to her original destination when John's done and tell her not to come back until I tell her. Go with her."

---

Fury nearly blinded her as, once again, Erika bounced on Keith's shoulder across the back yard, through the alley, and into the same garage as the last time. She wanted to scream at him—demand that he rip the tape from her mouth and untie her. What was the point? She got it now. Obviously, the danger wasn't past yet. She'd been saved by the "Agency" once, and she was grateful enough not to refuse help when it came again.

His eyes met hers as he laid her on the floor behind his seat—again. She tried, with every ounce of emotion she could infused into her features, to show him that she wasn't going to resist, but he shook his head. "Not now, Erika. Trust me."

As the van door slid shut, she could have sworn she heard him chuckle. So, her irritation amused him. Great. And how did he plan to explain her absence this time? It seemed ridiculous to assume that she could keep disappearing for weeks at a time without *someone* considering it unusual.

The driver's door shut, and the same stupid eighties radio station blared overly synthesized music into the vehicle. "Sorry, Erika, you can't assume someone will wake up enough not to overreact. I just found out that you're a target, so I came. I don't know where we're going yet or even if I'll tell anyone."

She heard something in his voice that she'd never noticed in the weeks she'd spent with him—fear, raw fear. Someone was after her; she'd seen it on the coast of Oregon, but then, he'd been confident. He'd been alert, cautious, even had a healthy fear of the consequences of bad decisions, but it was nothing like this. This wasn't the quiet, irritated Keith that had shot a man and then fought and shot another as just part of his job. This Keith was talkative and scared.

The myriad of questions that flooded her mind nearly drowned out his next words. "When we get to where I can pull off the road, I'll remove the tape, but it's going to hurt."

There—it was back. That was the tone she was accustomed to hearing. There was a comfort in hearing the warning and the authority in him again. Maybe he was just tired, and she'd misread him. Maybe she was wrong.

"So, you probably want to know why I'm here? I'll take that thump as a yes." His chattiness felt awkward—forced. The uncertainty she'd stuffed down returned. This was bad—possibly worse—than the last time, and the last time had nearly gotten her killed. "Someone infiltrated my last assignment. It took us a while, but we finally got him to tell us what he was after—sort of. You were next. That's all I know."

It might be all he knew, but Erika knew there must be more to the story. She heard something in his voice, and she didn't like it. That voice spoke volumes with each word, but it seemed to use an unfamiliar language. She'd have to wait until he took off the tape. She frowned, the tape stretching and pulling from the sides of her cheek painfully. Why would he take off the tape before they got somewhere? That would be an absolute violation of every protocol they ever used, and she knew it.

Wherever they were going, it wasn't back to the cabins. Of course, it'd be a little silly to take the same person back to a place they had been forced to leave. Obviously, the wrong people knew about it—or at least potentially did. She waited for him to tell her where they might go, but he didn't. Erika desperately wanted to be able to ask, but when he pulled the van over and crawled between the seats to remove the duct tape, she turned her head away from him.

"What?"

Erika whipped her head back and glared. He reached for the tape, but she jerked away again, shaking her head. "I don't get it. Don't you want that off?" She shook again. "Now you get all funny about the pain of the tape." She could only hope her face showed the absolute disgust she felt at those words. "Then what?"

With one last jerk of her head toward the driver's seat, Erika rolled away from him, hoping she'd made the right decision. The Keith Auger who had been her "protector" the first time would see her actions as proof of trust. With this Keith, who knew?

The drive seemed endless. She regretted her rash decision to stay a gagged prisoner. How stupid was that? Twice they stopped for gas, but after the second time, Keith's entire demeanor changed. He climbed back in the van, started it up, and pulled out onto the highway as if on auto pilot. "Okay, we're not far." He took a sip of water before he continued. "Look, Erika, this one's going to be worse for you—I think. I doubt you can leave; it's just an RV so it's tiny, and we'll be taking Navy showers so that it doesn't look like I'm using more water than a single guy normally would. I have to make it look like you're not even there when anyone from the park is around. I'm sorry, but it's the best place I can come up with."

Apologetic—not courtesy driven, but truly sorry for his decision—a new side of him. Erika didn't think she liked it. Confident, while irritating, comforted in a strange sort of way.

They arrived within minutes of the gas station. That was good. If Keith had completely freaked out, she could always try to escape and walk to the station. The van turned left onto an asphalt parking lot. He had chosen to bring her some place that public? It seemed odd—almost dangerous.

The van pulled off the pavement onto a dirt road of some kind and then stopped several hundred yards away. Keith hurried from the vehicle, and Erika waited for the door to open, but it didn't. There were faint scratching sounds outside, but she couldn't quite make sense of them. After what seemed like an hour, but common sense assured her was only ten or fifteen minutes, the door opened, and Keith beckoned her to scoot closer. "I'll take the ropes off here," he whispered.

The scent of trees... of *nature* filled her nostrils. But instead of hustling her inside, he did—he just worked on those knots. The moment he freed her hands, while he untied her feet, Erika whipped off the duct tape and hissed, "Are you insane? Get me in there!"

He retrieved her bag and his from the front seat and followed her into the RV. As she fumbled for a light, he grabbed her hand. "No lights," he whispered. "There can't be two silhouettes."

At first, that precaution seemed wise and simple enough. After all, it felt like he was back to his normal self—making sure her captivity felt like it. However, when her hipbone hit the edge of a table, that opinion changed. "I'm going to be black and blue!"

"Shh."

Keith dumped the bags and guided her to the "bedroom" of the RV. His breath tickled her ear as he whispered, "Straight ahead is a bed. To the left is the door to the bathroom. Just don't turn on the light."

With that, he was gone, the soft latch of a doorknob clicking behind him. She tried to glance around her in the

darkness, but Erika saw nothing. Walking with her hands out in front of her, she stumbled into the bed, crawled up to the pillows, and pulled down the covers.
*Well, that was weird.*

# TWENTY-THREE

The new house was nice—almost too nice. In Claire's mind, it was downright palatial. The entryway alone was larger than her entire apartment. The stables housed horses that, to her surprise, they were encouraged "to ride whenever Brian can be spared from the house." The children took to it as if accustomed to white couches in "mommy's" living room and a kitchen large enough to service an entire restaurant.

Brian remained terse toward Melissa and Claire, but without Keith to interact with the children, he did manage to carry on necessary conversations with the little ones comfortably—in almost a freakish Dr. Jekyll and Mr. Hyde scenario. Each time Claire tried to engage his gentler side in conversation, he managed to switch to the "dark side" faster than seemed possible. His explanations of how to get to the next level of a video game were simple but thorough. However, when, just as he paused to let Jordan try it, she asked when they'd hear from Keith next, his reply was, "Don't know."

Melissa spent her time taking care of Katie and the baby and fretting over where her husband might be. Despite all of Claire's reassurances, the woman dissolved into a puddle of anxiety and worry. Jordan was left to his own devices—something that Claire suspected the boy expected. Thankfully, he had that first-born tendency to be responsible beyond his years.

Jordan heard the helicopter first, and raced outside to watch it land, sending Claire right behind him to ensure he didn't get too close. At the sight of Karen and John, her heart leapt. Did this mean it was over? Was Keith next? She hardly noticed as John grabbed his son in a hug certain to squeeze the life from the child.

Karen's head shook as she jogged across the grass to her side. "He had to go back to Erika. It's been a nightmare," she shouted over the deafening whirl of the helicopter blades.

Inside, Claire opened her mouth, ready to demand more information, but saw that John was obviously not there to stay. He hugged his wife, kissed his children, listened to the exciting things they'd done, laughed at his son's indignation over vehicular bathrooming, and then rose to go. "They let me come in for a minute since we were dropping off Karen, but we really need to get this to the Feds. They'll start driving you home the minute the FBI gives the okay."

Melissa demanded to be allowed to go too, but John shook her off, giving one last pain-filled kiss before he hurried out the door and into the waiting helicopter. The sounds of the aircraft slowly disappeared as it flew back toward Rockland. Claire nearly screamed as Karen picked up the baby and led Melissa back to one of the bedrooms, explaining the process of turning evidence over to the FBI and what steps they had to take to ensure that they were still safe, even after the criminals were arrested.

Jordan asked about dinner, and since Brian's idea of meals meant popping something with the taste and consistency of cardboard into the microwave and serving it with a can of soda instead of milk, juice, or even water, the task had fallen to her to try to provide something edible and semi-nutritious. If it happened to taste better than Styrofoam, she considered herself a success.

Karen came into the kitchen just as Claire fought the stove, trying not to burn the cubed steaks she'd found in the freezer. "Turn down the burner. You want to let them cook slowly or they'll be charred on the outside and raw inside."

"Even something this thin?"

"They were frozen, right?"

"Yeah."

"Take it slow. People try to cook everything instantly. The stove isn't a microwave. If you let things simmer a bit, they have a lot more flavor, and they actually get cooked."

Claire stared at the woman as if she'd come from another planet. "My mom has been trying to tell me this stuff for years. Why can't she say things that plainly?"

From the depths of an enormous French-doored freezer, Karen pulled a bag of stir-fry vegetables. "If we steam these and toss them with some Italian dressing, the kids'll probably eat them."

"Vegetables? I thought kids hated vegetables. I was going for protein and maybe some juice or something."

Karen shook her head. "I've watched Melissa. She makes her kids eat veggies. All we have to do is make them palatable, and vinegar does wonders for that."

"Kids like vinegar."

"With veggies, sure. That, and ranch dressing." Karen reached into the fridge for the necessary dressing. "I'd chop up a bunch of raw stuff, but I don't know if we're staying here or moving."

"What for?"

"Well," Karen glanced around and then lowered her voice. "It's a long story. I'm supposed to be taking you to Stanford, but we're not actually going."

"What about Brian?"

"He'll escort the Frielichs home or to protective custody—whichever the FBI decides—and we're supposedly going to Stanford, but we'll meet with Keith."

"What will Mark say about that?"

Karen glanced around the room, stepped through the doorway, and when sure no one could overhear, whispered, "We're not telling Mark in case he's our mole."

---

After the fifth time she snapped at him, Erika decided an apology might be in order, but she couldn't bring herself to do it. One minute he was the slightly terse, no-nonsense, wants-her-to-fight guy that she'd first met, and the next minute he became apologetic, nervous, and at times, visibly alarmed when any unfamiliar sound dared to surface. It unnerved her—stressed her—even more so than Corey had.

The fifth wheel was nice, though. She'd never understood the idea of a camper that was half the cost of the average house in some of the smaller towns around Rockland, but she had to admit, it felt almost luxurious.

Cherry cabinetry, granite counters, even the sleek black appliances looked as though they were right out of a home design show rather than in a camper stuck in an RV park. The bed she'd slept on was the nicest bed she'd ever used, and even the chairs were quality. It had a flat-screen TV, larger than anyone she knew owned, and it hung over a fireplace. The idea of a fireplace in an RV just seemed weird. Cool, but weird—like everything else that had happened in her life lately.

Keith's phone buzzed, and he answered it with an expression she'd have considered guilt-riddled if she didn't know better. Listening to one side of the conversation nearly drove her over the edge of her already precarious precipice. "We're here. We're safe, but—"

Most of what he said made little sense to her, but occasionally things clicked together. He wasn't checking in with Mark. That unnerved her. She tried to concentrate on the TV, but it was nearly impossible. At last, feeling a little desperate, Erika decided to make a bathroom run in hopes of hearing something from Karen. As she passed, all she heard was, "John's family." That wasn't very helpful.

By the time she returned, Keith stared at his cellphone looking more agitated than ever. "Okay, what's up? I'm not going to pretend I didn't hear half of that, and I did hear Karen say something about John's family. So, who is John, and why doesn't Mark know where we are?"

Keith fidgeted, clearly torn—why, she couldn't be sure. Did he not know, or did he not know if he should share? If she wasn't careful, she'd encourage him in the wrong area and it would definitely backfire. However, before she could decide which angle to try, he sighed, sinking into one of the chairs, and hung his head in his hands. "There's a mole, Erika. We aren't sure who it is, but there's a mole. There has to be."

"You think it's Mark?" The idea seemed preposterous. He'd been so confident in Mark's decisions and abilities. No wonder he floundered and flip-flopped. It wasn't quite as bad as if his god had failed him, but probably close.

"I don't want to think that, no. I just can't risk your life until I know for sure."

"Don't you think he knows how to find you?"

"Not here..." His voice didn't sound as confident as she knew he wanted it to. "Well, okay any place at all could be an issue, but this was the most unlikely. It's a remote enough idea that he might not think of it, and if he did, it'd be too logical, and he's trained us not to do the logical. I had to go over and over trying to decide if he'd come. I'm pretty sure he would eventually, but by that point, we'll be gone. If it's not him, no one will figure it out."

"How'd you know—?"

He jumped up and clapped a hand over her mouth. Whispering into her ear, he said, "Go into the bedroom and lay on the floor between the bed and the wall with the window. Go!"

Erika listened as he opened the trailer door talking to someone and telling them he was going outside and taking them off speakerphone. She was confused at first, but then nodded. It was brilliant, really. That'd explain a second voice easily. His next quip about awesome reception nearly made her giggle. Oh yeah, he was good. In one sense, he was best when danger was potentially imminent.

Seconds after the trailer door shut again, he stepped into the bedroom and whispered, "Come on out."

While she grabbed a glass from the cupboard, rinsed it, and filled it, Keith dug through a couple of drawers until he found a stack of post-it notes and a stenographer's notebook. Pens followed. He held both out to her and whispered, "Take your pick. We don't talk."

With the questions Erika had, she was sure they'd go through the paper in no time. She grabbed the notebook and then, upon second thought, swapped it out for the post-its. She'd make every inch work for her. Before she even sat down, her hands started scribbling. "How do you know there's a mole?" His answer took a couple of minutes to write and filled most of the page from the notebook.

His evidence was irrefutable. Someone had known about the safe house and had tried to hurt either him or the guy John. It made sense that he was the target since the guy also had known about her. She hadn't expected anything quite *that* creepy. Strange men being sent after her made Erika feel violated. The irony of that thought sent her into a fit of giggles that nearly sent Keith through the roof. He punched on the TV, and forced himself to laugh, making her attempts to stifle her hilarity futile.

"What?"

The words across an entire sheet of paper annoyed her. Couldn't he see that the limited supply was going to drive her nuts, or was that his objective in the first place? Writing even smaller, as if by doing so she'd make a point, Erika's response earned her an exaggerated roll of his eyes. "Don't try to force a laugh again. You sounded like a cow in the throes of labor. Also, quit wasting paper!" She hesitated, and then wrote, "How long do we stay?"

His answer was swifter this time, telling her that he'd struggled more about what to share with her than the fact that there was a problem at all. "Karen is going to join us with my cousin Claire. Claire is at risk from the same people you are, so keeping you together will make it easier."

"How did your cousin get involved? Did they know she was your cousin?" As she wrote, Erika realized that it was exactly what had happened. "They used her to try to get to you or tried to get to her to get to you?"

Keith nodded. His pen hovered over the paper and then he wrote, "After we sent you home, Mark suggested I recruit Claire for the Agency."

As odd as it seemed to recruit someone so randomly, particularly someone who was under threat, Erika didn't know how they chose who they chose to work for them, so she missed the subtle message Keith had tried to send. However, as he waited, obviously expecting a different response than, "Did she want to do that?" he watched her closely.

"Oh, is that why you think he might be moleish? Is that unusual?" He nodded. Several times, he started to write again, and each time he hesitated. At last, Erika scribbled three words, peeled off the sticky note, and slapped it on the note pad. "Just write it!"

"I don't think it's him."

She tried to imagine why that would be so upsetting but couldn't. After coming up blank several times, she gave up and wrote, "Why does that bother you?"

He had his answer half-written even before she finished. "Because if it's not him, we're in the dark and don't know how to proceed. We know what Mark might do."

"Oh, but you don't know what someone else might do because you don't know who. Do you have options?" Her hands began to cramp—already. It seemed odd how such a little amount of writing could bother her so much so soon.

"Exactly. If we had a name, or even a few names, we'd have an idea of what to do or not to do. Right now, we're in limbo."

Erika's mind swam with ideas. While she thought, Keith stood and opened the cupboards, searching for some kind of food. He pulled out canned tamales and wriggled it as if asking if she wanted it. Nothing sounded more revolting, but she nodded. She'd be a pill about the food choice later. Meanwhile, she started making a list of everyone she'd ever heard of connected with Keith and the Agency.

Mark
Karen
Corey
John
Claire
*Helicopter pilot from second cabin*
*2 guys and 1 girl from Oregon*

She pushed the list across the counter and took the spatula from him. "Who else?" she whispered.

Keith thought for a moment and then added a few more.

Justin
Jill
Anthony

He hesitated long enough for her to take the pen and write, "What?"

He flipped the pad over and wrote again. "Well, technically, anyone from the office or even the building COULD be. Not likely but could."

With one hand holding the spatula, and the other scribbling, Erika wrote, "Scale of one to five, what are the odds of any of those?"

Only Karen got a zero.

# TWENTY-FOUR

"Where is he, Karen?" Mark's voice sounded stern, but slightly amused.
"He isn't telling me."
"So, he thinks one of us, most likely me, is the mole?"
"He's not ruling anyone out. So, until the mole is caught, he's hiding." Karen hated to have to say it. It sounded so disloyal and disrespectful to the guy who had gone to lengths she was sure they couldn't imagine to keep them safe in the past.
"Good. I hate it, but good. I've got to keep looking. You know that, right?"
She sighed, allowing him to hear her frustration with the situation. "I know. So does he. If it makes you feel any better, I know he really doesn't think it's you. It's just—"
"He's doing his job. I just have to do mine too. Now that John's family is in protective custody, I'll send you looking for him too."
"Sorry, Mark. I'm going off grid too. I have to protect Claire just as he has to protect Erika. If I could meet with him, we'd switch, but you and I both know he's not going to meet."
Mark swore. "I trained him too well."
"That's why he's the best."
"He thinks you're an option too, doesn't he? That's just insane."
"No, insane is trusting emotions rather than accepting the reality that any one of us could be. Anyone with any contact to or within the Agency—even the people at Mayflower could technically be the mole. He's being smart." Karen hated lying, but she had to do it. If Mark had crossed any criminal lines, the slightest mistake could cost several people their lives. Lives weren't optional. "However, if I can,

I'm going to convince him to meet and switch. I know he'd feel better if he could keep an eye on Claire."

"He won't do it, Karen."

She forced herself to sigh again, trying to make it sound just a tad irritated and very disappointed. "I know. However, he sounds a bit freaked, so maybe…"

"I've sent Jill and Anthony back to Helen."

"Oh!" Karen hadn't even considered that angle. "That's good. We blew it not asking Mike about that. Keith heard Erika and took off."

"He did the right thing. We've got Mike. We'll get it out of him."

Something felt wrong. Even as they talked, Karen grew more uneasy until she realized what it was. Mark was dialoguing for the purpose of dialogue. He kept her talking so he could get someone there to follow. She'd fallen for a simple trick that even rookies didn't miss. Her mind swirled as she answered questions and asked her own. She had to be fast, but how? Then an idea occurred.

"Hey, Mark. How can we get funding? I have some cash, but it isn't going to last long. I mean, it feels weird saying, 'You could be a mole, but I need bucks,' but I don't know what else—" Mid question, she cut the power to her phone.

She doubted that he'd buy it, but maybe if she tried calling back ten minutes down the road and then backtracked the other way. That'd work. For the first time, she saw the wisdom in not using the implant tracking devices the Agency had considered. It had seemed like such an excellent safety precaution, but now…

"Claire? Gotta get. Come on!"

Claire jogged down the stairs two at a time. "I've been waiting for you! Keith won't wait if we're late."

"I know. That's why I told him half an hour later than I plan to be there. Let's go."

Halfway down the drive, Claire asked the question she'd wanted to for years. "Karen, why doesn't Keith ever have a girlfriend?"

The Mall of America parking lot-slash-garage seemed excessively public to Erika, but Keith had insisted that public, at a time like this, was imperative. He wouldn't tell her where they were going or even if they were really meeting up with Karen and Claire, but from his demeanor, she assumed so. Each day that passed with this Keith made her less confident and more nervous than she'd ever been in her life. She didn't mind his surliness or the silence that hovered over his uncle's trailer—those she could stomach.

What terrified her were the moments when he gave her an apologetic look or actually voiced how sorry he was that they didn't have the support she should be able to expect in their circumstances. When he'd refused to tie her for the trip to Minnesota, she'd nearly gone crazy until he'd said, "I won't leave until you agree to ride as a passenger. This isn't the cabin, Erika. I need you to be able to protect yourself if something happens to me. Before, I had no doubt that I could protect both of us. Now, I'm just reasonably confident. That's not good enough."

As they pulled into the massive parking lot across from the mall, he'd reached into the console between their seats and passed her a gun with holster. "It's a tranq. Strap it to your leg under your jeans. If it's a woman, shoot three. Man, go for five."

"What—"

"Just do it, Erika. I need you to tell me you'll do it if you have to. If the initial shots don't stop them within three steps, shoot again. If you fear for your life, shoot until they're gone. Just promise me you'll shoot."

"What if you're the one scaring me?" She'd meant to sound sarcastic, but it came out terrified.

"Oh, man. I'm so sorry."

"Stop saying you're sorry!" She had a few expletives ready to fire at him, but the look on his face—the utter dejection—made it impossible. One thing her father had taught her was never to kick a man while he was down. Regardless of her flaws, Erika knew she was better than that.

"You're right. I'm not good at rogue. I like having the security of knowing that there's someone absolutely invested in me and the safety of our client. That doubt kills me."

"You have someone, Keith. You've got your god. You have to believe he's watching out for you, or why would you even believe in him? If you need someone to back you up, look there."

Erika looked as stunned as Keith did when she realized what she'd said. He pulled into a parking spot and shut off the engine. Seconds ticked past as he mulled her words in his mind, differing emotions flitting across his face with each new train of thought. "You're right. I keep doing that. I put my faith in people instead of the One with the real power to protect me."

His words sounded like some kind of mumbo jumbo, but she didn't care. The confidence was back, and even if it only lasted until they were on the road to wherever their next destination was, it'd work. That was what mattered. "Okay, so now that we've recognized the Almighty is here and ready to zap the crooks with his laser vision or whatever he has, now what?"

"We wait for Karen. She's watching the entrance. She'll be ready for us."

"Do we get out?"

He shook his head. "Not yet. Just keep an eye out for Karen. Claire is young, not too tall, blonde, and pretty. No idea how she'll be dressed—"

"Why aren't we changing how we look? You know, dye hair, change hairstyle, grow a beard—"

"I don't think a beard would look good on you, but we don't do that because—"

"People expect it."

The first genuine smile she'd seen since he'd escorted her to the airport spread slowly across his face. "You're getting it." A glance at the rearview broadened the smile. "They're here. Grab your bag and let's go."

They each reached into the back seat, grabbed their bags, and hurried from the car. A young woman, hardly looking old enough to be out of high school, threw herself at Keith, weeping about being worried and stressed. Erika wanted to slap sense into the girl until she saw Keith whispering something. Whatever it was, the girl's face seemed to relax and that changed his entire demeanor.

"Erika, this is Claire. We've got to get going." Keith, back to business, made everything feel much calmer.

They strolled to the trains and just off the platform, a man approached. Erika was on high alert, ready to pull out her gun and unload it into anyone who came too close or looked suspicious. Keith, on the other hand, seemed quite calm as he traded both sets of car keys for the one in the man's hand. It felt almost like a drug deal—two people passing goods as they intersected. Weird.

They hardly chatted as they rode the train to the airport, which made Erika feel even more self-conscious than ever. Karen yawned twice, and Claire hung her head in her hands, making Erika wonder if they'd had a long drive. Keith's lazy, "Sure will be glad to get *home* and away from stores," told her that it was all part of the ruse.

"Stop whining. You got to see your game."

"And they lost. Seriously? You fly a thousand miles to watch a game, the least they could do is win."

"Sore loser."

Keith grinned at his cousin. "Darn tootin'."

"Man, Keith, you've gotta learn to swear a little. Darn tootin' sounds like a kid who hates that he farts so much."

"Whatever. Let's just get checked in. It's still another hour until the flight leaves." Keith glanced at his watch as if disgusted with the time.

Erika listened to the banter, her mind swirling at his use of the word "darn." Hadn't he considered it no different from its predecessor? Why the change? His eyes met hers over his cousin's head and she grinned, knowing. An act. He'd put on an act, using words that offended his sensibilities, to protect her. In the right scenario, he could probably fling out a string of expletives to make any bathroom stall artist proud.

Once inside the airport, Keith went to check their flight status, while Claire made a beeline for a coffee kiosk. Karen dragged Erika into the bathrooms, passing her a note just as she entered a stall. Erika stared at it, confused. *Stay in here for five minutes, exit out the terminal one—Lindbergh—and take the light rail to terminal two—Humphrey—parking. First Row. Green Ford Focus wagon. 249X9A2.*

After a week of little sleep and more emotional turmoil than he'd dealt with in ages, combined with a twelve-hour drive in a car full of jabbering women, Keith had collapsed into bed, spent. Nine hours later, he crawled from the covers, awake, but nearly as exhausted as he'd been when they'd arrived. As he opened the door, Karen's voice hit him in the chest with a blow that felt physical. "Claire, if you'd seen it, you'd see why he's so rattled."

"I watched him all the way here. He's just—weird."

"Have you ever had to threaten someone when your job is to prevent that kind of thing? Have you ever had to hurt someone to try to protect someone else?"

"But that doesn't make sense. He's had to shoot people before. He said he had to beat up a guy who tried to attack Erika."

"That's another thing all together. Self-defense or direct defense is easily reconciled with your conscience, Claire. Torturing someone, no matter how important, goes against everything in Keith's make-up. It kills him."

"Torture? Keith?"

"In his mind, slugging someone repeatedly, pretending to look forward to it or enjoy it—that's torture. He's still reeling from it. I can see it in him, and I can't help. He needs the kind of comforting that you get from family or a girlfriend. I'm neither."

Claire's next question nearly choked him. "Have you ever told him how you feel about him?"

Laughter, mercifully natural and free, echoed around the empty kitchen. "I'm not in love with Keith. I care about him, sure. He's a great guy, but he's brother material for me."

"I don't know why women are so blind to him!"

"They're not, Claire. He just isn't around enough to give anyone any encouragement. This is a tough job. The biggest drawback is the loneliness. Very few agents have families, and those who do usually don't stay married for long."

"They choose the job over their families?"

189

Keith cringed at the answer he expected Karen to give but relaxed as she said, "Yep. Most do, but Keith wouldn't."

"So, you're telling me I need to take it easy on him."

"I'm telling you that your cousin just spent days trying to protect someone, found that person being choked, had to shoot the attacker, and then had to beat the guy to find out information that probably saved Erika's life. He's kind of had a rough week, okay? If you'd been through all that, what would you need?"

"Okay, fine! I'll give him one of my famous neck massages and maybe he'll open up."

"He probably won't, Claire, but knowing someone cares will do more good than talking about it. Keith isn't a talker. Some people decompress by talking. Keith isn't one."

A sound behind him sent Keith spinning, his hand on his gun. Erika stood in her doorway, just a few feet behind him, tears streaming down her face. Stuffing down an inward groan, Keith shuffled toward her, backing her into her room and quietly shut the door. "You okay?"

"You hit someone?"

Everything in him wanted to pound something until it shattered into tiny pieces. He did not need Erika afraid of him—not now. "He tried to choke my client to death. It didn't take much to figure out that he was really after me."

"So, you hit him to get him off the guy? What's the difference between that and the guy who jumped you in Oregon?"

When it came to protecting clients, Keith had no compunction about lying. He couldn't tell his mom that he liked her hairstyle if he didn't, but he could tell an endangered woman anything if it'd keep her calm and stress-free. One look in Erika's eyes, and Keith knew the best choice this time was the truth. "No, what Karen was talking about happened a few days later. The guy, Mike, wouldn't talk. We tried everything, but time was ticking, and we knew if we waited much longer, and there were any other targets, those targets wouldn't be there by the time we got the information we needed."

"Targets such as me?"

"Such as you. Yeah, Erika, I hit him. He was tied in a chair, I made sure I sounded menacing and like I almost anticipated the chance to pound him, and I literally slammed my fist into his face—twice. Had he not spilled everything then, I'd have hit him a dozen more times—until he was unconscious even. I was not going to stop until he told me what I wanted." His voice shook just a bit on the last word despite himself.

Fresh tears poured over her cheeks as Erika stared up at him blindly. "That's how you found out that you needed to come for me?"

"Yeah."

Erika's arms went around him. Keith stood, unmoving for several seconds, uncertain what to do. Clients rarely hugged them—even grateful ones. It just wasn't "done." When she didn't let go, he patted her back awkwardly, murmuring reassuring and random comments, but Erika refused to let go.

At last, she sniffled and said, "Thanks."

"What for?"

A giggle, a sound that seemed absolutely out of character, escaped before she shrugged. "Doing your job? I think I understand a few things now. You really had me freaked out."

"I did?"

"Yeah, but now I get it more. It wasn't just about you not having Mark to fall back on like you thought. You had to do something that revolts you. You were probably fighting the whole two wrongs making a right thing. Me, I'm just grateful you did it. I'd probably be dead by now."

She wiped her tears away with the back of her hand and stepped away awkwardly. "Sorry. You'd better get out there and let your family hug on you a bit. I'm not family and we both know you're not into dark spiked-haired girls with chips on their shoulders."

"Karen doesn't know what she's talking about. I'm fine."

"So, you'll be grumpy again?" Erika crossed her arms as if skeptical.

"I'm never grumpy."

"Hogwash. You were a walking bear at the cabins and in Oregon."

"Okay, if you say so. I don't know what you're talking about, though."

Erika reached for the doorknob and twisted it. "I'm going to point it out every single time you snarl, growl, frown, or in any other way show how irritated you are."

Keith followed with a shrug. "You do that."

# Twenty-Five

"Just why are we in a house a few doors down and behind mine?"

Karen gave Keith a warning glance as his eyes rolled heavenward and turned to Claire, asking, "Why do you think we're here?"

"She lives near here?" Claire's eyes sought Erika's for confirmation.

"You can see my yard from the kitchen window if you stand on the sink."

Claire glanced at her cousin and then Karen before nodding. "They don't expect us to come so close to where people might be looking for her. It's like the old 'hide it in plain sight.'"

"Isn't this a little too close for comfort?"

"Yes." Keith and Karen spoke in unison.

Erika sighed. "Hiding in plain sight. I forget."

"It's not quite that simple," Keith explained. "That can be as dumb as doing the opposite of what's expected. If you always make the unexpected decision, then the decision you make will be expected."

"Then why are we here?" Claire looked as confused as Erika felt.

"Our options are limited—more so than Mark thinks. This is one of those places that he'll think of and yet probably be sure we wouldn't risk. It's too close to home, but we really have very little choice." Karen spoke confidently, but Erika sensed there was more—and there was. "Erika, you need to call your parents."

"Okay. Why?"

"They need to leave."

Dread filled Erika's heart. She'd never imagined anyone coming after her family, but Karen seemed to be implying that it was possible. "Why are they after me? I didn't do, see, think, feel, take, or touch anything!"

"Focus, Erika. You have to come up with a convincing reason to get them to go away. I think you should have them mention the mountains on Facebook or something—say they're on an internet and technology fast—and then go to the lake until we come get them."

"What do I say? 'Hi, Mom. Someone is after me for no good reason, but since they can't find me, they might come after you, so I need you to go camping for the next week or so. Don't take any cell phones or use your credit cards.'"

"That'll work." Keith pushed a pre-paid cell phone across the table.

"Are you nuts? Tell me why you would do this if your kid called."

"Because my kid wouldn't be a prankster teen, but a responsible adult who apparently had something go wrong."

"And when they ask about the police?"

Keith glanced at Karen, and upon receipt of silent approval, he turned back to Erika and clenched his fists. "Okay. Then we do it this way. You tell your parents you've been kidnapped. This is true, right? You tell them that if they do not follow orders, you will be killed."

"My father will not pay a ransom. He doesn't believe in rewarding criminal activity."

"We won't ask for a ransom, but trust me. Lofty ideals are great in theory, but when someone says they have your daughter and she sounds terrified you will do whatever is necessary to ensure her safety." Keith nudged the phone again.

"Sound scared."

"Sound scared out of your wits."

"I failed drama in high school," she warned.

"You also never showed up for class." Karen didn't look impressed. "Seriously? It's an easy A, and you don't even show up?"

"Give me the phone. Sheesh."

As she'd predicted, James Polowski refused to follow the orders of the so-called kidnappers, but Erika's, "Daddy, please!" sent his wife into hysterics. After arguing, threatening, and eventually Erika's panicked shrieks, the man agreed to take their little pop-up trailer and stay at Lake Danube until Erika was delivered.

"He's calling the cops now," Karen said dryly as Erika pushed the phone across the table. Keith took it into the kitchen and smashed it with a hammer, pulling the card from the pieces.

"Cops! Wha—"

Keith hastened to reassure her. "That's okay. They'll patrol the Fairbury area, waiting for the drop off. You'll have to drive there yourself when this is over, but that's okay. Anyway, the point is, they're gone, and now they'll have police protection. It's perfect."

"Your picture will be all over the news. You can't leave again." Karen's words weren't very encouraging.

"So, what do we do?" Claire seemed bored already now that the call had been made. "How do we know when it's safe to go?"

"I'm going to drive to Chicago and call Mark from there. We need information. I'll be back as soon as I can." Karen acted as if she said similar things every day. She strolled into her room, retrieved her duffel bag, and backed the car from the garage.

Claire tried to convince Karen to let her go too, but the woman refused. Frustrated, she stormed into the house, down the hall, and slammed the door to the room she'd claimed as her own. With a shrug and a wave, Karen drove down the street and rounded the corner.

Seconds later, a call came through on Keith's generic phone. "Someone is at Erika's house."

---

"Glad you called. Is everyone okay?"

"Dandy." Karen didn't like the small talk. It seemed almost insulting to the man who had personally trained her.

"Good. Jill and Anthony have Helen in Florida."

"Florida! Why?"

Mark's voice sounded weary. "She didn't feel safe going back to Fiji, Australia was out in her mind, and that left here. At least Florida doesn't make sense."

"Since when does the client decide where they will and won't go?"

"Since she freaked, and since I cannot find who is leaking information in my organization."

"Well," Karen asked, hoping she didn't sound too accusatory, "have there been any more bungles? Is there any evidence that someone has information they shouldn't?"

"Not lately. I'd give anything for Keith's insight. Have you seen him?"

"You know I'm not going to answer that. Mind if I take a look at whatever information you have?"

"I'll upload the files I have. Do you know the password?"

"Text it to me when we get off." Karen hated leaving her phone on that long, but he'd probably already figured out where she was. Why freak about it now?

She turned down a side street and backtracked. She needed a library. "Okay, Mark. I've got to go. If you get any news, send an email to my phone. I'll pick it up in a few days."

"No. Check it once a day. I'm serious. Don't risk your life. If someone figures out where you are, you could be in as much danger as any of us. We're all sitting ducks until we find this guy—or girl. Twenty-four hours between calls is too long, but don't wait any more than that."

"Gotcha. Send it to this number, too."

The traffic nearly drove her insane as she crawled along the streets toward the nearest big box office store. She wasn't accustomed to being so unprepared. Buying a USB drive would cut into their ready cash, but it was necessary. Keith had a knack for catching what others missed, and with a potential mole in the Agency, Mark probably wouldn't let very many of the staff near anything remotely sensitive.

With thumb-drive in hand, she strolled into the Blackstone Library, charmed by the neoclassical architecture. Karen immediately realized her mistake. In a predominantly black neighborhood, she looked like a beacon advertising how out of place she was. For a moment, she considered finding a less conspicuous choice, but decided that she'd likely make more of a memorable impression if she left than if she just finished her business and left naturally.

Two terminals were open, but both were too exposed to risk opening anything even just long enough to download onto her thumb-drive. She grabbed the nearest book on the new release shelf and plopped down comfortably in a chair and glanced at the cover, barely stifling a groan. *Deep Thirst* wasn't exactly her idea of a good read. It seemed as if Americans had revived the ridiculous melodramatic gothic novels of the nineteenth century with the latest craze of vampires and zombies—particularly when the books romanticized them.

It took an hour, one she didn't think she had, but at last, the most shielded terminal was empty. Quickly, Karen slid into the seat, found the URL for Mark's library of files, and downloaded the one marked Keith's Birthday Wish. Funny. For a moment she wondered, was it actually his birthday soon? She'd have to ask when she called Mark again.

That thought comforted her. *Call Mark again.* Keith wouldn't trust it, and he shouldn't, but her gut instinct assured her of Mark's innocence. It was both a relief and a disappointment. Mark being the mole would have been a nightmare. He had access to information Karen couldn't begin to know where to find, but it would have meant the end. Found. Done. They'd all be out of jobs, perhaps, but still, it'd be nice to know the search was over. Knowing he wasn't a traitor to the people he was paid to protect was even better news. He had the ability to help them, and he understood their actions—even if he didn't like them.

Fifty miles outside Chicago, Karen called Mark's office, smiling at the relief in his voice. "Got it. You can take it down."

"Did you get to look at it?"

"Nothing secure around here, but I'll find a way to get it to Keith somehow. Speaking of Keith, what's with the title? Is it really his birthday soon?"

"No. I just thought if you got it to him, it'd make him smile. I love to watch that guy work."

Karen hesitated, the cautious side of her waging war against her more confident side. "Mark, I know it's not you."

He didn't speak for so long that Karen wondered if she'd lost the connection, but at last, his voice, almost a whisper, echoed throughout the little car. "Thank you, Karen." She could almost hear him swallow and then grinned as she realized what he'd say next—and he did. "Don't get soft. Keep yourself suspicious of everyone—even me. It's your job. I trained you to do it right."

"Did I give you my location? I think not. I'm just telling you that I know it's not you. I thought you might like to watch me gloat when it's over and I can say, '"See, I told you."'

---

The palm trees outside her condo seemed obscenely clichéd. All of it did. She'd only agreed to "protection" in order to keep suspicion at a minimum. Thus far, her histrionics had done their job. Jill and Anthony spent the better part of each day reassuring her that everything was fine—just fine.

The true problem was that nothing was really fine. She sensed the difference from the first day they'd contacted her. Anthony was skittish, and Jill snapped at him almost incessantly. Anyone who watched them from afar would have thought they were a couple entering year seven of marriage— "the year of doom" her mother had called it.

She'd tried to project herself as nearly panicked at the idea that someone could be searching for her, but it was time to gather whatever information she could about Erika. The more days that passed, the harder it would be to come out unscathed. Ready to bump the plan to the next phase, she stumbled out of her room, trying to look bleary-eyed. "What about Erika? Is she safe? Do they have her under protection again? I forgot about Erika! I can't believe—"

"We've got her. She's fine. There's nothing to worry about." Jill tried to sound soothing, but her words came out impatient.

"What did I say?" If the woman was going to lose it, she might as well use it to her advantage. "I don't understand why you're so antagonistic toward me. You come, tell me I'm in danger again, and then snap at me!" Helen fought not to glow with pride. She should get an Oscar for that performance.

"Sorry. We're all on edge."

"Why?"

"It's hard to explain." Anthony sent a warning glance at Jill and offered Helen a glass of tea.

"I don't like that stuff. Water's good. So, maybe it'd be better if I just talked to Erika and told her that this is my fault. She's probably so confused. I didn't want her to know, but now I'm not so sure. I've totally messed up her life for the past couple of months."

"Well, Mark doesn't think she needs to know. He thinks it's dangerous for her if she knows." Anthony pulled out a bag of prepackaged salad greens and dumped it in a colander. "Want some salad?"

"Sure. Got avocado and tomato?"

"Cucumbers?" The man opened the fridge and rummaged through the crisper drawers.

"Besides," Jill interjected, clearly put out for being overridden. The couple had operated like a seamless machine the first time, but now they were at odds at every turn. "We don't even know where they are. Keith took her off grid."

That was interesting news. "Why is that?"

"Mole."

"Protocol." Anthony glared at Jill. "It's protocol. Jill's always seeing gremlins behind every action. She needs a vacation."

"That's—" Jill stopped herself. "You're right. I don't know what's gotten into me. I'm tired, I guess. I'm sorry. I think I'll go lie down."

Helen wanted to demand to know more, but she put on her most sympathetic face and, taking advantage of her older status, put an arm around Jill and led the younger woman down the hall to her room. "A nap sounds good. I'm sure everything will look better when you wake up. I know I always see things through black colored glasses when I'm stressed."

When she returned, Anthony looked up. "It's nice of you to be so understanding. You're paying us to take care of you, and instead, we just fall apart. I've been a bear lately."

"You have been hard on her. That won't be good for Erika if whomever she's with is grumpy. She doesn't have the patience for it."

"Keith never gets grumpy. He's the eternal optimist. Always smiling, joking, laughing. That's Keith."

"I don't understand how things work. Is it really protocol to go off grid when there's a second abduction?"

"It's protocol to go off grid when anything seems off. Since we don't know the target right now, we have to do things a little differently."

"But how will he know when it's safe to bring her back? He can't just keep her out there forever. I don't think I'll ever understand your business." Helen popped a cherry tomato in her mouth and went to find the TV remote as if she hadn't asked a question. She'd learned long ago that people answered questions they normally wouldn't have if you acted as if you were just thinking aloud.

"Mark probably has a way of contacting. It'll take longer, of course, but it's just how it's done. Don't worry; Erika won't be out there a day longer than necessary. Meanwhile, we've got someone taking care of your place for you."

She flipped through several channels before shutting off the TV again. Helen only had one more question for him, but discovering how to ask it would be tricky. One word out of place and they'd get suspicious.

Helen ate her salad, picking pieces out and drenching each in salad dressing before choosing her next bite as if creating the perfect forkful was her only concern in life. Her silence was bothering Anthony, and that was a very good thing. At last, she dropped her fork onto her plate, feigning the loss of a battle with self-will, and lifted tortured eyes to Anthony's concerned ones. "Do you think—is it possible." She swallowed hard. "I mean, I just wondered if maybe we should be off-grid too."

"Oh," Anthony assured her calmly, "don't worry. We are. I only check in with Mark every three or four days. The way we have to go about it is so circuitous that no one can track us. The Agency doesn't even know we're in Florida."

Genuine relief washed over Helen's features as she picked up her fork once more. "Well, that makes me feel better anyway. I'd hate for my last expenditure to be an ineffectual protection detail—no offense."

# Twenty-Six

"What are you looking for?"
"Anything that looks out of place, no matter how small." Keith hardly paused to answer as his hand scribbled another note onto the large legal pad.

"Are those the normal things or the anomalies?"

"Anomalies." His forehead furrowed, and his jaw set rigidly as he added another item.

Erika read the line and frowned. "The fact that I asked to talk to Mark is an anomaly?"

"Yep. Most people never do—not even in exasperation. I know it means nothing to you, but I have to add it in case it triggered something in someone else."

"Mark." The name dropped from her lips like an anvil on stone.

"Well, not just him, no. But, it is another mark against him."

Erika grinned. "Cute."

Looking up from his files, Keith shook his head. "What?"

"A mark against Mark—I just thought it was kind of funny."

There it was again—the terseness. It was back. She anticipated the tone of his response before he opened his mouth. "Yeah. Do you need something?"

"I need you to note that you've gotten grumpy again. This is the tenth time since you challenged me to note them."

"Well, it's duly noted."

Erika glanced at Karen as if to say, "See, it's not in my head." Karen's face just registered complete shock. When she said that it was out of character for him, she must have meant it.

Before Erika could ask another question, Keith whirled in his chair, seeking Karen. "Hey, this doesn't say. When did Helen contact us? I need everything from the first call through the night we took Erika. Can you get that?"

"I could just drive to the office. Mark wouldn't know if it'd been a few days' drive or a few minutes."

"If you did that, you couldn't come back here. The risk—"

"Yeah. I was thinking about taking Claire too, but that'd leave you guys unprotected."

"Why Claire?" Keith glanced toward the room where his cousin generally lay on the bed curled in fetal position waiting for the "nightmare" to end.

"She has knowledge of Anastas' organization. She might see something that we don't."

"Take her. Just don't bring her back. You'll have to be vigilant, but maybe you can lose a tail. He flipped the pad to a new page, scribbled some directions, and pulled a key from his pocket. "I managed to find Uncle Ted's spare key in the RV. Take her there if you manage to escape scrutiny. Otherwise, don't risk it."

"Are you sure?" Karen glanced at Erika who listened to the entire conversation with great interest.

"We need a break—fast. Every day that passes is a day these girls can't get back. Every day that passes, gets the mole more information. We've got to stop this."

"Are you okay with that, Erika?"

"Sure. I've put up with this grouch before."

"I'm not a grouch!" Both women snickered at the growl in his voice. Keith glanced up, "What?"

"Let's just say your voice belies your words."

"Belies?"

Erika smirked and crossed her arms. "You know, makes a liar out of you?"

"Since when does Karen use words like 'belies'?"

"Since you stuck her in a house with nothing but books from the nineteenth century." Karen tossed a mock leather-bound copy of *The Count of Monte Cristo* onto the table, jarring Keith's pen.

"Whatever. Just get going. Don't change your clothes and rub the back of your hair on the headrest all the way there. Make sure you smooth your clothes as you get out of the car."

"I know how to do this stuff, Keith. It's not like I'm a trainee." Karen's voice trailed off as she wandered down the hall to give Claire the good news. Adventure awaited them in Rockland.

From her perch on the futon that was just as uncomfortable during the day as she was sure it was at night, Erika ignored her book in favor of watching Keith as he scribbled line after line of things that probably meant nothing. As the silence settled around him, she watched his features relax. It was hard to tell just what he was thinking. Unlike most people, his face gave away nothing.

Claire burst from her room, her duffel swinging over one shoulder, her purse in hand. "We're going! I actually get to *do* something. I'm so excited. This is what I thought this job would be like, not sitting around here waiting to get our heads blown off if we glance out the wrong window."

Keith's grin was infectious. He jumped up, hugged his cousin, and glanced over her head at Karen. "Take care, both of you. Neither of you is expendable."

With a glance at Erika, Karen grabbed Keith's pen from him, flipped the page up, and scribbled a note on it. Keith glanced toward Erika before looking at Karen. "What?"

"Just don't forget."

Keith pulled the sheet from the pad, crumbled it, and tossed it at the trashcan next to the garage door. It missed. He started to rise to toss it properly, but Karen shoved his shoulder back down. "I'll get it. Take care, you guys. Don't get lazy."

Once the two women were gone, Keith slowly immersed himself in his work again, but the absentmindedness was gone. This Keith was driven, focused, and yet attuned to everything around him. A dog barked outside, and he shifted. A kid cried, and he jumped up, peeking out the curtain to make sure it was something he could continue to ignore. The work went slower, but Erika saw a new determination in him. It was almost as if now that he was without backup, he was even more determined to get her out of there.

*He doesn't like me. I annoy him*, she thought as she watched the process. *I wonder why.*

Just as she was ready to go take a shower, Keith glanced up at her. "I've almost finished this. I want you to think of everything that happened from the minute you stepped into the airport until we came back for you. Everything. Think about who you worked with, who you talked to at work, who called your cell phone, your house phone, everything."

Minutes later, he rose, shut the laptop, and ambled down the hall to the bathroom. The second the door shut, she jumped and raced across the kitchen. Unfolding the wadded yellow paper, she read Karen's words. *Be nice to her. You're like a different person around her, and it's making it hard for her. Be nice.*

It still made no sense. From that first day, he'd been stern, almost fierce at times. She could tell he had a sense of humor, but he never relaxed enough around her to show it. The only time he'd been nice was at the trailer and until Karen had joined them. Then, immediately it was as if a weight lifted—for about twenty-four hours. He'd be even less relaxed now that he was solely responsible for her safety.

She dashed back to the futon and made sure she was dragging herself off it as he returned. "I'm going to take a shower and then I'll give you a rundown of everything I can think of, okay?"

"Sure. I'm going to make a sandwich. Want one?"

There it was again—that infernal politeness that she knew was genuine, but it had none of the warmth behind it that he showed Karen and Claire. "Yeah. That'd be great. Thanks."

"You could have asked what was in the note. I'd have told you."

*Busted.*

---

Keith felt immense satisfaction at the guilty look on Erika's face. It'd been a guess—an intuitive one, perhaps, but a guess, nevertheless. However, Karen's admonitions lately had put him on edge. Erika hadn't seemed to complain about him until after one of Karen's visits. Apparently, she'd commented about some sort of difference she'd noticed. Whatever it was, he needed to be on his guard. He had no excuse for making Erika's stay any more difficult than it already was. The girl had to be ready to scream with frustration.

As the water came on in the bathroom, he pulled out the lunchmeat, bread, lettuce, tomato, and mayo. They'd run out of mustard packets days ago. He liked mustard, but there was nothing he could do about it. As he worked, he considered the different cases he'd worked over the years. Erika really was a good sport. She didn't freak, even when she wanted to.

The difference in his expectations now compared to the last time he'd guarded her glared—acutely. He'd been determined to keep her fighting—wanting her to push the envelope to stay antagonistic toward him. She'd needed that then, but, although she was still an abducted client, she worked with them to keep her safe. The stress level alone was different.

Terse, stern, scowl—those words made no sense. He'd never been what you'd call jolly, but Keith was a pleasant guy. No one had ever considered him anything but friendly and companionable. It seemed strange that anyone would say something like that about him, but even Karen had seen it. It wasn't just Erika's imagination

Before Keith could work through the accusation, Erika came out of the bathroom, towel drying her hair as she did. "Man, I love a good hot shower."

"Me too. Your sandwich is there." He pointed to a plate with the butter knife before digging it into the mayonnaise jar.

Erika stepped into the garage and tossed the towel into the dryer. She'd set it for five minutes on the highest heat. She did it every time. It was brilliant. She used the same towel every time she showered and hadn't washed it yet. Keith had been tempted to sniff it to see if it'd gone sour, but the idea seemed a bit creepy—stalkerish in a not-stalking sort of way.

"Okay, so what do you need to know?"

Her voice jerked him from his mildewing musings. "Oh, well, why don't you try to tell me everyone you talked to, everyone you can think of, since you've been home. The mail you opened, the messages on machines, where you went after or before work—anything."

"Well, I called my friend Yvonne from the airport. I knew she'd be ticked off that I hadn't invited her on my 'trip.'"

"And was she?"

"No, she thought I went with Brent and didn't want to admit it or something."

"Brent?" Keith assumed it was the man in the photos but waited for confirmation.

"A guy I met. Yvonne wouldn't think twice about taking off for two weeks with a guy she hardly knows. I figure it's a recipe for disaster. Can you imagine how miserable you'd be if you found out you hated him?"

"Yeah." Keith took a swig of his tea and then grinned. "It's much better to be chained up in a cabin in the middle of nowhere with a stranger."

"Safer anyway." Her smile seemed odd at a time like that. Who smiles at the memory of being shackled and locked in a room "for your own good?"

"I was really ticked at you."

"I know. I was glad."

"I still don't get that." She chewed slowly, thoughtfully. How did someone do that? Keith didn't understand her.

"It sounds weirder than it is. The angrier you are, the more you're likely to fight. You need to fight. The minute captivity seems like a reasonable 'norm' you're already becoming a victim. It's best if you fight."

"Well, technically," she argued, grabbing a handful of raisins from a box on the counter and sprinkling them over her sandwich. The idea made him shudder. "I was a victim. I was kidnapped. What else do you call me but the 'victim' of a kidnapping?" Her air quotes would have been cute if he hadn't seen a raisin peeking out from a bite of her turkey and provolone.

"How can you eat that?"

"It's good. Try it." Erika offered her sandwich, but Keith recoiled as if she offered him snake innards.

"I'll stick to my plain, mustardless sandwich."

"What does mustard have to do with anything?"

Keith shrugged. "I just like mustard and we're out of packets."

"I've got some at home. I could run over after dark—"

"Not on your life." He polished off his last bite of sandwich, dusted his hands over his plate, and shoved it to the side. "So, what next?"

Erika told about her first day back at work, about talking to missed customers, about the online class she considered taking, the research internship she'd considered, and the guy who tried to pick her up in the produce department. "He was a creep-and-a-half. Too bad."

"Why too bad?"

"He was great looking—everything I like in a guy, but man, you could tell he'd heard that you 'pick up women' in the produce department, so he stood around almost like a vulture, just waiting for someone he didn't consider revolting to arrive."

"You're kidding."

"No." Erika snickered. "I watched him for a bit while I was picking over the asparagus. Then I decided I had to have a bell pepper."

The familiar furrows formed on Keith's forehead. He knew they were there and could almost hear his mother's warning that he'd have premature wrinkles due to that habit. "Why bell pepper?"

"Because he was standing next to them. I had to see if I passed muster."

"Well, that's ridiculous. Of course, you did."

"Well, listening from this end, sure. You knew he tried to pick me up, so of course, I did, but from where I stood, the guy was pretty picky. I almost wonder if he wasn't getting desperate."

"Fishing for compliments?"

"Huh?" She blinked, obviously trying to make the connection.

"Well, you acted like maybe you were his 'desperate move,' so I wondered if that was my cue to tell you that you're not desperation material or something."

"Nah. We both know I'm not your type. I don't think I was his type either. That's why I thought maybe he was desperate. He'd been eying blondes."

"So, what made you decide he was creepy?"

"He asked if I wanted to go out for coffee—and then mentioned the shop. It just felt weird, y'know? I mean, it was just one of those odd coincidences, and I wouldn't have thought anything of it, but when I said no, he got really pushy. I hate that."

He knew he'd gone tense but couldn't prevent it. "Pushy how?"

"Oh, you know how jerks like that are. You say no; they say how come? You say you're not interested; they say just one cup. Most guys won't try past three, but this guy wouldn't stop until I walked away—see? Desperate."

"Do you remember what he looked like?"

"Oh, yeah."

Keith didn't like the way she said that, but even more, he hated the fact that he didn't like it. What kind of nonsense was that? Erika was a client, not a Christian, and most definitely not his type; therefore, he was likely pulling a reverse Stockholm Syndrome type thing where he felt loyal to her. Great. Ugh.

"Well?"

She shrugged. "Well what?"

"What did he look like?"

Unexpectedly, she stood, pulling him from the barstool. "Yeah, about your height give or take an inch. Build too. His hair was darker, and his nose was more prominent. I think his jaw was more angular somehow, but really, he looked a lot like you. That's how I noticed him in the first place. I was sure you were going to take me back, and I was ready to run."

"Sorry."

"What for?"

"I didn't give you the option of running."

Taking her plate to the sink, Erika rinsed it and then turned, leaning against the counter. "You did the right thing. No, I don't like it any better than I did, but I appreciate it. It's frustrating, nerve wracking, and a little scary, but it's nice, too. I feel safe."

"Okay, what else?" Keith made a note to see if the store had any kind of surveillance tapes they could procure.

"I'm telling you; I had a boring week. I went out to the Pizza Zone, read a book, surfed the internet, talked to Helen about her renovation scheme—"

"Helen the owner of your house?"

"Yeah."

"I thought she lived in Australia this time of year."

Erika nodded. "She does, but she wants to do renovations and had questions for me. I guess she even considered coming back early this year, but work won't let her."

"What does she do?"

"International trade. I don't really understand what all it is, but I think she makes pretty good money."

"But," Keith objected, trying to respond as natural as possible, "no offense or anything, but your house is just a decent suburban type house. It's not all that big, the furniture is nice, but it's not expensive, and you don't even have granite!" He forced himself to sound excessively indignant, hoping to sound like he was teasing.

"Perhaps that's the point of the renovation?" After several seconds rummaging through the cupboards for the pre-packaged chocolate chip cookies, Erika added, "Besides, it has to be expensive to keep two houses in two countries. Maybe she's just frugal."

*Or trying to keep a low profile*, he thought. "What day was that?"

"I think about three or four days before you came back for me."

Warning bells flashed like beacons in Keith's mind. While Erika rambled on about something to do with the pool cover and dinner at her parents' house, he did the mental math from the time he'd dropped her off at the airport, when Helen had gone back to Australia, and when Mike would have gotten the call to go after them. Unaware that she'd stopped talking, he grabbed the notepad and pen from the table and backtracked, flipping through several things, pausing, taking notes, and reworking the timeline. The result, he didn't like—at all.

# Twenty-Seven

"Well, the names I remember most were all out of Columbus, so you probably have those." Claire's mind whirled trying to remember anything and everything she'd heard or seen in the short amount of time she'd spent with Alek and while at the salon. "I mean, people say things they don't mean to when they think you're clueless, but Alek didn't talk to me about just anything."

"Did he ever talk to someone on the phone when you were there? Ever mention cities or states he'd visited? A grandma in Poughkeepsie?" Mark's tone was insistent—almost demanding.

Karen frowned at him and started to argue, but Claire's expression changed from discouraged to thoughtful. "He did have to take a call from Australia once. That was weird. I remember because it was really late at the club and he had to go outside. He said the time difference was hard to work around."

"That doesn't make sense. The time is eighteen or nineteen hours different, not twelve." Karen gave Mark a meaningful look, but before he could respond, his phone buzzed. "Keith! What are you doing calling me?" He listened for a second, before opening a document on his laptop and typing, HE WANTS TO KNOW HOW EVERYONE IN FLORIDA IS. Seconds later, his fingers flew across the keyboard again. HE SAYS THAT HELEN CALLED 3-4 DAYS BEFORE YOU GOT THE INFO FROM MIKE.

"Well, I'm calling Anthony now. Just give me a second, and we'll see. We've been going a few days between calls and just having a one letter text message as a ping for security. No one is picking up."

The whole room heard Keith's voice explode just before Mark switched it over to speaker, "Get someone in there, now!"

"Do you really think—?"

"I know. I just know. It's Helen. Tony and Jill were the moles—just not consciously. They kept our client abreast of the situation, only she was the criminal too."

Mark whistled low. "Normally, I'd tell you that you were reaching, but just before you called, Claire remembered a phone call that Alek got from Australia at about one in the morning our time."

The room erupted in chaotic discussion of potential motive, leaks, and the best course of action. The women hardly noticed when Mark stepped outside the door to make a call, but eventually, Keith asked for him. "What does he think of all this?"

"Dunno, he stepped out to call I think."

"He's not back yet?" Keith's voice grew concerned. "I'm outta here. Call me at the other number when it's safe to be in contact. Just a precaution, but I gotta go."

The phone disconnected without another word. Claire looked nervously at the door as she whispered, "Does Keith really think—?"

"No, but his job is to protect Erika—even when it doesn't make sense. Possibly especially when it doesn't. He's just doing his job."

Seconds ticked by without the accompaniment of actual clockworks lending their rhythmic cadence to the process. Again, Claire whispered, "Should we go?"

"No. We'd never get out of here without being followed or stopped anyway, so on the off-chance Mark is corrupt, we need to look like we have full confidence in him."

"Do we?"

Karen's laugh filled the room. "I do. I don't know about you, but I do."

Before Claire could respond, Mark pushed the door open and the look on his face spoke for him. Claire's eyes flitted back and forth from the faces before her, trying to decipher what they meant. At last, Mark took pity on her and shook his head. "The agents protecting Helen are dead, and Helen is gone." When Keith didn't respond, Mark glanced at the phone on the desk as he pocketed his private one. "He's gone?"

"Yep."

"So, what does this mean?" Claire whined. "I don't understand what is going on!"

Ignoring Claire, Karen zeroed in on the problem, her mind working swiftly. "We have to capture Helen. The problem is, how?"

"Someone was at her house, remember?"

"You went by Erika... um, Helen's house—wait. Keith was at the transfer house? That's where he was?"

"He wanted us close in case we had to trust you in order to protect them."

"Smart. I didn't even consider looking there. We have no new cases that'd use it..." He shook his head, clearly impressed. "That's really smart."

"Well, if you'd put in the alarm system like he suggested, he wouldn't have done it. The logs...."

"Maybe he didn't really leave. I mean, wouldn't that be the best way to hide? Make it seem like you went, but didn't?"

"Now you're overthinking things, Claire." Mark sank into the chair, folded his hands, and waited for the girl to meet his gaze. "You can't just do the opposite of what you expect people to do all the time. It works sometimes and in some situations, but if that's all you do, you become predictable. You can't be too random, because—"

"—designed randomness is really just a pattern." Clair rolled her eyes. "Keith told me."

"I think this time he'll take her to some place that Helen won't think of—not some place I won't."

"Right." Karen stood, grabbed her purse, and pointed out the window and down the street. "We'll be at the Colonial. Clean, nice, not too cheap, not so expensive it's flashy... just call."

"Thanks, Karen. Stick with Karen, Claire. She won't fail you."

Just outside the door, Karen thought of another question and pushed it back open, but the sight of Mark leaning with his head in his hands, shoulders shaking, caused her to turn and lead Claire away again. She'd ask later. Besides, she needed a shower where she could release all the grief-filled emotions that she had been trying to stifle.

---

Even as he spoke the words "gotta go," Keith pointed to the bedrooms as he started shoving his papers into a laptop case. She knew immediately what it meant. Erika knew the second he disconnected the call by the crash of the phone. Her guess—rolling pin to it. He'd have the SIM card in his pocket. She still didn't understand why they were so determined to destroy perfectly good electronics. SIM cards were all they needed, weren't they?"

"Get everything you'll need and fast," he called as he carried the first load into the garage. She knew it by the sound of the door bumping hard before it latched. The sensation was an odd one—she knew the quirks of the house already.

They'd been lazy here. Oh, sure, the clothes were kept in the duffel, the dirty ones in a pillow case, but little things like shampoo bottles left on the corner of the tub and hairbrush on the counter—those things were asking for trouble, and now she understood why. At the sound of the door, she called out, "Can I take a few of the books?"

"Sure. Make sure you get *Magic Mountain* and *Great Expectations*."

"Why those?"

"Money in some of the pages." Keith's voice startled her from the doorway to the bathroom. "I'll take that. Oh, and *Pride and Prejudice*."

"Bet that's your favorite." The joke fell flat and only seemed less interesting with the scowl on his face. "You're grumpy again."

"I'm just thinking. Get the books and let's go."

Erika did notice a change in him. As she crawled into the very back seat of the van, buckled up, and laid down, she realized what it was. He was calm—almost deadly calm, but calm. That unnerved her more than anything else.

The van was piled with blankets, food, books, and just

about everything else you could want for a long trip. She'd wondered if they were going to run far, but she didn't know where and she hadn't yet asked why. That bothered her—deeply. Since when did she allow any guy, regardless of his life-saving abilities and history, to dictate where she went without even asking? It was ludicrous.

"Keith?"

"I don't know."

"You don't know what?"

His grin in the rearview mirror was even more unsettling than his customary scowl. "I don't know where we're going. I doubt we're going anywhere."

"We'll just keep moving?"

"Yep."

"Have I thanked you yet?"

"Don't, Erika. Remember—"

"Yeah, I know. I'm a victim." Yes, she knew it, and Erika was quite sick of being reminded of it. "But the fact remains that you still put yourself on the line, and I still don't understand why. Why are we leaving? What did I say or Mark say that—?"

"If you haven't figured it out, I'm not going to tell you on the off chance that we're wrong. The more you know—"

"Yeah, yeah, I know. The more danger I am in. I'm sick of it."

"I know." His features reassembled themselves into the grim face she'd grown accustomed to during her stint in "captivity." Then, as if the light went on, Erika understood.

Disgusted summed up her personal assessment of cluelessness. She felt betrayed by her own intellect. No one had ever called Erika Polowski vain, but she certainly entertained no false modesty either. She knew when a man was interested and either accepted it or rejected him—a simple process of elimination. Nice, interesting men received some measure of encouragement, and all others she simply disregarded with an obviousness that left no doubt of her lack of interest. Simple, but effective.

Keith occupied a category all his own. Had he not been religious, she'd have put him in the "cream of the crop" camp, alongside a very few others. Unfortunately, the religion thing made her uncomfortable—particularly since

Corey was probably correct. Guys like Keith probably didn't even consider women who weren't religious, too. It only made sense, and she respected them for it. What was the point of having a religion in the first place if it was so easy to toss aside for something else? There were less restrictive hobbies out there.

The guy had probably been chewing himself out for even noticing her. Well, she could be flattered that he did anyway. A glance at the mirror showed only his eyes—focused intently on the rush hour traffic surrounding them. It occurred to her that some of the stern intensity of his eyes showed most in their color. Steel gray, noticeable even as far back as she was, they seemed to reflect harshness and coldness that she otherwise wouldn't have expected.

"Keith?"

"You okay?"

"I'm good. Um, I think you need to remember something." She had to choose her words carefully, but he needed to change some of his thinking.

"What's that?"

"Yeah, I'm a victim here. I didn't ask for this, and I was taken without my consent. But, Keith, if I hadn't been, I'd likely be dead. Sorry if it offends you, but I am grateful, and it's a good thing that I am."

---

Irritation washed over him anew as Erika reminded him of her obligation toward him and the Agency. She was right, and he hated it. He hated every bit of it. This oddly placed loyalty drove him to the brink of insanity and back again--repeatedly. Karen was right; he was grouchy.

He had to get a grip. His job required him to protect people. He hadn't felt as guilty about Mr. Bruner, and Donald was an old guy who probably couldn't handle the stress as well as someone Erika's age. Regardless of how distasteful aspects of the job could be, it was imperative that he regain control of his issues and get back to being the professional he'd trained to be. Time to grow up.

He glanced in the rearview mirror and started to tell

her to lie back down on the seat, but something in her made him stop. What was the point anyway? Darkness would surround them soon, and there was no reason to make her feel even tenser than she already was. This'd be over as soon as someone found Helen. He had to hang on until then. Just until then.

Erika's voice interrupted his thoughts. "Keith?"

"Yeah?"

"Why do religious people read the Bible?"

The answer came before he had a chance to consider his words. "Because Christians believe that the Bible is God's recorded Word for mankind."

"What does that even mean?" Each word was smothered in disbelief and confusion.

"It means that we believe that every word in the book was written to tell us what God wants us to know about us, Him, and how to connect to Him." It sounded even more convoluted than his first explanation, but Keith had never been comfortable explaining his faith. The biggest failure of his Christian walk was, in his opinion anyway, his inability to be ready to explain the "hope within."

"Okay, so what does *that* mean?"

"Why do you ask?"

Her laughter rang out through the van. "You aren't very good at convincing people to believe things your way."

"Well, you're right. Then again, I don't do that, so that might explain why."

"Why not? I thought the point of being religious was to get everyone else to be religious too."

For the next mile, Keith considered how to respond to her. She was focused on religion, but he needed to find a way to explain that religion was only a small part of what his faith meant to him—all without preaching. Frustration mounted, and as he glanced in the mirror, the look on her face told him that she had already started to lose interest.

"Erika, it's not that simplistic. What you see as 'religion,' I see as a relationship. There is religion too, but the point is man's need for God."

"Why? Why do we need God?"

He swallowed, his mouth going dry. At last, a new idea came to him. "Have you ever wondered why there is so much evil in the world?"

"Um, who hasn't? That evil is partly why rational people don't waste their time with the idea of an all-loving God." Then, as if she realized what she'd said, Erika added, "I'm sorry, Keith. No offense."

"None taken. That's just the point, though. It's because mankind doesn't have God filling their hearts that life is the way it is."

Before she could respond, Keith swerved and slammed on his brakes. His eyes widened, and he shouted for her to hold on as a car full of teenagers, careening out of control, slid sideways into the van. It rocked over on two wheels, hesitated, and then dropped to the highway on its side.

Glass shattered, and Keith hung from the shoulder belt. That would hurt when he released it, but he had no choice. "You okay?"

"Yeah. I'm just hanging here, but I'm upside down."

"I'm coming."

He released the belt, tried to land on his back instead of his head, and nearly succeeded. Scrambling to the back, he tried to support her as he unhooked the seatbelt. They stumbled through the glass to the driver's door and he prepared to hoist her out. Just as she flung the door open, he whispered into her ear. "It's dark enough that you can hide. Find some kind of building, shrub—something—and hide. I'll find you. I'll whistle Dixie when I'm looking for you. Go."

# Twenty-Eight

"Ignore me when I call for you. Go!"

When Keith sent her from the scene of the accident, Erika was sure she'd never see him again. Part of her, that self-preservationist part of every human, listened without question. Fleeing seemed not to be an option. However, once hidden by a ditch filled with debris, she had second thoughts. Without Keith, the chances of survival, if they were being hunted, dropped nearly to non-existent. The desire to return grew heavy—nearly overwhelming—but he'd been right each time he'd given her an order. She couldn't ignore him now.

His voice called to her. "Where are you going? What—what about your stuff! Come back here! You can't just leave the scene of an accident...."

So that was his angle. Okay, she could work with that. The nearest building was a crumbling barn, but she knew he'd be livid if she went to hide out in such an obvious place. That thought made her smile. She was learning to think like him.

On the chance that anyone watched her, Erika continued toward the barn, hoping to slip out of sight behind it. Her feet tripped over ruts in the field, sending her sprawling over the rough ground, but she didn't hesitate. Back on her feet, with her stomach scraped and bleeding from contact with sticks in the ground, she continued to stumble across the field until at last, she reached the barn. From there, things looked dire. There simply wasn't anywhere else to hide.

Several hundred yards away stood a large tree—oak, if her knowledge of trees was remotely accurate. It seemed risky, but the barn was so obvious, she had to try. Although tall grasses grew behind the barn, Erika chose not to try to hide. She'd get there faster if she just hurried. It might be the wrong move, but she was comfortable with it. Trying to hide in the grass, crawling on hands and knees would only cause pain and make her more vulnerable in the end—or so it seemed.

Two garter snakes, obviously placed there by evil forces to draw attention to her as she squealed like a little girl, sent her dancing across the meadow even faster than ever. Wading through the grasses proved to be harder work than she had expected, and Erika arrived at the tree exhausted and drenched in perspiration. The highway was so far away now, that even the lights flashed more like dots than bars. Surely, no one could see her now.

After circling the tree a few times, Erika chose the most comfortable looking branch and began her climb. Near the trunk, several branches up, there seemed to be a fork that'd allow her to rest her back against the tree without having to dangle her legs indefinitely. She just hoped it'd work.

---

Erika had expected to sit up there for half an hour—an hour at most—but this was ridiculous. It'd been at least two or three, and she desperately needed a restroom. Her brilliant idea of chugging all the liquids she could stuff down her so that Keith would let her out of the van semi-frequently had backfired—badly. If he didn't arrive soon, Erika would be forced to climb down the tree.

Despite her protesting bladder, Erika managed to remain perched up there much longer than she'd anticipated. Just as she stretched her leg to work the blood back through it before attempting a descent, she heard the faint whistling of "Dixie" coming from the opposite direction she'd expected.

Her eyes strained to see, but through the leaves, in the slight duskiness that approached, and with her body screaming for relief, she found it hard to focus. Seconds later, Keith passed right beneath her, still whistling and meandering across the field as if he hadn't a care in the world. She didn't know if "Dixie" was a popular song during the War Between the States, but she couldn't resist whistling back a few bars of the "Battle Hymn of the Republic."

She hadn't known what to expect, but an answering bar of "Dixie" followed by laughter wasn't it. "In a tree. I wondered, but I didn't think you'd actually do it."

"Well, I did," she grunted, "and now I'm not sure I can get out, and once I do, I've gotta have some privacy, so just go away."

"I wondered if those water bottles would bite you in the backside—so to speak."

"Oh, that was bad... really bad."

Once she started after him, calling his name, Keith returned, meeting her halfway. "The truck is back there. I brought it around behind just in case."

"So, you do think it was suspicious?"

He shook his head. "Nah, those teenagers were racing and there just wasn't room for three of us."

"So why the whole clandestine thing?"

Keith pulled a granola bar from his pocket. "Because there were news copters and at least one news van. We could have been seen."

"Argh! It's like we never get a break." Before she could continue her frustrated rant, Erika thought of something else. "Wait, where'd you get a truck?"

"I got the tow truck to drop me off at the office and slipped in. Man, I almost got caught several times—and I can't guarantee that Mark didn't just look away—stole the keys from the rack, and high-tailed it out of there."

"Okay, you've got some big, fat, hai—"

"Don't say it. Just don't."

She grinned. "Kiwis."

Keith gave an exaggerated sigh. "Oh, now who's talking bad?"

"You know, I could have way too much fun with this, but I won't—*probably* won't, anyway."

The truck wasn't anything like Erika imagined or expected. Leftover from the mid-eighties, the Chevy S-10 pickup had seen much, much better days. She was certain that with a swift kick to the undercarriage, the whole thing would disintegrate into a pile of rust and crumbling vinyl.

"Well, you certainly didn't choose luxury, did you?"

"I took what was cheap to drive and inconspicuous."

"Where to?" Erika sighed in relief that the inside, while dilapidated, was at least clean.

"To get you some food. If it has a drive-thru, it's all yours."

---

"Did you see that?"

Mark nodded, giving Karen a look that clearly said, "It's about time too."

"Do you think we should check the news?" Karen's hand reached for the remote.

"Good idea."

It took several minutes for the story to update, but at last, they saw the familiar van, crumpled and on its side near the Brookside exit. Claire strolled back into the room, arms laden with coffee, and shrieked. "Is that—!"

"Shh!" Karen grabbed the tray of paper cups before Claire decorated the carpet with them. "Do you want to freak out the natives?"

"This native is freaked! Is that or is that not my cousin?" As Keith turned to point across a field, his face showed plainly on the screen. Mark swore. "That just increased danger exponentially. If Helen is watching, she knows they were here." Once more, a few expletives flew out of Mark's mouth before he was conscious of them.

Claire winced, turning to Karen, surprised. "I always thought Keith was way too uptight about people and 'foul language,'" she exaggerated the words as she made air quotes, "but you do get used to not hearing it, don't you?"

"Sorry."

"No, it's okay. I was just surprised. I'm not exactly a virgin mouth myself. I used to use the most vulgar words like people overuse the word 'like.'"

"Well, Keith is right. There are usually better ways to express yourself, but I don't have time to think about that. I need to find a way to trap Helen and fast."

"He'll check in, Mark. When he does, maybe I should tell him I'll take Erika and we can see if Myra is ready for a stint. She could cut and dye her hair like Erika's and we could bait Helen. Make sure he gets seen somewhere?"

"Too many variables." Mark swallowed hard. It'd be a horrible thing to do, but it was the only thing that made sense. "I'm thinking you warn Keith however you can, and I report the truck stolen. Keith can try to run at first, and then when they're arrested, we're there to grab Helen when she tries to bail Erika and or Keith out."

"What makes you think she'll do it herself? Wouldn't she just send someone else?"

Mark shook his head. "She's not a professional, she's arrogant, and let's face it, Erika would go with someone that she knew and 'trusted,' right? As far as she knows, we don't know she's killed Jill and Anthony." The man's voice cracked, and he gripped his desk as he tried to stuff down his emotions.

"Okay. I'll tell him. Are you sure it's safe enough for Erika?"

"Aside from getting out, jail is likely the safest place for her. Tell Keith to have her hit the officer. We don't want them thinking she's a victim."

Claire listened to the plans around her and sank into a chair. The idea that her cousin, her perfect law-abiding cousin, was deliberately going to get himself arrested seemed both incredible and astounding. She had questions but couldn't bring herself to interrupt the conversation. They hadn't spoken this openly around her since she and Karen had left Keith.

Karen flipped open her cheap phone, punched a short message into it, and snapped it shut again. Why they insisted on using those outdated and boring phones, she couldn't understand. You didn't have to activate all the apps for a smartphone, but at least you had options! Claire dreaded the day she was assigned one.

"Wow," Karen sounded genuinely surprised. "That was fast. He's already responded."

"Call."

Karen put her phone on "speaker" and dialed the number. The phone rang twice before Keith picked up. "We're having dinner, what do you want?"

"Mark is going to report the truck stolen. When the police find you, lead them on as much of a chase as you can, and make sure Erika resists arrest."

Silence hung on the line before Keith said, "Helen will post bail, and you'll be there to capture her."

"That's the plan."

"Do I really have to resist arrest? How do I do that?" Erika's stunned voice clearly indicated that she was not prepared to make that kind of sacrifice.

"Kick the officer, punch him, try to run. Just make sure they don't think you were helpless to stop Keith."

"I can't have an arrest on my record, Karen. It's hard enough to get a job in my field to begin with. A record means death."

"Inside sixty days, that record won't exist."

Keith began to speak, but Erika interrupted him. "How can you be sure Helen will post bail?"

"We can't, but if she's in the area, she will."

"And we'll make it out of there alive?"

Mark and Keith, miles apart, grinned at the trademarked soothing smoothness of Karen's voice. "Because if we couldn't, we wouldn't do this. You just have to trust that we've kept you alive this long because we know what we're doing."

"So, kick him, eh?"

"That was the general idea."

A few muffled words, unintelligible over the phone, were then followed by Erika's laughter. "Okay, I'll do it, but you are my witnesses. Keith has promised me a real dinner with real food and real waiters and a menu that you don't get a crick in your neck to read—preferably one without prices on it, but I won't be that picky."

"Oooh, a date!" Claire's voice interrupted the conversation. "This is gonna be good."

"This is payback for all the lousy food your cousin feeds me," Erika countered.

"Look, get her fed and get on the loop. You've got an hour and then I'm calling it in. Just circle the loop until you see those lovely flashing lights. The local PD will handle the rest—almost."

"I love that almost. See you soon—I hope."

Erika's voice was cut off mid-protest. Karen grinned at her boss and Keith's cousin. "Oh, man. What I wouldn't give to watch this. It's gonna be good."

# TWENTY-NINE

"Here we go." Keith punched the gas, sending the car from sixty to eighty in less time than it took him to glance her way and wink.

Erika grabbed the door handle, pretended to cross herself, and tried to ignore the weirdness that accompanied that wink. "So, how do you say the hail Mary thing anyway? I think I'm going to need it."

"Dunno. I'm not Catholic."

"So, only Catholics do the Mary thing?"

"Dunno." He swerved, nearly sideswiping a florist's van that tried to cross three lanes to pull over. Cars parted like the Red Sea to give them space, but a few were either two deaf from blasting music or too lazy to bother.

"Do you know anything?"

"Yeah," he growled. "I'm going to have to keep this up, all along the loop, until we run out of gas, or I'm going to have to get off of here."

"You can't go into town. Someone could get hurt."

"I was thinking the New Cheltenham exit. There's such a long stretch of nothingness."

"Maybe. How much gas do we have now?"

"Quarter of a tank."

"And that translates into..." She knew she sounded peevish, but Erika didn't care.

"I don't know, maybe five gallons? It might be a twenty-gallon tank, but probably more like fifteen, so maybe four. Bet we aren't getting more than twelve miles per gallon at this speed."

Dismay flooded her voice. "But that's probably fifty miles before we run out."

Keith leaned forward and looked through the top of the windshield. "There's a copter up there. Can you see if it's news or police?"

"WRAN Channel 4. News."

"Good."

"I can't believe I'm going to be on the news for criminal activity. Do you know how many people will see me kick a cop! I'm never going to live this down. Sure, my police record may not exist in sixty days, but that news footage will!"

"The memory will be sketchy, and we'll give a different name. We'll take care of the footage too."

"What, you're going to send some agent into the WRAN building and steal it? You're not CIA, but you can do that stuff and get away with it?"

"Yes." His answer, while unsatisfactory and inadequate, came without hesitation.

"What does that even mean?"

"It means that we know how to take care of you today in a way that ensures you don't have to live in a witness protection type lifestyle for the rest of your life." To her amazement, his hand reached for hers and squeezed before he pulled it back to the steering wheel and swerved around thrown tread from a semi. "It's going to be fine. You've trusted us this far. Just a bit more."

"I'm trusting that you're going to keep me safe when a woman who wants to kill me is going to get access to me. I don't even know why she wants to kill me!"

"Well, let's say that if anyone else figures out that you do know why, you're dead, so let's keep it at the fact that she's not who you thought she was, shall we?"

"You're annoying."

Considering the grin he now sported, Erika got the impression that he didn't really care what she thought of him. "Good. Keep being annoyed. You're going to need that angst when we get pulled over."

"I wish there was some way to dump the tank. This is torture."

"Not to mention ridiculously dangerous," he agreed.

"Do they train you how to drive like this?" Considering her white knuckles, Erika was amazed at how well he drove at ninety miles per hour.

"Some."

"That means what, that you're amazing at more than this?"

He didn't answer. A police car entered the freeway just ahead of them and refused to let them pass. At the next on ramp, another joined them. "Looks like the cops are getting smart. We've got an eighth of a mile and then we're going to be forced to stop or hit them."

"Should you try to go around on the median?"

"I will, but I think I can get us stalled out if I do it right."

"So, it's almost over?"

He glanced at her as if she'd lost her mind. "No, it's just about to begin. The chase was the appetizer. It's time for the main course. Here comes the next guy."

"How'd they keep people from getting on?"

"Police blockades down there. We've created a traffic nightmare."

The cars ahead of them all decelerated, forcing Keith to do the same. Just as he started to jerk the wheel into the grassy median, three cars from behind and from the other direction converged, forcing him to stop. A glance at the side mirrors told Erika he wouldn't be trying reverse. They'd done a perfect job of boxing him in with nowhere to go.

"They're going to tell us to open the door with one hand in the air and the other hand opening it from the outside. Do it. Don't even for a second think about arguing until you are outside the vehicle and then start screaming at me. When the officer tries to keep you from moving toward me, then kick him, hit him, resist in any way you can, but not until then. Don't let them think, even for a second, that you could possibly have a weapon."

"What about yours?"

"Tossed it when we got the call."

"How did I not see that?"

Keith's eyes met hers as his hands went into the air at the order of the bullhorn. "You aren't trained to see it, but

I'm trained to hide it. It just means that I did my job right and you were protected because of it."

The order came to reach out of the car and open the car door. Erika gave him a thumbs-up and muttered, "Let's roll."

The effort Keith had to exert not to erupt into laughter was impressive. She saw his mouth twitch, his eye water, and his face went a little red. She'd finally bested him in something—small as it was. It felt good—really good. *That's what Donald Bruner liked. That's what Keith meant.*

Seeing the officer, gun trained on her, nearly sent Erika into a panic. All the times Keith had held a gun while giving her the freedom to wander around the house or yard were nothing compared to the raw fear that came with being surrounded by the men and women you've always trusted to protect you—with their guns drawn on you. She heard the words, "Step away from the vehicle, hands behind your head," and bile filled her throat. This was real. She was about to violate every rule she'd ever learned about proper behavior, civility, and honor for the people who put their lives on the line every day to protect her from people like she seemed to be to them. It was a crazy mixed up nightmare, and she wanted out before some creepy guy with chainsaws for arms and knives for teeth started chasing her.

A glance at Keith assured her it was time. As she pulled her hands behind her head, ready for the officer to wrench them into handcuffs, she started screaming at Keith. "See what you've done now! Why couldn't you have stopped! What did you do? This is insane!" Erika whipped her head around as the officer grabbed her wrist and said, "I am innocent! He took off and what was I supposed to do? I can't jump out of a car going ninety, can I? I want him arrested for kidnapping!"

"You can tell your story at the station, but until—"

"That's not fair!" She tried to wrench free, but when the man's hands held her wrist in a vice-like grip, she kicked his shins so hard, she nearly landed on her face. "Let me go!"

"That'll get you charged for assaulting an officer, though. Good shot."

"Not good enough," she muttered.

"Turn on the news. WRAN. Found her. Shall I go in?"

Helen grabbed the remote and clicked to the right channel and watched the replay of the dramatic car chase that ended in the arrest of a man she didn't recognize and her faithful house sitter, Erika. "There you are."

"Well, do I go?"

"No. I'll take care of it. I can easily say I saw it on the news, post bail, she'll let me walk her right out the front door."

"What about the man?"

"He's got to go, too, but wait to hear from me. If she insists on taking him with us, I'll have to. Hopefully, based upon that screaming match, we won't have to do that."

"Standing by."

The phone disconnected before her man finished speaking, and Helen went into action. She changed out of her jeans and t-shirt into tasteful slacks, blouse, and added a few good pieces of jewelry. With large sunglasses and an oversized designer purse, she looked like any trophy wife out for a shopping trip—exactly the look she wanted.

It took several calls to find the correct station, but at last, her taxi pulled up in front of the building and promised to wait. Getting inside to see Erika was much more difficult. The officers at the desk would give no information, and despite her pleading, none would take a message to her "friend."

Furious, she strode from the building and climbed back into the cab. "Where to, lady?"

"Just stay put. I need to figure out when the next hearing is."

"Won't be until morning, most likely. You can go ask—"

"They won't tell me anything."

The driver turned off the keys and opened his door. "I'll be right back."

"Thanks—"

"No problem. My mom had to bail me out plenty when I was young and stupid. I'd like to think there was someone there helping her back then."

As she watched the man enter the building, Helen shook her head. "Gullible idiot."

Despite her true thoughts, Helen gushed over his thoughtfulness between sniffles at the injustice as the man drove her back to her hotel. A morning hearing was the last thing she wanted to wait for, but she had no choice. "She's just a kid, you know? I mean, I saw her kick the officer myself, but anyone could see she was just scared. I hate to think this'd go on her record just because she panicked."

"Why was she in the car in the first place?"

"I don't know! She has good friends—responsible ones. For all I know, she was kidnapped or broke down somewhere and accepted a ride. It's just not like her." Helen felt as if she were giving an Oscar performance. Thankfully, her oversized sunglasses would make it impossible to identify her, and the Australian accent would resurface the second she stepped from the car. All in a day's work.

At the hotel, she tipped the driver generously, thanked him profusely, and rushed inside, giving every appearance of being distraught. The moment she entered her room, she dialed her contact. "Can't get to them before morning. Be ready. After spending the night in a holding cell, I think she'll be a bit more tractable than she would be right now."

"I could get both of them as they're being transferred if you like."

"No. It'd raise too many questions. There'd be a huge investigation over something like that. Just be ready to go in, bail him out, and dump him over the state line."

"Got it. About that other matter…"

"Yes, at that one, there are enough people who want Alek dead. Kill him on his way to arraignment. If there are others with him, get them too—particularly his lawyer—but make sure you get him."

"Got it. I have a new account number for you."

"Text it. I'm going to get something to eat and then turn in early. Don't call again."

Helen punched the end call button and selected another number. "Frank?"

"Yeah."

"I've given Gordon a job. I'll need clean up tomorrow. Are you available?"

"Too bad. He's a good guy."

Frank said that every time. "Well then, he'll get to go play harps and wear robes. He'll be in heaven."

"Ha. Ha. Hilarious."

"You didn't answer my question."

"I'm available."

"I'll email the account number. Who knows what he has in there, but it'll be considerably larger by noon tomorrow."

Frank's laughter always unnerved her. "And all mine too. How nice. I might have to indulge myself with a trip to St. Martin."

She'd put money that he meant Thailand or Bali. Frank always talked Caribbean, but his travel history showed a fondness for the more decadent portions of Asian countries. Then again, she didn't care. Helen Franklin cared about two things—money and power. What others did only concerned her when they threatened to upset the balance of either of those things in her life.

"You'll need to be in my house when I leave the courthouse tomorrow. Make a mess and make sure it looks like you wanted drugs. Shoot the girl with me. I'm going to faint."

Frank's teasing annoyed her. "Tsk, tsk. You're in the business of keeping girls alive and useful. This one must be quite a threat to you. I'll be sure she's gone. I'd hate to see my income dwindle." The line went dead.

Erika was a minor threat—nearly non-existent. However, considering she'd removed people for less, Helen wouldn't hesitate now. She'd find a new house sitter. A text message came through her cell phone that brought a smile to her lips. ARRIVED. 172. 4. 4. Four sick and only four dead. Not bad. Not bad at all.

Her fingers flew over the keys of her laptop, entering one hundred seventy-two pallets of Vietnamese cigarettes. Four were marked destroyed in transit and four damaged. All in a day's work. The shipment had been paid for by the Anastas syndicate and had been "appropriated" by Helen. Piracy at its finest—all the rewards with none of that unnecessary and brutish swordplay.

By tomorrow, her last loose end would be neatly tied—right around Erika Polowski's little neck. Once Frank was done robbing them, shooting Erika in the process, it'd be over, and she'd be free to move more of the merchandise into the Rockland area. With the new shipment coming into Columbus, they could afford to give Rockland an infusion of workers for the industry. Sure, the economy was in a recession, but some things always make the budget.

# THIRTY

"I don't understand! Why aren't we going in there and doing something? We can't just leave them in jail!"

Karen shook her head at Mark and frowned. "Look, Claire. We told you. This is a trap to capture the person responsible for the danger in the first place. If we go in, she'll know."

"Meanwhile, you've got my cousin locked up and at the mercy of a killer! Erika doesn't even know why this chick is dangerous. She could say the wrong thing at the wrong time and—"

"And you're going to have to trust that we know what we're doing."

"But Keith—"

"Will be fine," Karen assured her.

"Unless he's the mole." The young woman studied Mark's face for any sign of betrayal.

"Claire, come here." Mark's voice was quiet—a tone that Karen knew well. She stepped outside the door, listening as Mark worked his soothing magic on a distraught young woman. It was what made Mark so good at his job. He could take an angry, panicked, terrified, or absolutely confused person and have them calm and ready to do whatever he thought best in minutes.

A peek through the crack in the door surprised her. Mark held both of Claire's hands in one of his as he spoke to her. He rarely let himself show personal concern for a client. Perhaps the "training" she'd been given wasn't a cover to protect her. It certainly seemed as if Mark was going to bring her into their group. He only showed that kind of brotherly concern when dealing with the other women in his employ. Either that or—

Karen chose not to let her mind go there. It was dangerous and nearly impassable territory. She knew it when she accepted the job and nothing had changed. The work they did was important. Their ability to work around the law and protect the reputation of government agencies was vital to the safety of people who were targets of those who didn't care about laws or protocols.

A second glance through the door nearly choked her. Mark's arm was around Claire's shoulder, his thumb massaging the kinks from her neck. She had to stop torturing herself. Whatever Mark did was essential to the morale of the team. Only the team mattered—not her personal heartache—if it even was that.

"Karen, can you come in here?"

She pushed open the door, nearly hitting Claire with it. "Oh, sorry."

"Excuse me." Keith's cousin hurried from the room wiping tears from her eyes.

Glancing after her, Mark shook his head. "We need to start a rumor about a dying grandmother or something. She's going to cause too much curiosity. I think, somewhere beneath the emotional layers, she has what it takes, but if we can't teach her to control the emotions, she can't stay. It'd be a waste. She has excellent instincts."

"I'll help her."

"I knew I could count on you." Mark glanced at his cell phone before he asked, "Do you know if she has anyone close to her? A really close best friend, boyfriend, something like that?"

A lump rose in her throat, but Karen forced it back down. "I don't know, but I can find out."

"Do it. We need to know if that's going to be an issue. It's the one reason I don't object to agents dating. There isn't a security issue. I usually check those things, but we were in a bit of a rush. I know she did have a guy, but there were rumors about him taking off with the best friend. I need to know if it's true. I hope so."

"I bet you do." Shock flooded Karen's face as she realized she spoke aloud.

Mark's eyes searched her face for a moment and then shook his head. "If by that, you meant that I would be personally happy to hear she is single, you'd be wrong. Brian would be good for her."

"It's none of my business, Mark. You just seemed interested, and I found it amusing."

"She's too young for me. I'm more comfortable with women who—with other types of women."

Something in his voice made Karen snap her head up and draw her eyebrows together. The words were innocuous enough, but the tone—the tone was something else—almost hinting. Mark's eyes never wavered. Not ready to face the possibility of disappointment or worse, the mortification of revealing interest she'd kept so carefully hidden, she shrugged. "Aren't we all?" She choked a bit as she realized how her words sounded. "Interested in other—anyway. Did you say there was something else?"

Clearly ready to change the subject, Mark passed a dossier across the desk. "I got a call from a DA in Colorado. He says this man, Leo Hasaert, is likely going to need an extraction. He'll resist."

"The DA or Leo?"

"Leo."

Karen picked up the dossier. "He's one scary looking dude. He's the one we need to protect?"

"Possibly. We have to be ready. I'll have to go in with you if we go. Brian is on the Devore case and Keith is in jail. Anthony is dead and well, need I go on?"

"Yeah, with a man," Karen agreed, "I'm gonna need help. I can't possibly do that by myself—not with a man that built." She read farther. "Whoa. Bike gang? Murder?"

"He's not a threat. From what I've gathered from his boss, his preacher—"

"Preacher! Oh, don't tell me, he gets caught, pretends to get religion—"

"No, Karen." Mark's interruption normally would have annoyed her, but there was that tone again—the one that caught her unaware every time. "He became a Christian, spoke to his pastor or minister or whatever, and upon the advice the man gave, went to the DA with his information. He gave it freely. The appointed lawyer got him probation and community service for turning evidence."

"Well, it'd be awfully convenient if whoever wants him

dead would wait to move until we've taken care of Helen Franklin."

"Don't want to have to rely on me for backup, eh?"

Karen shook her head. "Quite the contrary. You don't want to have to rely on me. One look at that spider web in person and I might just run."

---

The concrete slab wasn't much more comfortable with the addition of the thin mattress. Keith shuddered at the thought of all the bacteria and the probable critters living in it. He spent most of his time standing or leaning against the wall, but at last was forced to sit. Desperate to avoid the probability of lice or bedbugs, he folded the thin mat in half and shoved it to one end of the "bed."

Prayer was his only comfort. This was the worst part of the plan—the hours that he couldn't see, hear, or even ask if Erika was all right. Keith tried to trust that she was protected in a building surrounded by policemen, but people died in custody every year; why not her?

A drunk in the next cell railed out against the police, his girlfriend, and God—not necessarily in that order. For a while, the temptation to start singing "Amazing Grace" or "It Is Well with My Soul" niggled at him, but Keith resisted. There was no reason to torture anyone, even a mean drunk, with his voice. Had he thought he could get away with it, he'd have whistled, but it seemed like a great way to irritate the guard, so he didn't.

As the night wore on, the cells filled. Domestic violence, a few more drunks, a few assaults, and an attempted murder all filed in and occupied cells on the small block. If they filled too quickly, he could be let go with just an order to appear. That would be terrible. He'd have to throw a punch or something if that happened.

How was Erika doing? Was she as terrified as he imagined, or had she moved into fury? He hoped she was good and ticked. It'd get her through the next few hours. Leaving was the worst part of the ordeal. Once they got past getting out of the courthouse where Mark and Karen would be waiting, they'd be good, but getting to there wasn't as easy as it looked.

He'd made it sound so simple—almost as if it were failsafe. Keith felt like a liar. He had no scruples about telling a client anything he had to say to keep the person trusting and listening, but this time it felt wrong. She'd gone from being an abductee to a willing participant in their charade to capture her pursuer. It wasn't the same.

Had Mark been able to arrange for Judge Bleakman to preside over the hearing? With Bleakman, they'd get off with a fine and community service, which Bleakman would sign off on thirty days later. It'd be simple. Mark had considered bringing Constance Jamison into the loop. She was known to be hard on prostitution, so this might be the case to do that if she was on the bench, but anyone else would mean trouble. He doubted he'd be sentenced to jail. Anthony had once. He swallowed hard at the memory of teasing Anthony. That would never happen again.

Erika had managed to kick one of the more easily influenced men on the force. Karen would be able to convince him that it had been the flail of a struggling, terrified woman rather than a deliberate connection of foot to shin.

The walls seemed to close in on him the longer he sat there. Tired, miserable, and concerned for Erika's safety, Keith just wanted the ordeal to end so they could get onto more important things. They had Helen to stop on several fronts—starting with Erika, of course.

---

Being arrested was truly the most humiliating experience of Erika's life. The search was mortifying, the photographing and fingerprinting degrading, but nothing felt worse than hearing the clink of the metal bars connecting with the latch on the other side. She was alone in her block of cells.

The room was narrow with only a nod at privacy for the toilet. Painted cinderblocks and a concrete ledge that masqueraded as a bed meant it was easy to hose down—to clean. One look at the thin mat on the ledge and she shuddered. She'd always had a difficult enough time relaxing in a hotel room; this was ten times worse—a hundred.

*I wonder what he's doing. Is his block empty too?* Her thoughts ran wild with ideas. What if Helen got herself locked up too? Could she somehow kill Erika as she passed to her own cell? Did she want her dead enough to make it obvious that she'd been the killer, or did it have to be covert? *What have I done anyway? I've never given her any reason to see me as a threat!*

She discarded her ideas nearly as quickly as they flitted through her mind. Each seemed more ludicrous than the last. It had to be drugs or stolen art. Nothing else made any sense. Erika tried to picture the plants in the backyard, but she didn't remember any of dubious origins. The house seemed free of anything of real value. The wall art were cheap posters framed at a craft store. There were no vases, no sculptures—nothing that would make someone suspicious.

It seemed insane that now that she knew who wanted her dead, she couldn't know why, but Keith had been adamant. If anyone suspected, she could be a target of a faceless foe. The whole thing seemed so melodramatic, but no one could doubt the seriousness on Karen's and Keith's faces. She even tried not to think about it as a gesture of trust and respect, but her naturally curious nature refused to be so easily appeased.

Just as she draped her mat over the half wall that semi-hid the toilet bowl, a new, terrifying thought came to her. Her picture was likely plastered all over the news—first as the kidnapped daughter of Tom Polowski, and possibly as the woman who had fled the scene of the accident. She'd given her name as Erin Polk, but how long would it be before they found that her fingerprints matched the driver's license of Erika Polowski? This was very bad. Giving a fake name had seemed smart at the time, but now...

Less than two hours after she'd been locked into the cell, Erika found herself led from it and into an interrogation room. Her hands shook, her knees wobbled, but at the sight of her parents, she threw herself into her father's arms. "Daddy!"

# THIRTY-ONE

Voices, all speaking at once, rose to such a crescendo that Erika found herself whistling to silence everyone. "Officer, can I speak to my father for five minutes alone?"

It took some convincing, but at last, the room emptied of all but Erika and her father. The moment the door shut behind the officer, Tom spoke. "Are you all right? When we got the news—"

The word news was all she needed. Pulling him close, she whispered in his ear. "Don't talk out loud, just listen. The guy I came in with—he isn't the one who kidnapped me. You've got to help me get him out, and we can't let it get on the news that I've been found, or the real kidnappers will find me and kill both of us—maybe even you and mom."

"What are you talk—?"

She clamped her hand over her father's mouth and used her eyes to try to impart some sense of the seriousness of the situation. "Shh! I'm not being dramatic, Dad. I'm serious. We've got to do something."

"Is this some kind of Stockholm thing?"

Erika sighed in relief. At least he was whispering. That could mean he was also listening. "No, Dad. I gave them a fake name and refused to talk. I bet Keith did too. Just help us, or someone else is going to get hurt." Then, as if they hadn't spent the last minute in hushed whispers that she hoped couldn't be recorded and amplified, Erika spoke aloud. "So, what happens next?"

"Well, they said you assaulted an officer. Considering the circumstances, I think the judge will dismiss the charges, but you have to see him."

She nodded, mouthing the word "good." "What about Keith?"

"Well, he tried to evade the police, and he did have you in the car. You've been reported as kidnapped."

"I figured you'd do that."

"So, did he take you or someone else?"

Her mind whirled. Should she name the real villain, or was that too dangerous? She opted for ambiguity. "I didn't see who kidnapped me. Keith helped me escape at a gas station and we hid for a few days, working our way back to Rockland."

"Where were you?"

"Somewhere around Chicago, I think." The ease with which she lied unnerved her a bit. Was this what it was like to be Keith? She knew he wouldn't lie about some things, but if it kept someone safe, he had no qualms at all. That seemed odd, but necessary. However, she'd never been accustomed to lying so freely.

"I'll go talk to the officer. Your mom wants to see you, of course. She's being a bit emotional about all this."

"Dad, her daughter was kidnapped. It's okay for mom to be emotional about that. Cut her some slack."

"I suppose."

"Dad…" she repeated warningly.

"Perhaps you're right. I don't see the point to it, but—"

"The point is that most people have emotions about startling events like this whether they want them or not. You always forget that you're the unnatural one, not everyone else. Just deal with it."

"Hugs and holding and…"

"And listening without trying to fix it. She'll be okay. She always is." Erika kissed her father's cheek. "You love her."

"Endorphins."

"Fine. You endorphin her. Go prove it."

Tom shrugged. "After the police. Your mom wants you anyway."

It took hours to convince everyone from her mother to the captain that Keith was not the enemy and that she needed five minutes alone with him. Even as it was, an officer stayed just inside the door, watching—protecting. One look at the suspicious expression on the woman's face, and Keith decided to try an unusual approach. The second he was within feet of Erika, he wrapped his arms around her, kissing her as if he'd been separated for months. "I was so worried!"

How Erika managed to recover quickly enough, neither seemed to know, but she did. As she hugged him again, she whispered, "You rescued me from a gas station near Chicago and we've been traveling for two days. I've begged them not to leak the news that I've been found. I said that the kidnappers would find me and kill us if it happened."

Keith pulled away slightly nodding. He mouthed, "Good job," before saying, "You're okay? They didn't hurt you?"

"They're the police. They're not going to hurt me."

He allowed himself to brush a thumb across her cheek, hoping he looked like the deeply in love man he tried to pretend to be. "You kicked the one guy. I know they don't take that kind of thing well."

"You're so cute!" Erika made an exaggerated roll of her eyes at the officer. "He's convinced you guys are going to pull a Rodney King on me just because I freaked a bit when they stopped us, and I kicked that guy."

"We don't assault citizens—even if they attack us. We'll fight you off if necessary, but a kick doesn't require that kind of force."

"Yeah. He's just a little paranoid."

"How long have you two been together?" The officer tried to act casual, and it was working with Erika, but Keith knew better.

He waited, unwilling to answer on the off chance that she'd told someone they were strangers. What he didn't know could kill their credibility. Erika shrugged. "We met on my vacation a few weeks back. When they dragged me to that dumb station the third day in a row, I just begged a gal in the bathroom to let me use her cell phone. Keith came the next day and helped me get out of there."

"Sloppy."

"Yeah, it wasn't anything like you see on TV. Those guys on TV are always on the ball, y'know? These idiots didn't seem to know what they were doing. I think they really thought Dad would pay up if they kept me long enough or something." She winked at Keith. "They don't know my dad. He's not the paying up type."

"Nah. Men talk like that, but when it comes down to their little girls being scared at a gun at their heads…"

"Have you ever met a man who didn't handle emotional females well?"

The woman nodded. "Yeah."

"Now, add a man without normal emotions, and that's my dad. See what I mean?"

The door opened, and another officer's face peeked in the door. "Look, we've got to get them in for more questioning. Are they done yet?"

"We're ready," Keith agreed. As they moved toward the door, he whispered, "Let me try to answer what happened from the station. You answer before."

The questioning went on for what seemed like hours. Any time they asked Keith a question about her captivity, he shrugged. "You'd have to ask her. She didn't tell me."

Each time they asked about a location, Erika shook her head. "I don't know. I was all turned around. Keith should know, though. He found me. I know I was close to Chicago though. They said something about that."

A few things didn't line up, but rather than making the officers come down harder, they seemed to take it in stride. They examined and cross-examined until both Keith and Erika were ready to collapse, but it worked.

"So, you ran from us so that you would get caught and have police protection?"

"Yes. It sounds weird, but we were afraid they might be watching police stations."

"Do you know how unlikely that is?" The officer shook his head. "There are too many stations between here and Chicago—"

"Look, we were scared. What do we know about it? All we could think of was to get caught so that we'd have police protection." Keith stammered and bumbled, trying to appear to have confused bravado. It was an Oscar performance. "Hey, can I make a phone call now?"

---

"Mark? It's Keith. Yeah, I'm in a bit of trouble." Keith listened for a moment and then continued. "Well, I'm going to need bail probably. The hearing is at nine o'clock in the morning. Can you set that up? Yeah, I know it's technically morning now, but hey."

Anyone listening to both sides of the conversation would be utterly confused. As Keith talked about the charges and the guestimate at bail, Mark informed him how they'd play out the capture. The effort it took to listen and comprehend the critical information Mark passed to him, maintaining a coherent one-sided conversation, all while trying to make it look natural and as if nothing were amiss nearly made him come undone.

It was time to sound desperate. "Mark, come on, you've gotta help me! I can't spend the rest of the week here until my arraignment!" He listened to Mark tell him to be ready to follow Erika to wherever Helen planned to take her and give instructions as to where they'd meet.

The walk back to his cell was awkward. He was used to people who expected him to talk, but the officer had no interest in carrying on a conversation. Instead, he started several awkward sentences and then muttered something about uppity cops who couldn't give anyone the time of day before he pretended to drop to the bed. The officer hardly noticed.

So, everything was in motion. In twenty-four hours, Erika's nightmare would be over, and the biggest name in human trafficking in the United States would be behind bars. Mark had enough evidence against her and the Anastas syndicate to put them away indefinitely. It wouldn't bring back Jill and Tony, but at least they'd get some justice, and their families could have some closure.

Alone, with the lights dimmed as low as a holding tank can be, Keith wrestled with his thoughts. He needed mentally to prepare himself for the following morning. There'd be no margin for error. Every word, every response, everything must be calculated to perfection. Even the slightest mistake could spell disaster, but his mind refused to cooperate. As he tried to reason out every possible scenario, the memory of his impulsive kiss assaulted him. He shoved the recollection aside for a later date, but when his next scenario failed, leaving Erika wounded or dying, that moment flashed before him again.

*Um, Lord, a little help here?* The thought was chased from his mind faster than he'd imagined possible. Had she responded out of interest or because she was that sharp on the uptake? He didn't know. Furthermore, he needed not to care. His job was to get this assignment complete without any more casualties, and that wasn't going to happen if he sat around his cell daydreaming like a teenager.

When he could think of no more scenarios, Keith moved onto prayer. It was a little easier to focus when he wasn't forced to push thoughts of Erika aside. Instead, he brought his questions to the Lord. It felt like cheating at first, but he shook that idea off as ludicrous. What was dishonest about talking to the Father of fathers about a problem? Wasn't that the purpose of prayer?

However, after his success with prayer, his relaxation techniques, designed to give his body maximum refreshment when he couldn't allow himself the luxury of sleep, failed. Miserably. Each attempt to bring his thoughts to calming things, gentle scripture, or lazy memories that always seemed to help him relax dissolved at the mental image of Erika's face. She hadn't hesitated—had acted as if it was the most natural thing in the world. That wasn't what bothered him.

What annoyed him most—what niggled at him as he tried to rest before the hearing—was the realization that it mattered more to him than a simple diversionary tactic ever should.

Helen waited for the hearing to end. She was prepared to pay the bail—had cash in hand—and it was just a matter of time before she'd have Erika out of the way for good. The man, Keith, might be a problem, but it couldn't be helped. If both came with her, though, she'd have to consider letting herself be shot. That sounded revolting, but the alternative was unacceptable. She could not afford to be under suspicion. Life was about to become very sweet again.

As case after case came before the bored sounding judge, Helen sent text messages flying to her "problem solvers." Gordon was on his way to her house now. Frank followed Gordon. The moment Erika was dead Frank would take out the robber and take a few months off to enjoy the fruits of his labors. She'd use someone else for Anastas. Despite what she'd told Gordon, that'd been the plan all along. He worked better knowing his cash flow wouldn't dry up anytime soon.

At the sound of Erika's name, she sat up and listened carefully. So, she was claiming kidnapping. Helen watched the judge's face as he listened to the recommendation of the officers. *Why is she even here if they don't want to press charges anymore?* The moment the thought entered her mind, the judge asked the same question.

The ADA shook her head. "We didn't learn this until she'd already been booked, and I had already filed the complaint."

"Dismissed. Um, next is Auger, Keith."

"Thanks for the ride, Ms. Franklin." To hear him, you'd think Keith had just been caught smoking his dad's cigars in the basement.

"Well, if you were helping Erika, I couldn't just leave you there, could I?"

A pinching squeeze caught Erika by surprise. "You okay?" Those words meant so much more, and she knew it. Keith was really saying, "Snap out of it."

"Yeah, I guess. I didn't sleep much, and it's been a rough week, you know?"

"Well, we'll get you home and you guys can zonk out for a while. I've got to pack. I'm so glad I was here. When I saw you on the news, I couldn't believe it!" Helen played her role well—too well. She nearly sounded like a community theater actress. Each word just barely overstated and with dramatic flair.

"I'm just glad he let me off with the ticket the one officer gave me. It could have been so much worse," Keith interjected when Erika still refused to speak.

Each mile, each block, and finally each house felt like a death march. The nervousness seemed to grow exponentially until she thought she'd come out of her skin. Any second, something could go wrong—something would go wrong. She knew it.

At the sight of the house, Erika's throat went dry. "The front door—it's open." Her voice sounded raspy, and she knew she looked as terrified as she felt.

"I really wish you'd told me about that latch. I'd have had it fixed. There'll probably be cats in there now. I hate cats," Helen hissed.

"What about the latch?"

"It's been slipping open. I've been home for three days, and every day I've found it open. It's annoying." Helen sent an annoyed glance at Erika. "I pay you to notice those things."

Keith sent Erika a warning glance, but it did no good. She was useless, and she knew it. He urged her toward the door, trying everything to hide her resistance. How could he be so calm? They were certainly walking into a trap. Where were Karen, Mark, and whoever else she'd hoped would keep her alive?

The moment they stepped from the entryway into the living room, a man turned, a gun pointing right at her. Helen stepped out of the way and said, "Well done, Gordon," before she dumped the contents of her purse onto the coffee table. "Make sure you take all of this. You're going to have to shoot me too. With him here, it's unlikely I'd be missed. Just be sure to get my side—even if you miss a couple of times."

"Her first?"

"No, him, I think. Don't want to risk him trying to tackle you, which—" she added after an appraising look at Keith, "it looks like he's ready to do now."

The man, Gordon, turned his gun on Keith. A shot rang out a millisecond before Keith and Erika dropped to the floor.

# Thirty-Two

With the weight of Keith on her, Erika was sure he was dead, and she was next. Fear flooded her heart at the idea of the finality of death, leaving her trembling. Screams ripped through the room, making it nearly impossible to know what to expect next, but Keith's voice, calm and strong, murmured, "Stay down. It's going to be okay."

Fury flooded her. At a time like that, he had the audacity to say everything would be okay. What kind of mindless nonsense was that? "Are you nuts? Are you bleeding all over me?"

"I'm not the one hit. Looks like FBI, but I could be wrong."

"You're not hit?"

"Nope. Neither are you. Shot came from the archway to the kitchen and caught Gordon, if that's his real name, by surprise."

"Who is screaming?"

"It's a toss-up between the guy and Helen. She seems a bit freaked out. I don't think this was the plan."

"We're really okay?" Erika knew she sounded ridiculous, but she didn't care.

"You can get up now. We've got all three of them."

"Three?" Erika and Keith spoke in unison.

"Yep." The agent gestured to a man in a business suit and fedora. Erika's first thought was, "really?" but before she could speak, the agent continued, "Not sure what his part is, but I suspect he was here to clean up."

"How nice," Erika groaned sarcastically as she accepted Keith's help up from the ground. "She wasn't going to let my parents find my body lying here."

"Yeah. That." Keith exchanged amused glances with

the man, leaving Erika even more irritated.

"What?"

"He's here to take care of Gordon, Erika," Keith explained. "For all we know, she'd have killed him or had him killed once he was out of the country."

"How do you know he'd go out of the country?"

"If you got paid good money to kill someone, would you want to put distance between you and the hit, or would you want to hang around and see if the police suspected you?"

"I thought—"

Keith shook his head. "I think you're overwrought. Why don't we call your parents? It's over, Erika. It's over."

"I've heard that one before," she muttered.

The subsequent snicker was hard to miss.

Seeing Helen, handcuffed and being led from the house, Erika became enraged. She broke away from Keith's side and stormed up to the woman shouting, "Why? What did I do? Whatever made you think I was any kind of threat to you? I was just a stupid house sitter. A house sitter! What could I possibly have said or done to upset the delicate balance of international trade?"

"You gullible—"

The agent jerked Helen away from Erika as another pulled Erika back into the house. "It's complicated and you don't need to know."

"I do need to know! This is insane. She almost killed me. Why? I have a right to know why!"

Arms wrapped around her from behind, dragging her down the hall and into her room. Keith pushed the door shut behind her and held onto her as she screamed and kicked. "Let go of me. I don't have to put up with this anymore. You know why; tell me."

"I can't. I'm serious when I say it puts you in danger."

Her anger dissolved into frustrated tears. "I just don't understand."

"I know." His arms relaxed. "Are you going to attack me if I let you go?"

"I might." His chuckle annoyed her. "What?"

"I always expect you to deny things like that, and you never do."

"If I deny it, will you let go?" Keith dropped his arms and waited, as if for some kind of blow, but she had no intention of making him less inclined to talk. When she was safely on the other side of the room, Erika turned to him and said, "So, am I safe now? No boogey men are coming after me? No assassins? No kidnappers—not even you?"

Before he could answer, Karen burst through the door, nearly knocking over Keith in her haste. "Are you guys okay? There's blood everywhere in there, and no one will say anything."

"How did you get in here?" Keith's stunned words told Erika it wasn't a common thing.

"Climbed through the other bedroom window after I was denied access." Karen glanced at Erika. "Sorry, I kind of destroyed a screen."

"I imagine Helen has more important things to worry about right now." The words sounded ridiculous even to her own ears. "What am I saying? I probably have to move, don't I?"

"Probably," Keith and Karen answered in unison.

"That's it. No more house sitting for me. It was a sweet deal when I had it, but forget it. It's not worth it. I'm going to rent me a nice little apartment near the coffee shop—some place that I can walk to..."

Karen shook her head. "I don't think you've checked the rents around there. Even a studio apartment would take up most of your paycheck."

"Well, I'll find something. I'm not dealing with this anymore."

With a wink at Karen, Keith said, "Well, you could always ask Mark for a job. He pays very well, and you rarely need a home to go to."

"That's just sick, and you know it."

The door pushed open before Keith could respond, and the agent in charge entered. "Who—what is she doing here?" Pointing at Karen, the man jerked his thumb. "That's it—"

"She's with us. I told her to come in."

"Well, we said to stay out."

"It's not her fault that she thought you'd changed your mind. If you've got a problem with it, then charge me. She's just doing her job."

"You people are bizarre. Let's go. We've got a long night ahead of us—all of us."

Erika glanced at Keith. "Is he serious?"

"You can't imagine."

"Can I pack a bag?"

"Lady, this is a crime scene. You can't touch a thing. Nothing."

"My purse?" The shake of three heads prompted a string of expletives that made Keith wince. It felt good—really good—to make him as miserable for once. "Fine."

---

The modest house in Marshfield had that charm of decades of family living that newer houses never managed to achieve. The driveway had handprints near the garage door, planter boxes, repaired and with layers of paint, held overgrown flowers, and the welcome mat was frayed at the edges. Karen loved it. The Polowskis lived in exactly the kind of house she'd shared with her parents. There'd be a piece of furniture, probably one that Mrs. Polowski hated, somewhere in that house that the man clung to as if it held everything together. There'd be school pictures on the walls—pictures of a little Erika with overgrown teeth and pigtails. All those things were gone for Karen now. She missed that.

Tom Polowski opened the door, a curious look on his face. "Is she needed again?"

Karen held up the bags on her arms. "Mark sent some things for her."

"Erika!" The man's loud voice sent echoes through her ears. "That woman from the FBI is here."

She smiled at his misconception but didn't correct him. What was the point? "I could just give them to you—Hey, Erika!"

"I didn't think I'd see you again."

"It's unusual, but Mark insisted." She held out a few bags. "I suggested gift cards, but he said you could return or exchange if you needed to, but this way you didn't have to go out if you didn't want to." She shook her head with an exaggerated wag, "Why do men always think that women respond to stress and stimuli in the same way they do?"

"Why wouldn't we think that?" Tom responded. "It's our only frame of reference. If I feel better after a jog, then when my wife is angry, I naturally suggest a jog to make her feel better."

"And what if your wife is angry that her favorite jeans are too small? How is she supposed to feel about your suggestion to jog then?" Karen couldn't help the temptation for a little gentle ribbing.

"All the more reason!"

"My father doesn't understand anything but pure logic—emotion never enters the equation. He would never imagine that someone would take that as a hint that she needs *the exercise to lose the weight that make the jeans too small!*"

"Why would that be bad again? If her jeans are too small, she clearly does need the exercise."

Erika opened the door wider. "Come on in. This could take a while." She led Karen into the living room and pointed to the couch. "Just don't take Dad's chair, and you're good."

There it was—a needlepointed monstrosity of a wingback chair that should have seen the dump decades earlier. "That's a very unusual chair."

"Dad, that's a polite way of saying, uglier than the neighbor's bulldog."

"Then why doesn't she just say it? No one thinks the chair is nice to look at, do they?"

Karen felt the heat of embarrassment creep up over her face. She hadn't meant to be rude. "I—"

"Don't worry about it, Karen. Dad has something off in his wiring. The emotional and social cues centers of his brain—whatever they're called—"

"It's the—"

"We don't care about the semantics, Dad. Anyway, his got unplugged or were never connected. He just doesn't 'do' emotion, he's a bit over-analytical, and common courtesy is his idea of lying." She giggled. "Can I tell her about when you met Mom?"

"Why not? I don't care."

"Mom! Mooommmm..."

Mrs. Polowski shuffled down the hallway, waving her hands to dry nail polish and with a towel wrapped like a turban around her head. "Oh, it's um... Kay—"

"Karen. Nice to see you again."

"Karen's boss sent a few things over for me, and she met Dad. I was just going to tell her how you met."

"Oh, this I've got to see. I never get tired of the expressions on your next victim's face."

"Well," Erika said, tucking her feet under her, "Dad met Mom at a restaurant where Mom was a waitress. He told her she was pretty."

The pause told Karen she was expected to say something. "Sounds normal enough."

"Well, he came back in every night for a week. On Friday night, he asked her if she wanted to go out for ice cream when she got off work. Since he'd been kind of rude about things all week, Mom was a bit put out with him, so she said, 'Why'?"

"I still think that's a ridiculous question," Mr. Polowski interjected.

"Well, Dad just stared at her as if she was the stupidest woman on the planet and said, 'Because I want to start a sexual relationship with you.'"

"What!" She couldn't help it. Karen's eyes bugged out, and she whipped her head around to see if the elder Polowskis were in on some kind of joke. Although Mrs. Polowski giggled profusely, Mr. Polowski's face was a study in boredom. "Did she slap you?"

"Yes. How do people always guess that? I know, you say that it's a natural response, but I think it's ridiculous." The man shook his head.

"Well, I've never heard anything like it. I thought Erika was joking or something."

Tom shook his head again. "People are always surprised, but what else would you call it?"

"A date?" The compulsion to answer overrode the feeling that it was a wasted suggestion.

"And what is a date?"

"Dad, you're not Socrates," Erika protested. She turned

to Karen, shaking her head, and sighed. "Dad, as blunt as it is, does make kind of a good point. That's all dating really is, right? If you didn't want it to get to an intimate relationship—"

"Sexual, Erika."

"Oh, Dad, it's just so crass when you put it that way. Let me tell it." She shook her head and started again, "Anyway, Dad's point is that friendships don't have that goal. Anyone can be friends at any time, but 'going out' is kind of supposed to lead to marriage which is really legalized sexual relationships."

"And commitment... and love..."

"Endorphins." The Polowskis spoke in unison.

At the sight of Karen's wrinkled nose, Erika continued. "Dad can't comprehend love, so to him, it's all endorphins. I have to remind him that he's not the normal one—we are."

"Sad."

"Thank you!" Erika pumped her fist.

Anxious to get out of the strange household with odder ideas of relationships than she'd ever heard, Karen stood. "Well, I have to say, that's the most unique 'how we met' story I've ever heard. I really need to get going, though. Technically, I'm working today, so I have a lot of things to do." She grabbed a few of the bags. "If you don't mind, I'd like to show you what is in here, so you know what we got and where. Is there—"

"Come on into my room." Once the door was shut behind them, Erika smiled. "Don't worry. One of the good things about not having proper emotions is that you don't get offended. Dad doesn't understand a lot of the time, but he doesn't get worked up about things. I remember I always wanted to tell *him* about things when I knew they weren't going to like what I had to confess."

"No yelling, eh?"

"You got it."

Karen pulled several receipts from her purse. "I didn't get gift receipts, so you could return them yourself if you wanted. They were paid for with cash, so you're good. I could have told you that out there, but this..." Karen dug a small blue plastic bag from inside a Macy's bag. "Keith sent this. I didn't think your father would understand."

She watched as Erika pulled out the small leather covered Bible and frowned at it. "He—"

Erika shook her head. "He's not going to do it, is he?"

"What?"

"Well, he promised me a good dinner. I know it probably made him uncomfortable, but I thought he'd keep his word. He seemed like the kind of guy who would."

"Why would it make him uncomfortable?" Karen's left eyebrow rose.

"Because he's attracted to me and doesn't know what to do about that." A snort escaped. "After all, I'm not cute, blonde, and religious."

"Look what the last one by that description did to him. He's broadening his tastes perhaps."

"But he sent this and didn't come himself. He's chickening out. I thought he was better than that. The Keith I thought I knew would at least call."

"The Keith I know," Karen agreed, "will... and he'll ask you out for that dinner like he promised." As she opened the door, Karen gave a meaningful look at the Bible. "Read it—or at least thumb through it. I'm guessing there's a note or something in there—well, if I know Keith there is."

Erika stared at the door as it closed behind Karen. She'd probably never see Karen again. Then again, she'd thought the same thing the previous day when she'd ridden home from the FBI building with her parents. Flipping through the thin pages of the book, she found one small sheet of paper. Karen was right. There was a note, but it didn't say anything about their dinner. Despite her pretense of not caring, she did. She'd finally met someone who was who he pretended to be and then he'd failed her.

The note confused her. Just a few short words, she didn't know what to make of them

*Erika,*

*"Here I give you milk to drink, not solid food; for you are not ready for solid food yet."*

*I dare you to read it.*

*Keith*

# Thirty-Three

In a city the size of Rockland, apartments become available on an extremely frequent basis. However, affordable apartments that are still available by the time a potential tenant has finished examining the place are much rarer than most renters suppose. After two weeks of getting nowhere, Erika began looking in Hillsdale, Marshfield, and Westbury. If the subway was in reasonable walking distance, she made an appointment to see it.

By the end of the third week, she wanted to cry. As she walked away from yet another shack masquerading as a reasonable excuse for an apartment, her cell phone rang. "Hey, Yvonne. Do you want to go drown my sorrows with me? Another dud."

"That's why I called. Didn't you say you were in Westbury today?"

"Yeah. I checked out three. One was decent, I guess, but the landlord was creepy. Kept ogling me. Yve, I've got to find a place, or I'll go nuts. I've taken to reading in my room to avoid yelling at my dad when he says something else that is totally inappropriate. I mean, it's Dad! What do I expect?"

"Well then, I expect you to take me out for coffee or dessert or even a nice steak would do."

"Why? What'd you find?" As she listened, Erika dug out the mini notepad she'd been making notes in all day and began writing. "Oh, that's just…" It took a few seconds to find her street on her cellphone's map, but her memory was correct. "Three streets over and a block or two down."

"They're asking six-fifty and that includes everything including cable—fully furnished."

"Well, that's kind of high, but not ridiculously so."

Yvonne's impatient voice snapped back at her, "Negotiate. I bet if you point out your years as a house sitter, you could easily knock off a hundred dollars a month."

"Yeah. Glad I got that reference for my file last summer when she talked about staying longer. Of course, if the guy tries to verify it, he'd have to call the FBI for how to contact her."

"Tell him upfront and remind him that her criminal activity doesn't mean that she didn't write an honest reference. Who you are doesn't change because she turned out to be a creep."

"Why don't I just have you negotiate for me? You sound better than I ever could."

"Hogwash," Yvonne protested. "You're the one with the mad people skills. Treat him like a customer that you want to buy a scone to go with his coffee and sell the deal."

"Okay. Fine. I'll call you if I get it."

Erika slid her phone shut and stuffed it in her purse. Yvonne was right. She was acting like a twit. "I know how to negotiate, and I know how to sell. I'll get this apartment if it's the last thing I do, and I'll get it for five-fifty. Period."

The last two blocks were short enough to prevent the doubts from resurfacing. As she rang the doorbell, she glanced around the yard. "Must be a basement apartment. I hate those. They're so dark. Might as well look, though," she muttered as she waited for the owner to open the door.

A man, hardly taller than herself and twice as round as anyone his height should be opened the door. Erika stifled the temptation to laugh. Every storybook description of a jolly grandpa danced through her mind as she took in the white bushy eyebrows, the two powder puff pieces of white hair on each side of his head, and the little clear round "Santa" glasses on his nose. He was too adorable for words.

"Hi, my name is Erika Polowski. My friend Yvonne—"

"Oh, she called and said you'd be coming. Come on in."

"You know Yvonne?" That was news. Her friend hadn't mentioned knowing the man—just that he had an apartment.

"Oh, sure. She dated my grandnephew for a while. Lovely girl, but not ready to settle down, is she?"

"Yvonne? No."

"Well, Gabe just moved out last week, and when she called to see if any of my friends had places, I thought it was perfect. Come on in and check it out. Gabe had it all designed for me and oversaw the work. He was very particular."

"Gabe Moretti?"

"Yes! You knew him?" The man led her around the side of the house and down a small flight of stairs. "See, it has a drain pipe that runs to the street. Gabe insisted on it so that the rain wouldn't come into the apartment."

"Mr.—"

"Moretti. Like Gabe."

"Great. I didn't realize it had a private entrance. I like that."

"Oh, it has everything. See those windows?" Mr. Moretti gestured to large windows along the west side of the house. "Gabe had them doubled in size. Said a dark house would be miserable."

"Seems like—" Erika stopped mid-sentence. The apartment was amazing. The furniture, the appliances, even the window coverings were better than she'd hoped to find. Yvonne had to be wrong about the price. "Yvonne said the rent—"

"Six-fifty, all inclusive. That might even include meals sometimes. I tend to cook too much still. Might as well share it with a tenant than eat it every day for a week." At the uncertain look on her face, he added quickly, "Not that I'd expect to eat here or for you to come eat with me, but there's no reason you couldn't stop in and grab a plate when you got home sometimes. It'd save you cooking—"

"Are you for real? Is this a joke? Is Yvonne hiding somewhere or something?"

Almost panicked sounding, the man backtracked. "I didn't mean to make you uncomfortable. I just feel sorry for people who have to work hard all day and then come home and cook. If that's not something you'd like to do, I can work harder to learn to cook for one."

"Well, for that price—"

"I could drop it to six hundred, but I really—"

"No."

Erika could see that the man was crushed. As she tried to formulate an acceptance of his original price if it included food now and then, the man sighed. "I do that. I'm sorry. I just love young people and I get a little carried away when I've got a chance to have someone around the place. I promise I won't be a bother. I hardly came down here when Gabe was here, and he only came up for dinner a few nights a week. I'm really not as pushy as I sound."

"No, no. That's not what I meant by no. I'll take it. At six-fifty and dinner when you cook too much. Just call me on the way home and if I'm not busy, I'll eat with you and do the dishes too. I'm just a bit overwhelmed. If you saw the dumps I've been walking through every day. If I like it, it's too expensive. If I can afford, it, the place should be condemned. I saw one place that literally pulsated with the beat of the music from the cars that circled the neighborhood all day. Freaky."

"You'll take it? Let me get the contract."

Mr. Moretti hurried toward the door, but Erika had one more question. "Oh, when can I move in?"

"Do you have a suitcase with you?"

Her laughter filled the little living room. "Oh, I'm going to like you. I'll move in on Saturday. You've just made my month."

"And you've just given me hope that I can repay the loan I took out from myself to remodel this place."

"Well, I'll do my best. How long did Gabe live here?"

"Three years."

"Well, he probably made a healthy dent in it himself!" Erika glanced around the room, her eyes lingering on the leather couches and the large flat-screened TV.

"Oh, no. I couldn't charge family rent! I'll be right back."

Erika frowned at those words. She'd never liked Gabe, and now she liked him even less. Good riddance to a jerk.

Erika clicked the remote, plunging the TV screen into darkness. Why didn't the networks come up with something reasonable to watch on Wednesday nights? *It's all pathetic!*

She reached for the latest Alexa Hartfield mystery and tossed it aside. Either the woman was losing her touch, or Erika needed a change of genre. It seemed stale and uninteresting. The magazine she'd brought home was more advertisements for things she'd never buy than articles about things that didn't interest her.

For the third time that week, she wandered through the four rooms of her apartment, anxious to find something to do without resorting to another trip to a movie or the mall. Her mother had "diagnosed" her with a serious case of ennui. Even that seemed too exciting for the disinterested feeling she had. It seemed as though that now she'd accomplished her latest goal, finding an apartment, there was nothing left to do but exist.

A glance at her watch told her it was too late for the library. She could try the bookstore in the mall. Maybe they'd have a new TV series or a book—or maybe she should go read some nice political blogs to get her blood boiling. There was nothing like reading a bunch of right-wing hot heads to stir some life into her.

Next to her laptop sat the Bible Keith had sent her. The cryptic note, still stuck in the same place where she'd found it, continued to annoy her. What did he mean about solid food or milk? Was he calling her a big baby?

She grabbed the Bible and the laptop and carried it back to her favorite chair. Maybe if she Googled the right combination of words, there'd be some explanation. It was probably some religious terminology that those with an "in" understood. Church types always seemed to speak their own language—kind of like little kids who want to be able to insult the people around them without those people knowing.

It took a little searching, but she found what she thought he was trying to tell her. None of it made sense, and the worst part of it was that she couldn't just call and ask. Anger welled up in her heart again as she remembered his broken promise. The meal didn't mean that much—not really. No one would expect a guy like Keith to toss aside whatever rules there were about dating people who weren't religious—there had to be rules. People like him had rules for everything.

Then again, she hadn't had any illusions of it being an actual date. He'd promised her dinner in a difficult circumstance. It was supposed to be a fun, "Hey, we're out of this mess now" kind of celebration, not some big deal. As she remembered his entire curt demeanor, she sighed. It was about the attraction. He wasn't going to risk it again. It was too bad, too. He was a good-looking guy—a nice one, when he wasn't letting you wander through the woods tired and hungry or tackling you when you tried to escape.

A word on the opposing page from the note caught her attention. Adultery. She hated that word. Yvonne's parents had been through the ugliest divorce she'd ever heard of because of adultery. Even her own father, with all his bizarre ideas, had a simple outlook on marriage. You kept your word. You promised to be faithful, now do it. If you can't promise to do that, then don't get married and say you will.

Premarital sex didn't bother Tom Polowski, but extramarital received the same passionless condemnation that murder, corruption in politics, and bad service at restaurants did. "It's wrong" spoken in nearly a monotone as if bored. Just thinking of it made her smile and frown at the same time. Men like her dad were rare—no, not the lack of emotion. Men today seemed more interested in serving themselves than honoring promises—kind of like Keith. The irony would have been amusing if she wasn't so irritated.

The word adultery pulled at her again, so Erika began reading the section from the beginning. It was short—simple even. It was powerful. She'd heard that Jesus was a pretty good guy. One of her friends had a mother who talked about how Jesus forgave this and forgave that. Here it was in black, red, and white. The woman was caught and told to knock it off. Erika snickered at the thought that followed. "Knock it off before he knocks you up is more like it."

Google sent a few dozen links on adultery when she typed it into the search bar. Some verses were harsh. Killing a person for adultery seemed a bit extreme, but a small part of her resonated with the idea. If capital punishment, which she had always opposed, was the sentence for adultery, Yvonne's father would never have strayed. People liked to live. It didn't sound like the Bible people had a backlog of cases to drag out the sentencing either.

One verse made no sense. Adultery and friendship with the world didn't make sense. If she could have, she'd have called Keith and demanded an explanation. That thought sent the Bible flying across the room. Her anger grew as she realized she'd let her emotions override her self-control. Unlike her father, Erika valued emotions, but like her father, she respected people who were able to control them. She rose, picked up the book, smoothed the rumpled pages, and set it on the bookshelf where it belonged. She'd ask around and see if anyone at work wanted or needed a new one.

---

"How long are you going to make her wait?"

Keith shook his head. Why did Karen always ask it like that? "I'm not 'making her wait.' I'm giving her time to see what the Bible is all about. I thought it'd give us something to discuss."

"She's going to see you as someone who breaks his word."

It was true; he had to accept that possibility, but Keith had prayed like crazy about how to go about the dinner, and this was his solution. He didn't know if it was prompted by the Holy Spirit—some kind of perfect timing thing—or if he was just subconsciously stalling for whatever stupid reason that'd be. "Well, I never said when. As long as I ask within a semi-reasonable amount of time, she can't say I broke my word."

"It's been two months. Isn't that a bit excessive?"

"She's been getting settled. I'm being patient—waiting."

"You're stalling. Call." Karen shoved his phone across the table. "I'll go see how Allison is doing."

"She won't thank you."

"I know. Isn't it great? They are so cute."

"When people say opposites attract…"

"Yeah," Karen agreed. "Look at you and Erika."

"She is not attracted to me."

Laughing, Karen strolled from the room. "Well, I don't know about that. You could be right, but you sure are attracted to her."

"Go check on our latest prisoner."

Hours later, Keith's fingers hovered over the buttons on his phone, before he slid it shut again. He might be a fool—probably was—but until he felt a green light, he wasn't calling. Period.

# Epilogue

For the third time that morning, Erika thought she saw Keith out of the corner of her eye. The first time, she'd been a little excited. As annoyed as she was, it was still an interesting prospect. She hadn't lost her curiosity about that friendship with the world and adultery thing.

The second time, she'd snapped at Jason and Myla both. Actually, if she were honest with herself, she'd have to admit that she humiliated Myla with her peevish remark about reserving flirtation for when they were off work. The girl hadn't been the same since, and Jason had subsequently avoided both women.

Now, furious at the idea that she could be so discomfited at the mere thought that someone she wanted to talk to could be avoiding her, Erika stormed out onto the sidewalk, glanced around her, and marched back inside again. Ignoring the line of customers that nearly reached the door, she strode through the back, into her office, and looked for something, anything, that she could break.

Remorse flooded her seconds later. What kind of manager was she? They were down two baristas, and she was throwing a temper tantrum like none she'd ever seen. Taking a deep breath, she opened the office door and charged back to the counter. "Next!"

For thirty minutes, the customers poured into the shop and then hurried back out again, anxious to make it to their next train. Once the store emptied, she glanced at the clock. "Hey, you guys, go on your breaks. I'll take care of it. We've got twenty minutes before it gets bad again."

"Are you sure?" Myla seemed doubtful but eager to leave. "Todd isn't here and—"

"Get out of here," Erika joked as she made shooing motions. "Go somewhere and get a change of scene. I'll be fine."

A glance at the serving area made her wince. Dropped lids, crushed cup sleeves, and drizzles of whipped cream littered every surface. With a glance at the door to be sure no one was coming, Erika grabbed a fresh towel and washcloth and started cleaning. A puddle of spilled coffee right in front of the register had nearly sent all three of them sprawling, but in seconds, she wiped it up and tossed the dirty rag in the bin. Just as she pulled herself up behind the counter, two familiar eyes smiled at her.

"So," Keith Auger, kidnapper extraordinaire quipped, "I do believe I owe you a steak dinner."

Irritated, Erika grabbed the can of whipped cream and sprayed it into his face. She waited to see what kind of response he'd have to that, and then shook her head when he asked, "Should I take that as a hint that you want dessert too?"

"You should take it as a hint that I don't live by the adage, 'better late than never.'"

"Name the restaurant."

"Marcello's in Fairbury. Oh, and I have questions for you."

Keith's knowing smile answered several unasked questions. "I thought you might. Friday?"

Erika nodded. "Do you need my address, or am I still on the watch list?"

"I could get it, sure, but I'd rather you gave it to me."

For several seconds, Erika searched his face for something, although she wasn't quite sure what. After what seemed like an excessive pause, she nodded. "Good answer."

"See you Friday, then?" If she didn't know better, she'd swear he was actually looking forward to it.

"Why did you take so long?"

"That's an answer I'm not sure you want to hear."

"Try me."

She watched him wrestle with himself for a few seconds and then frowned as he shook his head. "Nope. If you want me to tell you why, you'll have to ask me after dessert. On Friday. I'll pick you up—assuming you ever give me your address—at five-thirty."

"I'll barely make it home. No time to change."

"Then you can keep me waiting. Don't women love to do that?"

Laughing, Erika nodded. She scribbled her address on a customer rewards card just as Myla and Jason entered the store, ahead of the first caffeine addicts from the next train, sending her into work mode. "Don't be late. I've waited long enough."

"I'd say we both have. See you Friday."

Erika watched him leave the store, turn to head toward the subway, and then pause. He gave her a slight wave before he disappeared from sight.

*Now that's promising. He kept his word after all. Maybe real religious people do exist. Maybe.*

Don't miss the second book in *The Agency Files: Mismatched!*

# CHAPTER ONE

The sleazy bar oozed with the slime of a biker haven. Ernie pulled into his usual parking spot and jerked on the emergency brake before turning off the engine. Loud music blared in the cool Colorado air as a group of men exited the building. He watched them, but none stumbled. Good.

Inside, he accepted his usual glass of Coke from the end of the bar and wove his way through the customers and regulars to the paneled hallway plastered with posters of women wearing too little to leave anything to the imagination and advertisements for beer. He found the last door on the left closed and locked. A keypad accepted his access code. The light turned green. All was well.

Once inside, he closed it again, turning the deadbolt even before he turned on the lights. A glance around him assured Ernie that nothing was amiss. Things remained a bit skittish after the mess with Leo.

Unlike the rest of the bar, this room boasted clean and modern décor. Sleek stainless office furniture butted against beige walls. His chair was a masterpiece of ergonomics and luxury. Contemporary lighting kept the room bright and a splash of artwork on one wall added visual interest. The laptop—the one that never left the building—sat on the desk, ready for him to login.

His cellphone buzzed and a glance at the screen flashed one name. JENk. He ignored it. There was no news yet. As he typed in his sixteen-character password, Ernie muttered, "I swear they want information before it happens now. The world isn't going to hell in a hand basket; it's flying there at the speed of light."

Reports cascaded onto the screen at the touch of his mouse. Emails flooded his inbox, most going into the junk folder that he still had to comb for coded messages. Google popped up with his browser, taunting him with the temptation to "feel lucky." His fingers skimmed the keys and hit enter.

The entries popped up as he typed and the final tally for the day was 139,431. Ernie scratched out the previous day's number and wrote this below it, replacing the sticky note on the edge of the monitor. "Up sixty-three. Maybe today."

A single knock preceded the sound of keys in the lock. His boss stepped into the room. "You're in early. Got anything?"

"Just got here. Looks like an increase on Leos though. Maybe we'll find something."

"Del talked with his mother."

Ernie nodded. Though it didn't surprise him, it did bother him that some chick had to die because her son ran his mouth. "I'll see what I can find out." He hesitated before asking the obvious question. "Del sticking around to see if Leo shows up for a funeral?"

"That's the idea." Jenk left the room with a silent order hanging in the air. *Get me the reports and see if any of the new Google hits pan out.*

According to the previous night's sales report, "beer" was up by twelve percent and for no apparent reason. He punched a number on his phone and waited for a reply. "Hey, Roman, you need to boost production by fifteen percent." Without a word, he disconnected and went back to his lists, highlighting the places that Jenk needed to read.

Three printed emails went on top of the pile. Twenty-two minutes later, he had the extra entries finished and Google closed. Another bust. Jenk wouldn't like that. He pulled out his phone, hit the button for JENk and sent a text message. "No news."

Papers in hand, he strolled down to the boss's office and knocked. "Got the reports."

Jenk called him in and held out his hand for them. Unlike Ernie's office, the room was more like a man cave, complete with state of the art HDTV and leather seating. Again, however, it looked out of place in the shabby building. "What do we have... an increase in beer. Good. Did you call Roman?"

"Told him to have fifteen percent more next week."

"That'll give us samples—good thinking. I've got a new kid. Thinks kind of like Leo did. Speaking of Leo..."

"Bust. Nothing there. One email is from the informant at the courthouse—the one from TTYL@letterbox.com."

"TTYL?"

"Text-speak for talk to you later. It's a dummy account, of course."

"What's it say... hmm. Good. Follow up on these. See if there's any reason to visit any of them."

"Will do." Ernie pocketed the list of towns across the country where Leo might be, certain that it was a waste of time.

"Got anything else for me?"

"That's all."

Jenk passed back the stack of papers and nodded his dismissal. "Shred 'em then."

An hour later, another message from JENk arrived—a one-letter text. K.

# Keep Reading

### The Agency Files

*Justified Means*
*Mismatched*
*Effective Immediately*
*A Forgotten Truth*
*Hashtag Rogue*

### The Hartfield Mysteries

*Manuscript for Murder*
*Crime of Fashion*
*Two o'Clock Slump*
*Front Window*
*Silenced Knight* (A Christmas Mystery "Noella")

### Sight Unseen Series

*None So Blind*
*Will Not See*
*Ties that Blind*

### Meddlin' Madeline Mysteries

*Sweet on You* (Book 1)
*Such a Tease* (Book 2)
*Fine Print* (Book 3)
*Dead Letter* (Book 4)
*Byrd's-Eye View* (Book 5)

Made in the USA
Coppell, TX
04 December 2023